# HALF THE BATTLE

SAINT VIEW PSYCHOS #2

ELLE THORPE

WWW.ELLETHORPE.COM

VI.

Editing by Emmy and Studio ENP

Proofreading by Karen Hrdlicka.

Photography by Wander Aguiar

Cover Design: Elle Thorpe

*For Shellie, who has beta read almost all of my books. Thank you for all of your advice and encouragement.*

# 1

## BLISS

"*V*incent!"

The rain poured over Caleb's lips, which twisted in an ugly snarl. "This guy? For fuck's sake. I told you he was a faggot. Is he retarded too? Just standing there, watching like a pervert? You want to watch while I pound her, buddy? Go right a-fucking-head."

He yanked at my pants while I struggled to fight him off. I rammed my elbow back, finding some meaty part of his gut, but it was like he didn't even feel it. He only tightened his grip on the back of my neck and slammed me face-first into the side of my car again.

Pain splintered through my cheek and nose, taking the brunt of the hit, then spread through the rest of my body. My ears rang. Blood dripped over my lip, the metallic tang seeping its way onto my tongue.

Caleb was too big. Too strong. The scotch spurred on his anger and hate.

Vincent stood on the other side of the car, a beacon of hope I couldn't reach. I screamed his name again.

He pressed his hands over his ears, his expression tortured.

"Gonna take what I want from your used-up cunt, and then I'm gonna leave you out here to die, like the stupid bitch you are. Everyone will be better off when you're dead at the bottom of those cliffs, Bethany-Melissa. They'll rule it a suicide, and I'll tell everyone you did it because I wouldn't take you back."

"Vincent!"

I could see the internal battle. The fight between good and evil he wrestled with. It was all-consuming, tensing every muscle in his body, the pain of it written in the agony on his face.

Vincent was everything good and sweet.

Scythe was everything manic and unpredictable.

If Vincent let him out, there was no telling what he'd do.

Caleb pushed at my pants again, dragging them down my thighs so roughly the material ripped. He already had his fly open, and his erection rammed against my backside, searching for a way to make me pay.

Panic surged. The touch of his skin against mine repulsive and terrifying.

I couldn't do this again. Let him take me. Abuse me. Hurt me.

Tears rolled down my face while I stared at Vincent, knowing I had to save myself.

Even if it meant hurting him.

"Scythe," I begged between sobs, hating myself for even uttering it.

His gaze snapped to mine.

It was too late to go back. "Scythe!"

The change was instant.

His hands fell away from his ears. The tortured pain in his expression disappeared, replaced by a slow-growing grin.

In a heartbeat, I realized exactly what I'd done. The hope disintegrated into fear.

Vincent wasn't in that smile. Vincent was gone, letting Scythe out to play.

He moved so quickly I barely saw it.

Caleb, distracted by screaming at me while he tried to force his dick between my legs, definitely didn't.

Not until Scythe's blade was at Caleb's throat.

"What the fu—" Caleb's howl of pain cut off his question.

His grip on the back of my neck disappeared, as did the sick feel of him trying to invade my body. I spun around, sobbing with a mixture of relief and terror while I fumbled with my ripped clothes, trying to get them back on.

Scythe and Caleb were similarly built. But there was no doubt who had the upper hand. Scythe wrapped a muscled arm around Caleb's neck, dragging him back across the mud and away from me. A silver blade clutched in Scythe's hand glinted in the moonlight. It idly traced a path down Caleb's cheek, drawing blood as it went.

Caleb howled.

"How unsurprising. He cries when cut," Scythe murmured. "You hurt my friend, Caleb. What made you think that was a good idea?"

Caleb's feet slipped from beneath him, and his fingers scratched and tore at Scythe's forearm. He tried to speak, but the arm around his neck only tightened, until the only noises Caleb could make were splutters.

Scythe stopped a few feet away, entirely calm as he squeezed the life out of the man I'd once loved.

I did nothing to stop him.

Caleb's face purpled while Scythe played with his prey, letting him have only enough oxygen not to pass out. A small smile of enjoyment ghosting his lips the entire time.

Blood trickled down Caleb's face from the cuts Scythe made there, and I wiped at my nose, feeling no sympathy for the man when he'd thought nothing of making me bleed.

Caleb stopped fighting. I wasn't sure if it was because of the lack of oxygen or because he realized he was at Scythe's mercy and fighting was just a waste of energy.

Scythe rolled his eyes. "I hate when they give up so easily." He loosened his grip on Caleb's neck.

Caleb sucked in raspy breaths, his fingers grabbing at Scythe's forearm again.

"There we go. He's back." Scythe held the knife out to me. "You ready?"

I didn't move. I stared at the blade and then at the man offering it to me. "Ready for what?"

"It's your kill. This rain isn't letting up any, so the quicker we do this, the quicker we can go home. Vincent's dog has probably shit all over my carpet by now. Annoying. I never would have let him get that thing."

I'd known it, of course. I'd seen the distinct change in mannerisms. But hearing Scythe talk about Vincent like they were two entirely separate beings was disturbing.

I shook my head. "We can't kill him."

"Yes, we can. It's really pretty simple. One quick draw of a blade across his neck, and hey presto, he's bleeding out in the mud."

There was a gleeful joy in his voice that sent a shiver down my spine.

Caleb whimpered. "Bethany-Melissa. Please. Call off your pit bull. He's insane."

Clearly.

Scythe's eyes narrowed. He turned the blade over in his fingers while he studied me. "Have you forgotten what he did to you?"

I hadn't.

Not for a second.

I stepped in, ignoring the offered knife, and clenched my fingers into a fist. Then sent it right into Caleb's gut.

He let out a groan and tried to double over, but Scythe held him up, interest flickering in his gaze.

I rammed my fist into Caleb's gut again, hitting the exact same place.

"Fucking bitch," he gasped between hits.

My next punch was right to his nose. The sound of bone breaking more satisfying than I ever would have thought it.

If my hand hurt, I didn't feel it. Adrenaline coursed through my body, taking away any pain, and bringing with it the desire to make him pay for every hurt he'd caused me.

"Take the knife," Scythe said around a grin. "So much more satisfying. Hurts your hand less too. Trust me."

I stared at him. My fingers trembled.

"First kill is the hardest. They all get easier after that. You'll see."

I shook my head. "I'm not killing him."

"Fine. I will." His grip on Caleb's neck tightened, until Caleb's eyes rolled back and his body went limp.

Scythe dropped him unceremoniously into the mud.

I screamed, staring down at Caleb's body, twisted awkwardly on the ground. "Vincent! I mean—Scythe..." I looked up at him in horror. "Is he...?"

Scythe squinted at the body at his feet, squatting beside him and rolling him onto his back. "Dead? Not yet. Just unconscious. I couldn't stand listening to his sniveling and moaning anymore." He cleared his throat. "Please, Bethany-Melissa," he mocked. "Make the bad man stop. Honestly, the secondhand embarrassment was killing me."

With a single slice of his blade through cotton, Scythe cut away Caleb's shirt, exposing his chest and stomach. Then he pushed to his feet, striding to where I stood.

He pushed the knife into my hand. "Take it."

I stared up into big brown eyes that somehow no longer belonged to Vincent. "I can't."

Scythe's eyes darkened. "He's called you fat. Ugly. A waste of space who nobody would miss."

I swallowed down the emotions his reminder brought up and nodded.

He walked around me slowly, his voice a low growl in my ear. "He's ignored you. Cheated on you. Made you feel like an object. Treated you like you were his property."

I nodded again, knowing each word was true. "Every day."

"He's hurt you. Emotionally. Physically. In every way possible."

A tear slid down my cheek. "Yes."

Scythe's eyes hardened. "Don't you want to hurt him the way he hurt you?"

I should have said no.

I shouldn't have wanted to.

But instead, my fingers tightened around the knife.

Scythe's eyes glinted with pleasure. "Good girl."

Caleb stirred at my feet. "Bethany-Melissa?"

"That's not my name."

Scythe chuckled behind me, his body warm even though drenched by rain. "Carve it in his skin so he remembers."

I glanced back over my shoulder at him. "What?"

I was stalling, but some part of me wanted to. Because all I could see in my head was Caleb ignoring me at every dinner party we'd ever been to. Caleb screwing someone else while I stood there and watched. Caleb shoving me up against the banister and taking what I hadn't offered.

Scythe's lips brushed the side of my neck, his palm sliding down my arm until his hand covered mine. My knees sank into the mud, and rain slid beneath my soaked clothes, but when Scythe held Caleb down with his free hand, I didn't stop him.

I didn't stop him when he guided my hand to Caleb's chest, or when he pushed down, forcing me to cut into Caleb's skin in a thin, clean slice.

Caleb's screams echoed through the night. He twisted and thrashed, but he was too oxygen starved to put up any real fight. I watched the blood pool around the shallow cuts.

Scythe's gaze met mine, strong and steady. "He was going to leave you raped and beaten at the bottom of the cliffs."

Blood rushed my ears in an angry roar.

"I hate you," I whispered to Caleb. "You don't deserve to live."

He screamed again when I dragged the knife around his chest, carving out the shape of a B, an L, and then an ISS.

Head cloudy with hurt and fear and memories, I dropped the knife on his chest and pushed back onto my feet, stumbling away.

His blood coated my hands. I wiped them on my pants and stumbled backward, staring at the marks I'd made on his skin.

I'd cut him. Hurt him. Horror filled me at what I'd done.

Scythe raised an eyebrow at me as he picked up the knife. "You sure you don't want the honor?"

"Let him go."

Scythe squinted. "Nah. That's no fun."

Something hysterical unleashed inside me. "I said let him go!"

Scythe paused at my scream, as if considering his options. Then he shrugged and gazed down at Caleb. "It's your lucky day, friend. The lady says to leave you breathing. So I will." He leaned down close to Caleb's ear and stage-whispered, "For now. But I can't wait until she changes her mind. Because when she does..." He drew the dull, back side of the knife across Caleb's throat.

The smell of urine filled the air.

Caleb's sobs grew louder, but I couldn't bear to look at him. My heart thumped too loud at what I'd done. Caleb would go right to the police and report me, and the evidence would be right there on his skin.

But I couldn't kill him. And I couldn't let Scythe do it either. That wasn't in me.

Carving my name into someone's skin shouldn't have been in me either, and yet I'd done that. I had no idea who I even was anymore.

I stalked away to the edge of the cliffs, no longer worried about Caleb throwing me off them when he was a crying, bleeding, pissed-himself mess on the ground.

Below, the waves crashed hard against the cliff face, sending spray up high enough to mix with the rain. I poked and prodded at the ground, fighting back fresh tears while I searched for the keys he'd thrown.

I just wanted to leave. To go home, get in a bath, and pretend none of this had happened before the police would be at my door with a warrant for my arrest.

Behind me, my car engine cranked over. I spun around, finding Scythe behind the wheel, the window down despite the weather. "Would you like a ride?"

I had no idea how he'd gotten my car started, but I was hardly surprised that starting one without a key was in his wheelhouse of talents.

I'd never wanted a ride more in my life. Which was saying something, when the man offering one was entirely capable of killing me in an instant.

I strode back, retrieving the bag of money I'd mistakenly brought with me, and stepped over Caleb.

Scythe didn't make a move to get out from behind the steering wheel, so I took the passenger seat.

The inside of my car was warm and dry. Clean. Like nothing had happened all around it. Like Caleb didn't cry and scream through the windows, feebly banging a fist against the car and begging me not to leave him out here to die.

That was rich, considering he'd been planning to do the exact same thing to me.

"Where to?" Scythe asked.

I watched him clean Caleb's blood off his knife, wiping it on the bottom of his shirt. And yet I still found myself saying, "Anywhere but here."

## 2

## NASH

They were taking too long.

The crowd in Psychos bar was thick, filled with all of War's motorcycle club buddies and their ladies, but I watched the door like an eagle watched a field mouse. Every time it moved, I was on my feet, peering through, looking for Bliss and Vincent.

Something was wrong. I could feel it in my gut.

The next time the door opened, War strode through with Hawk at his side, and a cheer went up. "Here he is!" The group of bikers swarmed him, slapping him on the back as he shouldered his way through.

War shook off the greetings of his fellow club members, making a beeline for the bar. He grinned, resting his elbows on the bar top. "Hey, Nash. Bliss around? And can I get a beer, please?"

"She's out with Vincent," I said through gritted teeth. I hadn't forgotten Bliss emerging naked from the private room she'd been in with War. Jealousy coiled hot inside me. I didn't move, too busy staring down the door, willing it to open again.

I should have been the one to go with her.

It should have been me and her in the private room.

Instead, I'd let War and Vincent take those roles. While I stood back, always the nice guy.

Nice guys finished last. Every fucking time.

Rebel sighed and took a beer bottle from the refrigerator, popped the top on it, and placed it down in front of War. "Take a deep breath, Boss Man. She's fine."

War finally picked up on the mood, his fingers clamping around the beer bottle, his gaze darting between me and Rebel. "What's happened? Why wouldn't she be fine?"

Rebel glanced at me when I made no reply but then went ahead and answered for me. "She went out to meet our dealer. She hasn't come back."

War reared back. "What the hell?" He pinned me with a glare. "You let her do that alone?"

"We were swamped here," Rebel explained. "Vincent went with her."

I shook my head, pulling a cleaning cloth off my shoulder and throwing it down on the bar top. "I'm going after them. They've been too long."

War abandoned his beer instantly. "I'm coming too."

Rebel glared at both of us. "Neither of you are going anywhere. You," she focused on me, "are letting your crush rule your head." She turned to War. "And you brought all these people here. We're way over capacity and a security guard down, so the two of you are not running off, leaving me with no staff, no security, and a roomful of bikers who are hell-bent on getting drunk.

Stop thinking with your dicks. She's a big girl and perfectly capable of looking after herself. Vincent is scary as hell when he wants to be. They've got this. I know you both want to be the hero who swoops in and rescues the damsel in distress, but mark my words. She. Does. Not. Need. You."

She had a point.

War obviously saw it too, because he sank back down onto his barstool. He took a swig of his beer, swallowing several times while he eyed me. "You have a crush on her?"

I glowered at him.

He chuckled, sitting back, and folding his arms across his chest. "Well, that's new. I wasn't even entirely sure you were into women."

I frowned at him. "You thought I was gay?"

"I've been coming in here since before I was even legally old enough to drink and I ain't ever seen you with a woman."

"You ever seen me with a man?"

War shrugged. "Fair call. So, what? You just... don't?"

"Pick up women at work? No. I don't. Because I've got some sort of moral compass and that's unprofessional."

Rebel and War both stared at me, then burst into simultaneous laughter.

"We run a sex club in the back room, Nash. I had customers doing shots out of my belly button last week. I don't think professionalism is a required skill to work here."

War laughed and nudged her. "He's just trying to cover for his lack of game. Is this what I have to look forward to when I hit forty? Shit, I'm already over thirty. Is it all downhill from here?"

I flipped him the bird. "Fuck you. I'm not forty."

"Yet," Rebel singsonged. "Your birthday is coming up."

I hardly needed reminding.

The door opened again, and War and I glanced over expectantly. He turned away when it wasn't Bliss, but I swore low under my breath, catching War's interest again.

He took another glimpse at the woman in the doorway, then turned back to me. "What's wrong? You know her?"

I sighed as the woman caught my eye and zeroed in on me. "Yeah, I know her. She's Bliss' mom."

Rebel groaned. "Goddammit. She knows she isn't supposed to be here. I knew she'd turn up out of the woodwork and start sniffing around."

Kim strutted over wearing too-tall heels, a too-short skirt, and a top that barely covered her small tits. Her face was gaunt and lined with more wrinkles than came with being in her fifties. She'd made no attempt to hide the track marks on her arms.

She was nothing like Bliss, who was all shiny hair, curves, and sunshine smiles.

Kim squeezed in at the bar next to War, looking him up and down slowly like he was a piece of something delicious she might want to take a bite out of. "You after some fun tonight, honey?"

War raised an eyebrow, then turned to me as if to say, what the fuck? This is Bliss' mom?

I rolled my eyes. "Knock it off, Kim. You aren't gonna

be coming in here trying to make money. Axel never allowed it, and nothing has changed."

Her face crumpled. "My baby boy. How can you even say his name so casually?"

Rebel rolled her eyes at Kim's dramatics. "Maybe because you never gave two shits about your baby boy, except for what he could do for you."

Kim's fake tears dried immediately, and she shot Rebel a scowl. "You still work here, skank? That'll be the first change I make when Psychos is mine."

Rebel folded her arms across her chest, never one to back down from a challenge, but I cut in before she and Kim could start pulling hair. "What are you talking about?"

Kim stared me dead in the eye. "Where's my daughter?"

"Question of the night," War muttered around his drink.

I ignored him. "What do you want with Bliss?"

"I heard she's back in Saint View and claiming the bar as hers."

"It is hers."

"Did Axel actually have her name in the will?"

I ground my teeth together because we both knew he hadn't. The business had gone to Bliss as his next of kin because Kim couldn't be legally found. That was the only reason Kim wasn't in jail right now. Because she had an uncanny ability of sniffing out the cops and avoiding them at all costs.

Kim looked like the cat who got the cream. She knew full well she had the upper hand. She ran her finger along the bar top, picking up water droplets as she went, only to flick them at me. "Tell my daughter I'll be back for what's mine. She has no right to keep it from me."

She pushed her bony hands off the bar top and took a few wobbly steps back.

Anger roared inside me. This was the woman who'd spent years neglecting her kids while letting her boyfriend pimp abuse them. She'd been happily bought off with five hundred dollars when Bliss' dad had taken her in. And the things that Axel had endured...

I slammed my eyes closed on those memories. But I couldn't stop my tongue from moving. "You can't just let her have this one thing, can you? Haven't you caused enough damage? You've already given her a lifetime worth of trauma."

Kim stopped and stared at me. "I did no such thing."

My mouth dropped open. "Did you forget the way you didn't feed her? How her hair was always full of lice? How you never took her to school? What about how you were ready to let your pimp boyfriend have her? If Axel and I hadn't got her out, how long would it have been before she was working a street corner with her mother? Would you have even waited 'til she was eighteen? Would sixteen have been good enough? Maybe fourteen? Twelve?"

Axel and I had never told Rebel, or any of our other staff, about what had gone down when we were kids. They knew he was estranged from his mother, and that if she showed up, she was to be led politely to the door. But this was the first time Rebel had truly understood why.

She shook her head at Kim, disgust written all over her face.

I was sure it matched the look on mine.

War swore under his breath. "That's fucking messed up."

I hadn't meant to blurt out Bliss' truth for everyone around me to hear. It hadn't been my story to tell, and I owed her an apology, but it had slipped out in the memories Kim invoked.

It was why Axel had never let her come here. And why I would do whatever it took to keep her away from Psychos, and away from Bliss.

Kim pinned me with a glare. "You think you're so much better than the rest of us, don't you, Nash?"

I shook my head. "Just you."

Fire sparked in her eyes. "You're a liar. Do your friends know that? Does Bliss? Do they all know about what you did? About why I know for a fact you're no better than me?"

I vaulted the bar, landing on the other side in front of her. "Shut your mouth."

She cackled in my face and wiggled her fingers at me. "Oooh. Did I hit a sore spot?" Her laughter cut out as abruptly as it had started. She peered around my shoulder at War and opened her mouth.

I couldn't let her say it.

She was right. I was no better than her. I never had been.

In fact, I was worse.

"Please, Kim," I murmured, low enough I prayed War and Rebel wouldn't hear.

She stepped in and patted me on the chest, her hand lingering there longer than I was comfortable with. "I'll keep your dirty little secret for now. But you tell my daughter I want to see her. And Nash? If she has any stupid ideas about keeping me from what's rightfully mine, then maybe you should have a word with her? You know, in exchange for me keeping your secrets. I'd hate for everyone to find out exactly how similar you and I truly are."

## 3

## SCYTHE

*T*he urge to kill rattled around my skull, unsated and unhappy about being stopped before we'd got to the good part.

That had never happened before. I had no idea what to do with the feeling now that I couldn't run my knife blade across Caleb's throat and watch the life drain out of him.

More's the pity. I would have so enjoyed it.

I glanced over at Bliss huddled in the passenger seat. Her bare feet were tucked up beneath her, her arms holding on to her knees like they were the only thing keeping her from falling apart.

I frowned. "Is everything okay?"

She looked at me like I was insane and then went back to rocking slightly on the seat.

Right. That was a negative.

Vincent roared inside my head, order after order, each one coming so thick and fast I had to squint to make sense of them.

*If you so much as hurt one hair on her head, Scythe...*

I rolled my eyes. "So dramatic," I murmured.

But I knew he wouldn't shut up unless I gave him something. And Vincent could be incredibly vocal in my head for a man who didn't say much when he was in control. "I'm not going to do anything, okay?"

Bliss glanced over at me, like she wasn't entirely sure she believed me.

Well, that was insulting. I hadn't been talking to her anyway.

And fine. Maybe I didn't have the world's greatest track record. I had been known to kill things Vincent loved just to antagonize him. So I couldn't really blame him for being shouty when I was within stabbing distance of the one thing he loved more than anything.

He went quiet at that thought, like he hadn't even quite realized himself.

I chuckled to myself. But I was willing to throw the guy a bone since I had kind of shoved him out viciously, without even a chance to say goodbye.

I could take care of her better than he could.

I just had to prove it so he would shut up, and so she would stop looking at me like I was Jack the Ripper.

I was in a different league to that guy. He had no finesse.

"Ooh!" I flung on a blinker and swung the wheel hard, pulling into a driveway. We bumped over the gutter at speed, coming to a halt behind another car, waiting in line.

Bliss turned huge eyes on me. "What on earth are you doing?"

The car in front of me inched forward, and I let my

foot off the brake to keep up with them before I answered. "I like Big Macs. I'll get two. And some fries. And a chocolate shake. What would you like?"

I waited for her to answer, creeping the car forward, a few inches closer to the drive-through window.

She didn't reply. But her eyes were bugging out.

"My treat?" I offered.

"Scythe!" she yelled. "Have you seen my face? Or your hands? Our clothes? Caleb has probably crawled his way to the police station and given our descriptions. They're probably at our houses right now, waiting to arrest us."

I shrugged. "Yours maybe. Not mine. The police have no record of me, and they're so incompetent they couldn't find their way out of a paper bag."

Vincent roared in my head so loudly I winced. "Jeez, fine. That was bad form. I apologize. Don't worry about the police. Caleb won't say anything. Or I'll kill him. It's really very simple math, Bliss. Now, how about some nuggies?"

*McNuggets*, Vincent corrected.

But I could tell he was pleased I was feeding her because he'd stopped yelling for half a moment. I smiled smugly to myself and pulled up to the window, giving the young boy my most charming smile while I ordered.

As interested as he would be if taking a math test, he repeated my order back, not even turning in my direction.

I gave Bliss a knowing look, but she was too busy staring out the opposite window, trying to cover up her bloodied face and hands and clothes.

I picked up our food from the next window, a young girl handing out the bags while she talked into a headset.

I reached for our drink tray, and she paused, noticing the blood on my hands. Her gaze traveled to the dried blood on my shirt.

Her eyebrows drew in. "Bit early for a Halloween party, isn't it?

I shook my head. "My friend and I love Halloween. We celebrate all year round."

The girl shrugged, like she'd heard crazier, and passed over our drinks. I took them, handing them toward Bliss and nudging her with the tray when she didn't make a move to help.

"Bliss. A little help, please?"

Stiffly, she turned around and glared at me, trying to communicate something by making her eyes wide.

I had no idea what she was trying to say.

She took the cup tray though, and I wished the drive-through girl a pleasant rest of her evening.

I navigated my way out of the McDonald's parking lot and back onto the road. Then I held a hand out to Bliss. "Lay one of those Big Macs on me."

"You haven't even washed your hands." Her gaze rolled over me. "Also, you do realize you're completely insane, right?"

"Glad you noticed."

My stomach growled. But Bliss wasn't giving up the food until we got home and cleaned up, so I put my foot down harder on the accelerator, twisting through the darkened streets until we were back in Providence and parked in front of my house.

I took half the food from her, inhaling the delicious burger aroma, and made my way up the porch steps to my front door. Or Vincent's front door. Everything always felt like his when I broke through at first, but it wouldn't take long for me to make it mine.

If I got to stick around, that was. Which for now, it seemed like I was. This was the longest I'd had free run in what felt like forever, and with a bit of luck, Vincent's voice would fade day by day, until he was locked neatly back in a little box.

An intense amount of small dog barking came from the other side of the door, yipping and yapping and then growling. I sighed. "Vincent's keys are back with the car he smashed up because he can't drive for shit. I'm guessing the house keys were on that too. Wait, please."

Bliss barely had the energy to stand, let alone argue. She slumped against the side of the brick house, her eyes blinking too slowly.

An unfamiliar trickle of emotion wormed its way through me, but I ignored it, dumping the food down on the step and then gazed around the garden. I narrowed in on a large rock that bordered a flower bed. "That will work."

In two quick strides, I had it in my hands, and in the following second, I'd recalled all the baseball training I'd done in high school, which was the last time I'd been in control for longer than a few minutes. I pulled my arm back and then let the rock fly.

It smashed through the window of the living room, the tinkling of glass breaking raining down over the thump of the rock hitting the floor inside.

Bliss flinched away on instinct, sheltering from the spray of glass.

Vincent started up again in my head.

"Oh, for fuck's sake," I muttered. "It's not my fault you don't have a spare!"

*I do!*

I glanced to my left at the little safety locked box attached to the wall. It had silver buttons for a code. I didn't know what it was, but I punched in my birthday, hoping for the best.

It sprang open, a set of silver house keys on the other side.

I laughed as I plucked them out. "Oops."

Bliss didn't comment. She just followed me through the door, fingers clutching the brown paper bag of food.

On the other side, Little Dog went crazy, skittering around in excited circles at my feet, dragging her pink cast around the floor with her. She was happy to see me. Her excited yips and tail wagging told me that much.

I crouched to pick her up and check her over. She licked my face.

I crinkled my nose in disgust. "And that's enough of that. Out you go. Go play in the traffic." I set her down outside on the front step and closed the door.

Bliss yelped and slapped a hand across my chest, shouldering me out of the way to yank the door open again. "Scythe!"

"What? What did I do?"

Little Dog sat obediently on the front step, right where I'd left her.

I frowned at the dog's clear lack of intelligence, but Bliss scooped her up, holding her to her chest. "Hey, sweet girl. Are you okay?"

We both ignored the broken glass and the rock sitting on the living room floor and put the food down on the kitchen counter. My stomach rumbled again, but Bliss was already rummaging through the bags, and I had enough manners not to snatch it right out of her hand. She pulled out a Big Mac and unwrapped it.

"Hey, that's mine—"

She fed it to Little Dog, who looked like all her Christmases had come at once.

I gaped as the tiny animal's slobbery tongue darted out and licked all around my burger.

Bliss glared at me, daring me to say a word.

I didn't.

She put the dog down on the tiles, and the rest of the burger into her little silver dinner bowl. When she straightened, she eyed me, her eyes more focused now that some of the shock had worn off.

"You really aren't Vincent, are you?"

I shook my head. "Nope." I let the P pop.

"Is he coming back?"

I paused, considering my answer. Then went with the truth. "His voice in my head is strong right now. But it'll fade, day by day, until it isn't there at all."

"So that's it? He's just...gone?"

I shrugged. "He's there. He's just not here."

"I'd really like him to come back."

I shrugged. "You and him both, sister. But I'd like global warming to end and a never-ending chocolate sundae with sprinkles, but we can't all get what we want, can we?"

She swallowed hard. "So, what? Am I just supposed to start calling you Scythe now? Tell everyone we came up with a fun new nickname for you?"

I grabbed her arm, fingernails digging into her skin.

She yelped, her eyes going huge. Frightened.

"You can't call me that around anyone else. No one, Bliss."

"Why not?" she whispered. "People are going to realize pretty quickly you aren't Vincent." She shook her head. "You don't even sound like him."

"I'll do better. But you can't call me Scythe. There are too many people who would want me dead. And if I'm dead..."

"Vincent is dead."

"She catches on quick!" I let her arm go.

She immediately shrank away from me.

Dammit. I'd forgotten I was supposed to be making her like me. Now I'd gone and scared her. Again. I fought the urge to roll my eyes. Instead, I poked around in my brain, trying to work out what Vincent would have said. Because she was right. I was doing a poor job of sounding like him. "Would you like to get cleaned up? I'm sure Vincent—I mean, I—have a T-shirt you can borrow or something."

She hesitated for a moment, and I couldn't blame her. My moods were like whiplash, and worse as I tried to orient myself with being in control again. I knew parts of what went on in Vincent's life, just like he knew parts of mine. But there were plenty of things we kept hidden from each other.

Some by necessity.

Some just because I liked to torture him a little.

Bliss looked down at her blood-covered clothes. "Yes, please. Are there towels in the bathroom?"

I shrugged. "One would assume so."

She nodded and moved toward the stairs.

"Want me to sit in and talk to you while you have your bath?"

She stopped and spun around. "What? No!"

I squinted at her. "Vincent did."

Her cheeks went pink. "I knew Vincent wouldn't take a peek. He's a gentleman. You..."

I couldn't help the grin that spread across my face.

I was anything but a gentleman.

# 4

## BLISS

*I*n Vincent's extravagant bathroom, I shut the door, checking twice that it was locked. Then I leaned on it, letting my head thunk against the brown wood, before a horrifying thought occurred to me. I whipped the door open again so quick it nearly hit me in the face. "Scythe!"

There were heavy footsteps, then he appeared at the bottom of the stairs, smug smile on his face. "Did you change your mind? I'm more than happy to wash your back for you."

If I'd had a loofah in my hand, I would have thrown it at him.

How was he so different to Vincent?

I wanted Vincent back. But for now, I was stuck with his arrogant, openly flirtatious, nothing-like-the-man-I-knew alter ego.

He was still sinfully sexy though. With his biceps popping, and his gaze running over my body in a way that Vincent's didn't because he was too polite. Heat rolled through me, and it was almost welcome, because I was so damn cold. Inside and out.

"You don't touch Little Dog while I'm in the shower. Got it?"

"Is that seriously what you called me back here for?"

"Yes! Do not hurt her again."

"When did I hurt her?"

"You put her outside to play in the traffic."

"Dogs need exercise."

I glared at him and tried to ignore the deep timbre of his laugh. It was new. I didn't think I'd ever heard Vincent laugh, but on Scythe, it sounded good. It lit up parts of me that really didn't need lighting up right now. "Just promise me you won't touch her while I'm having a bath. Please."

He sobered. "Little Dog will be just fine. I'll even give her some water."

I nodded, satisfied he wasn't going to try to kill Vincent's dog while I had my back turned.

"Just enough to drown in."

"Scythe!"

"It was a joke! Jesus, you're as boring as Vincent is."

I went back into the bathroom and slammed the door behind me. I couldn't wait for Vincent to come back. I refused to accept I was stuck with Scythe indefinitely. The thought was too hideous to bear.

With the door locked again, I moved to the bathroom vanity to wash my hands.

It took multiple pumps of soap and scrubbing to get all the blood and mud off. The longer it took, the more my hands shook, not from the exertion of scrubbing dried blood from beneath my fingernails, but from everything that had happened.

I'd carved my name in a man's skin.

Then left him for dead.

What if he didn't get himself off the bluff? What if he was bleeding out in the mud?

I hated Caleb. But I didn't want to be the reason he died. I didn't want to be the reason anybody died.

I finally raised my gaze to the mirror above the sink, and a gasp slipped from my lips. I didn't recognize the woman staring back at me. Her eyes were huge and scared. Her hair was like a bird's nest, caked with mud and stray sticks and leaves. I plucked them out with a rising panic that didn't ebb when I took in the state of my nose, lips, and chin.

They'd taken the brunt of the hit when Caleb had attacked me. It was a miracle he hadn't knocked out any of my teeth, but the rest of my face hadn't fared so well. I was swollen and bruised everywhere I looked, my skin a mottled mess of reds, purples, and blacks.

Any sympathy I'd felt for Caleb disintegrated. And his threats roared in my ears once more. *"Gonna take what I want from your used-up cunt, and then I'm gonna leave you out here to die, like the stupid bitch that you are. Everyone will be better off when you're dead at the bottom of those cliffs."*

Those cuts I'd made on his skin were shallow. They'd scar, but they'd heal. And I wasn't going to feel bad about them when he'd been planning to do so much worse.

I should have rammed the knife right through his ugly, black heart.

It was less than what he deserved.

I wiped at my face gently with the wet end of a hand

towel, but it stung so bad tears welled in my eyes. I choked on a sob, trying to hold it back.

"Tell me you've never been in a fight without telling me you've never been in a fight."

I jumped at Scythe's voice on the other side of the door. Then narrowed my eyes at it. "Are you sitting out there eavesdropping on me?"

He didn't answer. "It'll hurt less if you just get in the shower and let the hot water wash away the blood. You're just causing yourself unnecessary pain by trying to scrub it off with a towel."

He was right, and I'd been on my way to the same conclusion. I really wanted a bath, but I didn't want to be floating around in the filth that coated me either. The shower was the next best option.

I turned the shower on, waiting for the water to warm up.

"Naked yet?"

"Would you go away? You better not be trying to peep through the crack."

Vincent would have never. Scythe, I already didn't trust as far as I could throw him.

"Why would I bother when I can just look at the hidden camera footage?"

My mouth dropped open. "You wouldn't!"

He chuckled. "Enjoy your shower, Bliss."

---

*I* couldn't go home. There was no way I could explain the state of my face to my father or Nichelle, and I would terrify the kids. I sent Rebel a text, letting her know I was okay, and then crawled into a bed in Scythe's spare room, taking Little Dog with me. She snuggled onto her side of the bed and immediately started snoring.

I was exhausted, but I tossed and turned for hours, sleep refusing to come.

I wasn't the only one. Outside the room I'd claimed for myself, Scythe moved around the house. At one point, I heard the front door open and then close quietly. When I got up to look out the window, Scythe was stealing away down the street, another shadow adding to the many.

With him out of the house, I finally relaxed enough to get some sleep.

When the sun rose, I got up with it and snuck down the stairs to find my car keys. If Scythe had come back, I hadn't heard him. I searched the kitchen counter, only to remember the keys were lost somewhere over the edge of the Saint View Lookout. "Dammit," I muttered, ordering an Uber instead.

The app told me my driver would be twenty minutes, and I cringed, gazing down at myself in one of Vincent's oversized T-shirts and a pair of boxer shorts.

"Your things are in your bathroom."

I jumped a mile, spinning around to find Scythe sitting at the outdoor table silently, a steaming cup of coffee in front of him. He'd been so deadly still I hadn't even noticed him there, through the open doors.

"What things?"

"I went to your place during the night and picked up some clothes for you."

I blinked. "You went to my house?"

Panic clawed its way up my throat. I'd seen exactly

what Scythe was capable of last night. "The kids were there. My dad, and Nichelle..."

He leaned back in his chair, putting his booted feet on the table. "They were all there. I would have introduced myself, but I didn't think that would go down too well at three in the morning. Did you know your dad sleeps naked though?" He gave an overexaggerated shudder of revulsion that matched the expression of disgust on his face. "Your new mommy is either really into personality or solely after his money. Because..." He held up two fingers, only an inch apart.

I picked up an apple from the fruit basket on the countertop and threw it at him.

He caught it without blinking and took a bite out of it. "Thank you. That's what you were supposed to say, you know."

I glared at him, still tasting bile over the TMI on my father's penis size, and ran back up the stairs and into the bathroom I'd used last night.

An overnight bag was overflowing with clothes, and on the sink, he'd placed all sorts of things that he'd pilfered from my house. My toothbrush and toothpaste sat on the vanity, and when I opened the cupboard, my hairdryer, curler, and straightener were all there. The top drawer held my deodorant and makeup bag, which I pulled out gratefully, because it meant I could cover up some of the mess on my face. But first I needed to tame my hair. I opened the second drawer, searching for a hairbrush, and gawked at what I found there instead.

Heat rushed me, centering on my cheeks, but quickly turned into anger. I picked up the offending item and crashed back into the hallway. "My vibrator, Scythe! Seriously?"

"It appears to be ribbed for your pleasure," he called back. "You're welcome!"

Something that was a half groan, half scream of frustration pushed its way out of my mouth, but I didn't have time for it. I rushed to get ready, slapping some badly applied concealer and foundation over my bruises. There was little I could do about the swelling, but by the time my Uber driver beeped his horn and I ran downstairs and out to meet him, I was as presentable as I was going to get.

Scythe was already in the front seat, chatting to the driver about what they'd had for breakfast.

I slid into the back seat, glaring at Scythe. "Do you make it a habit of stealing other people's Ubers?"

"Do you make it a habit of going places without your bodyguard?"

The young guy who owned the car glanced at me in the rearview mirror and then back at Scythe. "She famous or something?"

"Or something," I muttered. "I'm headed to Psychos, in Saint View, please. Feel free to drop him anywhere but."

Scythe laughed, and my body did that hot flush thing it had done last night.

I ignored it.

"She jokes. She's not funny, but we let her think she is." Scythe elbowed the guy, his eyes darkening. "So laugh."

The driver laughed awkwardly, a flicker of fear in his expression when he glanced at Scythe.

Great. He'd probably leave me a bad rating thanks to Scythe making everyone uncomfortable.

We both got out at Psychos, and I strode ahead, not waiting for Scythe to catch up. It was early, but there were cars in the parking lot, and the doors were open.

When I walked inside the building I realized why. "Holy shit," I murmured.

The place looked like a bomb had hit it. In the middle, the lone three survivors stood—Rebel, Nash, and War—with mops and cleaning cloths in their hands.

All three looked up when I entered, Scythe close behind me.

My gaze met Nash's, and the signs of relief that swamped him were so instant and pure it had my heart thumping.

"Jesus fuck! What happened?" War strode across the mess of overturned tables and chairs and garbage that littered the floor. His boots crunched down on already broken glass, and then he swept me into his arms.

All of the stress and worry from the last twenty-four hours dissolved in his embrace. I pressed my face into his shirt, which didn't actually smell all that great, since he'd obviously been wearing it since the night before, but there was still a familiar comfort in him that I desperately needed. I held him tight, and he held me right back, keeping me up when my legs buckled at the release of pressure.

"What happened?" he growled, but I could tell it wasn't aimed at me but at Scythe.

"There might have been a slight mishap."

War's fingers grasped my chin, tilting my face up to his. And then he stared back at Scythe. "A slight mishap?

Her face is probably black and blue behind all that makeup, isn't it? I could see the swelling from across the room. Did you fucking do this?"

Instantly, I was thrown back to Vincent attacking War during the last party, ripping him off me while we were in the middle of having sex. That had been Scythe in control that day, and I didn't need a repeat of it.

I shook my head, putting a placating hand on War's chest. "Hey, no. He didn't. It was my ex."

War's fingers clenched into fists. "But it happened on his watch. He was supposed to be keeping you safe."

"I'm fine."

"You're not," all three guys said in unison.

I glanced past War to Nash, whose face was also like thunder.

Behind me, Scythe was attempting to keep his cool, but his body was tensed, ready for a fight if War or Nash brought it on.

The entire situation needed defusing. "What happened in here last night?"

If it were possible, Nash's mouth flattened into an even thinner line, but he moved his glare from Scythe to me, shooting War a dirty look along the way. "What didn't happen? Place got overrun with War's MC buddies. A couple of them got in a fight, which turned into all of them getting in a fight, which turned into them destroying the bar because we didn't have enough staff to stop it."

"Which is why I'm still here," War offered, expression turning apologetic. "And I'll be back later with cash to replace everything that got broken."

Rebel shoved her hands on her hips. "Good. Because

we've got less than two weeks to get this place cleaned up."

Nash sighed wearily. It was clear he hadn't been to bed yet. "Why the random time frame?"

"For the party."

I fumbled through my purse and held up the muddy bag of cash I hadn't delivered the night before. "No money drop-off. No product for a party."

Rebel frowned. "It's Nash's fortieth. There needs to be a party."

I blinked at him. "Is that true?"

He groaned. "Rebel, you're seriously a pain in my ass. I told you, no party."

"And I told you I don't care. You're having one. Doesn't have to be a Psychos party. Though knowing the dirty perv that you are, I figured that's what you'd like most."

I glanced at Nash curiously.

He didn't deny it.

"When is your deal supposed to go down?" War asked.

I shrugged. "I thought it was last night, but since that turned out to be unrelated, I don't know. He said by the end of the month."

"Today's the thirtieth," War mused. "Last day of the month."

I hated the uncertainty of all of it. "Maybe they don't want to work with us anymore?" Then a worse thought crept into my head. "What if they got caught by the cops? Just great, they're probably throwing me under the bus right now, and I'll go down for attempted murder as well as drug charges."

War and Nash and Rebel all turned to stare at me.

"What the hell happened last night, Bliss?" Rebel asked.

Scythe stepped in closer to my back. "Nothing you all need to worry about unless you want to be an accessory if the cops find out about it."

She shook her head quickly. War and Nash exchanged looks, but neither of them pushed any further either.

But I was back to worrying about it. It was another unknown. I'd been too gutless to end Caleb's life, which meant that now I had to live mine wondering when he'd retaliate. Maybe he wouldn't go to the cops, but I wasn't so sure he'd let me get away with everything I'd done without any sort of backlash.

That, coupled with my drug dealer problems, and I was just getting buried farther and farther.

Nash ran a hand through his hair. "Not to pile on, but there's something else you need to know, Bliss."

I threw up my hands. "Lay it on me."

"Your mother was here last night."

"Are you joking?"

"I wish I was. She wants her cut."

A stillness washed over me, gripping tightly. It was the same response my body had every time I'd seen her since she'd given me up to my dad. Even as a grown woman, that dread, the knot in my stomach that twisted until I was ready to vomit, it never went away.

Nash's voice was quiet. "Bliss? What do you want to do if she comes back?"

She'd come back. Of course she would. Because I was never going to be free of her. Or this town. How easily I'd been suckered back in. And how easily it had turned my life upside down.

But there was no exit strategy. Bethany-Melissa didn't exist anymore.

And Bliss wasn't going to lie down and let anyone take what was hers.

*B*y the time I got back to the clubhouse, after staying at Psychos for hours to help clean up the mess my men had made, most of the bikes had cleared out. I parked my bike up at the front and let Bliss get off first before I swung my leg over the seat.

Bliss winced as she looked around the compound. "This place is as trashed as Psychos was."

I toed at a beer bottle lying discarded on the ground. Then drew my leg back and kicked the bottle as hard as I could. "That's what days of nonstop partying gives you. Fucking ingrates. Good riddance to the lot of them."

"That's not a very nice way to talk about your family."

I glanced over my shoulder at the unfamiliar voice, my heart sinking and annoyance rising when I recognized the face. "What are you still doing here? Don't see none of your guys hanging around."

Gus, prez of the Vegas chapter, shoved his hands in his pockets. He was still trim for an old guy, his T-shirt tight across a solid chest and stomach. "Thought I might stay on for a bit."

"Why?" I asked, not caring that I was being rude.

Gus chuckled. "You're as blunt as your old man was. That's why I liked him. But he made me promise a long time ago that if anything ever happened to him, I'd be around to help you out."

I ground my molars and instinctively reached back for Bliss' hand, needing something to ground me. It was just like my old man to have no faith in me, even when he was fucking dead and buried. "I'll be fine."

"I'll hang around anyway."

For fuck's sake.

I switched from grinding my teeth to biting my tongue. With a curt nod of acceptance, I strode away down the path that led to my cabin.

Bliss trotted along beside me, trying to keep up with my longer stride, until I realized I was half dragging her back to my cave and slowed down so she didn't have to run.

"Thanks," she said. "What was all that about?"

We were well out of range of the clubhouse now, the surrounding woods swallowing it up from view. But I glanced around anyway, like there might be someone hiding in the bushes, ready to eavesdrop and report back to Gus.

The trees were quiet, nothing more substantial than birds sitting on branches to hear us. "A show of power and position. Gus Finazzo started the Slayers MC with my old man, back when they were both fresh outta the army with crater-deep chips on their shoulders."

"How come he isn't VP then? Or...co-president? Is that a thing?"

"Because my dad and Gus were too fucking similar and too messed up in the head to run anything together. Gus split a couple years after I was born and started his own chapter. But because he's one of the founding fathers, everybody has to kiss his ass."

She nodded. "You don't want to kiss his ass, I assume?"

I chuckled and pulled her in tight, dropping my hands to the curves of her backside and squeezing a handful. "I'd much rather kiss yours."

Fuck, she felt good in my arms. She let me feel her up, my palms sliding over the material of her skirt, and up higher to the indent of her waist. I gazed down, drinking in the sight of her and letting it fill up the hollow place that had opened when she'd been AWOL last night. "I missed you," I murmured.

"You only saw me a few days ago."

I dropped my lips to her neck. "Yeah, but I want to see you every day. You can't blow my mind the way you did the last few times we've been together, then cut a guy off. He'll go through Bliss withdrawals. And there's no rehab for that, except for the one between your legs."

She smiled, then winced, putting a finger to one of the little cuts on her upper lip. "Don't be sweet. Or sexy. Hurts too much to smile."

"I want to kill whoever did that to you. All you gotta do is say the word..."

I wanted to move up and take her mouth with mine. She'd spent all night with Vincent. And I hadn't missed the connection between her and Nash. I'd seen the way he looked at her, like his balls were in a fucking vise every time she was near. I almost felt sorry for the poor bastard because I knew how it felt to be barred up over Bliss Arthur. I had no claims on her. I knew that, and yet the second I'd seen her walk in the door of Psychos, with her face all banged up, knowing some other man had hurt her, I'd just wanted to touch her. Claim her all over again. Make her mine so no other man would dare lay a finger on her.

I kissed my way down her neck and over every inch of exposed skin left bare by the open buttons on her shirt. With deft fingers, I undid a few more until her bra showed, and I could lick the swell of her tits.

I wanted everyone to know she was with me. "At the next Psychos party, I want to fuck you in the main room. With everyone watching."

She sucked in a gasp, drawing back to look at me. "War..."

I dropped to my knees in the grass and lifted her skirt, rucking it up around her waist and flashing her panties. "Bliss..."

I put my mouth over her panties, tonguing them in a preview of what I was going to do to her clit.

She didn't fight me. She widened her legs without me prompting her to, and damn if that didn't make my dick hard. I pulled the silky material to one side, exposing her mound and the sweet slit below. "You're gonna let me have you out here, where any one of my guys could walk by at any moment, but not at Psychos?"

I licked her mound, her smooth bare skin warm beneath my tongue.

Her hand dropped to the back of my head, fingers running through my hair. "I don't work here."

"But I do."

"You like people watching you."

I ran my tongue between her folds, finding her wet and aroused. "I think you do too. That show you put on for me, riding your fingers while I watched through the door...fuck, baby. That was so hot."

"Maybe," she whispered.

I found her clit with my tongue, massaging the little bud at her center. "What was that?"

She moaned, her fingers flexing in my hair. "Fine, I like it."

I licked lower, pressing between her soft thighs to thrust my tongue into her pussy. "You like what? Tell me."

She groaned, and when I glanced up at her, her cheeks were pink. But she wasn't stopping me. I yanked her panties right down, exposing her completely, and dove between her legs again, licking every inch of her.

"I like the idea of people watching you."

I paused. "You mean us?" There was something she wasn't saying, and I wanted to know what it was. "Talk to me."

She bit her lip, gazing down at me. I still had my hands wrapped around her thighs, her pussy an inch from my lips, just the way I liked it.

But still, she held back.

"Spill it, Bliss."

She sighed. "You know how attractive you are, right?"

I was vain enough to have an idea. I'd never had a problem getting a woman into bed anyway, which was about as attractive as I needed to be in life. It hadn't taken me long to discover what women liked. I already had the bad boy biker thing down pat. I worked out because I needed it to keep my fucking head on straight, but the by-product was a trim body that women liked to touch. Throw in a few tattoos and a smirk, and that was about all it took for a one-night stand.

Which was all I really did.

Until she'd made me want repeats.

"I'm not as ugly as Hawk, so that's a bonus."

She smiled. "He's not ugly. You're a shitty friend."

Hawk was so stupidly attractive that anyone calling him ugly was clearly lying. "You're changing the subject. Spill it or I'm gonna leave you wet like you are with no orgasm until you do."

She laughed, then winced when her wide smile tugged at her healing cuts. "You could be doing this with Siren, or any of those other tiny women who hang around the clubhouse, but it's me. With my fat thighs and belly rolls. I like the idea that you want me and that you don't try to hide me away like some dirty secret."

Fucking hell. Women were insane. Like I gave a shit about a couple of belly rolls. She had curves I couldn't stop touching. She was soft and warm. Her tits over-spilled my hands. She was straight-up banging, and the fact someone had made her feel like shit about it only told me he had a small dick. "Don't talk about your thighs like they're anything other than my favorite thing to get between."

I grinned at the way she took the compliment. She needed to get used to it, because I wasn't gonna stop telling her how bad I wanted her. "You like the idea of me wanting you so bad I couldn't even wait to get you inside?"

"I still don't know about Psychos..."

I ran a finger through her juices gathering at her center. "How wet you are right now just talking about me fucking you there tells me otherwise, baby girl." I didn't say anything more. It was enough to know she was as into it as I was. And that having people watch us turned her on rather than terrified her.

I'd have her on that main floor at Psychos. Maybe it would take some time, but eventually, I'd have her so confident she'd be the one claiming me in front of an entire room.

Fuck. I was so pussy-whipped for her. I could only see it getting worse, but I didn't care.

I wasn't ready to give her up.

I stood and shrugged off my jacket and laid it down on the soft grass at my feet. I brushed my lips to the corner of hers, so desperate to kiss her but never wanting to cause her pain that wasn't the good kind. So I trailed my lips up to her ear and whispered, "Lie down. I want to make you scream my name so loud the entire club comes out to see exactly how badly I want your body."

She laughed, sitting on my jacket. "We're pretty far from the clubhouse. I'd probably need a megaphone."

I cocked one eyebrow. "That a challenge?"

"Maybe it is."

I leaned in and sucked her neck, right on the spot I knew she liked best. "I really want to spank you right now for that comment, but instead, I'm gonna get you fully naked. So if anyone does happen to walk past, they're gonna see every inch of you while I make you come.

That's your punishment." I undid the last of the buttons on her shirt and drew it down off her shoulders, then without waiting for permission, unclipped her bra straps.

Her breath hitched as the cooling autumn air touched her nipples, but then they were enveloped—one in my mouth, the other between two fingers. I pushed her back to the grass, sucking and licking and tweaking her until she closed her eyes and was writhing beneath me.

Movement to my left caught my eye, a flash of something that didn't belong.

I tensed, pulling away from Bliss' tits to search the woods.

There was someone there.

I couldn't see them, but I could feel their presence just as strongly.

"War," Bliss gasped.

My woman needed me, and I was going to give her exactly what she wanted.

But my dick strained behind my pants knowing someone was there.

I wanted to know who.

I lowered my head to run my tongue all over Bliss' breasts. I sucked her brownish-pink nipples, and tongued the swells, and buried my face in their valley. I pinched her and cupped her and squeezed until she was panting and begging me to move lower.

I looked up into the woods to find a man watching us. His dark-brown eyes locked on mine.

My compound was secured on all sides. I had men at the gates twenty-four seven and security along the expansive fence lines.

Yet somehow, motherfucking Vincent Atwood had

gotten himself in, following Bliss around like a lost puppy, taking his bodyguard job way too seriously.

Fuck, this guy was a pain in my ass. But at least this time he wasn't ripping me off her and throwing his fist into my face.

He'd caught me off guard the first time. That wouldn't happen twice.

But he could put a cork on his Bliss crush, because I wasn't stopping for him. Not when Bliss was laid out with her pink pussy dripping on my jacket and ready for me to take.

With my gaze locked on Vincent, I moved down Bliss' body, every kiss I pressed to her skin a fuck you for the last time he'd interrupted us. That wasn't happening today. He could turn away. Disappear in the same silent way he'd shown up.

To my surprise, he didn't.

My dick throbbed, begging to get in on the action. Begging to put on a show.

Fuck this guy. Fuck his crush on her.

Fuck the way he stared at me.

I lowered my mouth to her soaked pussy and did what I did best.

## 6

# SCYTHE

*I* wished I'd brought my wallet because the War and Bliss show needed to come with snacks and a refreshing drink.

Preferably one I could pour over my head to cool off, because they were turning up the heat.

I would have cheered for them if it hadn't been such an un-Vincent-like thing to do.

Back at Psychos, Bliss had run into War's arms, slamming so hard into his body I'd semi expected them both to crash to the floor.

She'd held his hand. Smiled at him.

She did those things with Vincent too.

But not with me.

With me she was standoffish. Wary or overcompensating with yelling. She shrank away from my touch.

I didn't want that.

So I'd tagged along, following War's bike in the Jeep I'd borrowed from Nash.

Nash didn't know I'd borrowed it, of course. But if you

just left your keys sitting around behind the bar for any old psychopath to grab, what did you expect?

I hadn't banked on the whole MC thing. I hadn't picked that up when I'd been glimpsing things through Vincent's eyes. But the fence was hardly a problem. There were obvious blind spots in the way their cameras had been set up. It had taken me less than a minute to find them.

There were always blind spots in surveillance. You just had to know to look for them if you didn't want to get caught. Which I hadn't. My plan had been to just follow War and Bliss quietly, at a distance, and watch the way he was with her, so I knew what I needed to do. I could imitate. I'd been doing that my entire life. Imitating other kids, knowing I had to in order to fit in. I was better at it than Vincent. He stuck out like a sore thumb with his stilted words and obliviousness of social cues. So the fact she liked him but not me really fucking grated.

*It's because you're completely insane.*

"Yeah, well, you are too," I murmured.

War glanced up, and our gazes locked. He watched me while he went down on Bliss.

Which was really fucking interesting. He knew I was there, watching, and he hadn't stopped. If anything, he'd turned the dial up.

He pulled back, sticking two fingers into his mouth, and then pressed them up inside her.

Her shout of pleasure went straight to my cock. Her tits pointed to the sky as she arched her back, her eyes closed, face blissed out with pleasure.

A surge of jealousy washed over me. It had been so long since I'd had a woman beneath me like that.

Vincent, the pansy, was probably saving himself for marriage, he was so fucking inexperienced. But I knew exactly what it was to have a beautiful woman beneath you, to feel her nails running down your back, and her fingers ripping at your hair while you tongued her clit.

Bliss had walked out of my house this morning smelling of fresh honeysuckle.

I'd wanted to lick it off her.

Pressure built inside me, War's fingers slipping in and out of her pussy, his gaze alternating between his work and me.

His smug expression left me in no doubt that he knew I was here. He licked her slick juices from his fingers, tasting every drop before continuing, riling her up until her hips bucked off the ground and she begged him in breathy moans to let her come.

My dick ached. My balls ached. Everything fucking ached to take his place. My erection pressed against my jeans, and I dropped the zipper, giving myself some extra room.

War put his mouth over Bliss' pussy again, and she shouted his name as she came, splintering apart out in the open air where anyone could see and hear her.

War didn't try stifling her shout. Instead, he undid his pants, freeing his cock.

My gaze dipped to his erection, but then he had her legs hooked up over his arms and was pushing inside her dripping core.

I clamped a hand around my dick.

She took him easily, throwing her head back while he pumped in and out of her body. The noises of sex filled the air—her moans, their skin slapping, the rhythmic motions intoxicating and doing nothing to help the need that stormed inside me.

I jerked my shaft slowly, torturously, fighting back the urge to go shove War out of the way and take my rightful spot between her legs.

It was agony to watch someone else have the things you wanted. I'd never been much good at sharing.

War's hips rolled, his biceps flexing while he thrust into her. He picked up speed, and I found myself doing the same thing, my strokes matching his.

She reached one hand between them, rubbing her clit. Her breaths came faster and faster, turning into pants of need and little, "oh, oh, ohs," as she neared another climax.

"Fuck, you're so wet, Bliss." War slammed his hips against her, taking her hard, driving in so deep her eyes rolled back.

"I'm going to come," she moaned.

I wanted to slam my head against the nearest tree in agony.

Her second orgasm tried to wreck me. I pumped my dick harder.

She screamed, the pleasure-filled sound echoing around the empty woods. War pulled out and gripped his cock, spilling himself all over her tits and belly, and then lower on her pussy. He massaged it into her clit, extending her orgasm until she begged for mercy.

Her eyes finally opened again.

I shrank back into the shadows, dropping my hand from my erection before she could see me.

War lifted her to her feet, kissing the side of her neck, and pointed to the cabin they clearly hadn't made it to before they'd got wrapped up in their need for each other. "Go get cleaned up. I'll meet you in the shower in a minute. Just gotta check on something then I'll mess you all up again."

She took her clothes from him and nodded, running across the clearing to the cabin like she was suddenly worried about someone seeing her in all her post-sex glory.

Too fucking late.

The cabin door squeaked when it opened and then banged closed behind her.

War zipped his fly and grinned in my direction. "Enjoy the show, you perv?"

I stepped out of the shadows, crossing my arms over my chest and leaning back on the tree. "Your technique could use a few pointers, but not bad for a beginner."

War jerked in surprise at my answer, but a grin spread across his face. "You think you could do better?"

"She wouldn't have had to rub her own clit if it had been me between her thighs." I shrugged. "Just saying."

War shook his head, his grin turning to laughter. "That so?" His gaze dropped to the bulge behind my pants. "So you're the expert in getting Bliss off but can't even get yourself over the line?"

"You upset you didn't get to watch me come too?"

Heat flared in War's eyes, and fuck if it didn't hit me low in the gut. The base of my spine tingled.

I needed to come. It was physically painful not to.

War's gaze rolled over me, slow as molasses. But then he cocked his head to one side. "What happened last night? You seem different."

My erection shriveled when I realized my mistake.

Vincent would have never done what I'd just done. He didn't give in to his basic bodily needs the way I did. The man probably never even jacked off. He didn't do banter. He didn't swear. And yet here I was, flirting with a man, my dick hard with thoughts of how I wouldn't have minded if he'd wanted to finish me off.

I was going to give myself up on the first freaking day. And of all people, War was the one who could never find out who I was.

Not after I'd killed his father.

Oops.

War's voice turned curious. "What are you doing here anyway?"

That was safer ground, and the truth was easy enough to give. I just had to phrase it in the way Vincent would. "It's my job to look after her."

"She's my woman. It's my job to look after her too."

That jealousy inside me flared. Bliss had said they were having sex. I'd been in Vincent's head enough to hear all of that.

She hadn't said anything about being his girl.

Not that it would stop me. Vincent would have respected those boundaries.

I saw boundaries and skipped right over them.

But War didn't need to know that. He needed to think I was Vincent, so I nodded curtly. "I'll leave then."

I could feel War's eyes on my back as I headed toward the section of fencing I'd come in through.

"Vincent?"

I almost kept walking, only realizing a beat too late that I needed to respond to that name. "Yes."

"How'd you get in?"

"Your security sucks—I mean, your security is lacking."

War's brows furrowed together. "It's state of the art."

It was a piece of shit that I could have got around at five years old, but whatever. I kept walking.

War called after me. "Next time I come into Psychos, if I buy you a beer, will you tell me where the problem is?"

I didn't look back.

I didn't want him to see the unexpected smile I had to force off my face at the idea of having a drink with him.

## 7

## BLISS

*T*he smile War put on my face hurt like hell and was probably opening up the cuts from last night. But it was worth it.

I'd needed to be in his arms. To be reminded what it was to be with someone who worshipped my body instead of trying to hurt it. I loved the way he always wanted me, no matter where we were or what I looked like. I knew my face was pretty messed up. There was only so much makeup could do to cover the damage, but War had been gentle where I wanted him and rough where I needed it.

I'd needed him to come on me. I needed somebody to take away every trace of Caleb's hands on my skin.

But now I was a sticky, happy, well-satisfied mess who desperately needed a shower.

I ran across the little clearing to War's place, feeling exposed now that his big body wasn't on top of mine. My ass jiggled when I ran up the steps, but for once, I didn't worry about whether War would notice. He'd made it perfectly clear that he liked my curves.

Maybe now, without Caleb around, I could too.

On the wooden porch, I dragged open a glass sliding door and slipped inside. I blinked rapidly, my eyes trying to adjust to the darkness after being out in the midday sun for so long.

"Jesus, is that his cum all over you?"

I yelped, clutching my clothes to cover my naked body, smushing them into the cum that was indeed all coating me.

Siren uncrossed her long legs and pushed her hands down into the big king-size bed. She stood gracefully in heels and an outfit that was ready for a party, not a Thursday morning.

I had no idea what was going on. "What are you doing here?"

She curled her upper lip in distaste. "I was going to ask you the same thing."

"This is War's cabin."

"Exactly."

The two of us stared at each other.

I was at a distinct disadvantage. She was taller than me in her heels, not to mention fully dressed, while I cowered, trying to cover myself. "War and I are together."

Siren let out a laugh that made me wonder if that's where she got her name, because it was loud and obnoxious. "Oh, sweetie. War is fucking you, but you aren't together."

I didn't say anything because she was probably right. This thing with him and me had already gone well past a one-night stand, which was a lot more than I'd expected from a man like him, but I was overstepping by saying we were together when we hadn't even had a conversation about it.

I didn't want to look like a fool in front of Siren though. And this entire situation was mortifying. "That's none of your business. I really think you should leave. Or go talk to War about it. He's outside somewhere."

She moved around his cabin, straightening a stack of motorcycle magazines on a side table like it was her place. "I'll leave. But, sweetheart, whatever you're expecting from him, let it go. He can't give it to you."

She was beginning to annoy me. I didn't need her mocking and patronizing. She was out of line being in here at all. I let my anger stiffen my backbone and take control of my tongue. "Because you know him so well? *Sweetie*, he ditched you for me. So while you're standing in a glass house, perhaps you shouldn't throw stones. If you want to hang out in here cleaning up after him, go right ahead. I'm going to have a shower. He'll be joining me, so maybe you could do me a favor and tell him to bring in a towel."

I moved toward the bathroom door, silently giving myself a high five for not being a complete and utter doormat. It might not have been the most cutting of comebacks, but it was probably as good as I was going to get.

I stopped when Siren laughed again. "He hasn't told you who I am then, has he?"

"Queenie did." And I'd filled in the blanks. She was an MC groupie. Always hanging around, getting off on the bad boy thing, and basically up for whichever of them needed a woman for the night.

Siren tapped a crimson nail over her matching lips. "You think I'm a club slut."

I wouldn't use that word because I didn't talk about other women like that. Even those I disliked as much as the one standing in front of me.

Siren stalked across the empty space between us and pressed her finger against my lips, smearing her lipstick across it. I jerked back, partially at the pain and partially because what the hell?

"Since you've clearly been misinformed, let me set the record straight." She stuck her hand out like we were meeting for the first time. Then dropped it when I didn't take it. "Fine. Clearly you have no manners, but I do. Siren Finazzo."

I'd only just heard that surname an hour or so ago. "As in Gus Finazzo..."

She nodded triumphantly like she'd just laid a winning hand on the table. "His daughter. Slayers royalty, sweetie. War has been promised to me from birth. I'm the woman who'll take his surname once he's done sowing his wild oats. It might not be legal yet, but I'm his old lady. And now that he's king, that makes me queen." She sniffed like I was a piece of trash. "And you're just the girl he comes on."

---

*J* let the warm water pour over my head and scrubbed at the mess War had made on my skin. Outside the bathroom door, War and Siren argued, but I couldn't make out the words. I didn't even want to. I just wanted to get clean and then get out of here.

The bathroom door opened, and War appeared, closing the door behind him.

I avoided his eyes, turning away so I didn't have to meet them.

The flow of water didn't hide his zipper drawing down, or his cut and shirt hitting the floor. The glass door on the shower squeaked when he opened it and stepped in behind me.

His arms circled around my middle, resting below my breasts. His chest pressed to my back, and I fought the urge to lean back into him.

"Whatever she said, ignore."

I shook my head. "It's fine."

"She doesn't own me, Bliss."

"But the two of you are engaged?"

He sighed, tightening his grip on me and burying his face in the side of my neck. "We aren't engaged. Our dads wanted it—"

"She clearly does too."

"Too bad. It's not what I want."

I shook my head, pulling out of his arms and turning to face him. "It's not my business. We don't owe each other anything. We had sex a few times. That's it."

He raised an eyebrow. "It's more than that and you know it."

Warmth sizzled through me. "What then? You want to be my boyfriend?"

He chuckled. "I've never been anyone's boyfriend. It could be fun."

I shoved him. "Be serious. You don't want that."

His gaze was steady on my face when he replied. "I don't? Or you don't?"

He was right. Or we both were. He might have joked about it, but I knew enough from what he'd said about Gus and his dad that if making Siren his old lady was expected of him, going against that now could be a huge problem for him, and for his club.

But I didn't want to commit to something either. I hadn't forgotten Vincent's kiss and the way Nash's gaze lit me up inside. I wouldn't commit to someone when I had feelings, or at least an interest, in others. I wasn't that sort of woman.

War took the cloth from my hand and soaped it up. Then he ran it across my chest and over my breasts. He dipped lower to my belly and then swiped it over my mound, cleaning off every trace of him. He let the water wash the soap off, then dropped the cloth to the floor, his eyes searching mine with every movement. I was sure I was as attractive as a drowned rat and that my bruises from last night were showing as my makeup washed away, but I loved the way he looked at me. It was with a gentleness I wouldn't have ever expected from someone who was the president of an MC.

His hand moved between my legs, washing the spot where he'd rubbed his cum into my clit.

I gasped, my whole body lighting up for him again.

"Can we just keep doing what we're doing?" He rubbed small, tight circles. "I like you. I want to get to know you better. And just so you know, I'm so fucking attracted to you that if you say no, I'm gonna be stalking your social media for photos of you to jerk off over."

It lightened the mood enough that I snorted. "Eww. That's disgusting."

He smiled, and dammit if my knees didn't go weak.

"I can't help that you do it for me." He leaned in and licked away the stream of water running down my neck. "So it's settled? We'll keep doing what we're doing for as long as we both want to."

I couldn't deny him, even with Siren's words ringing in my head. The thought of never having sex with him again—the first good sex I'd ever had in my life—was a pitiful thought.

His fingers slipped up inside me when I nodded yes, and I clutched his wet biceps, using them to hold me up while he stroked my G-spot.

"There's something else I need to tell you while we're laying our cards out on the table," he said against my neck.

"Are we seriously going to have a conversation while you're getting me off? Oh God, keep doing that."

He chuckled, doing *that* again. "Someone was watching us outside."

I jerked my head up to look at him. "What? Who?"

"Vincent."

My mouth dropped open. "No!"

War grinned. "Yep. Second time the poor guy has had to watch us going at it. He's beginning to make a habit of it."

"What was he even doing here?"

"Following you, of course. The guy has it bad for you."

I shook my head. "He doesn't. He just..." It had been on the tip of my tongue to say he just took his job seriously. But it was Vincent who was like that. And Vincent would have never just stood in the bushes watching. The first time had been a misunderstanding.

The first time hadn't been Scythe.

"I'm going to kill him," I announced. "Did he see everything?"

War laughed. "Everything."

"Even when you...?"

"Everything."

I sighed. "I need to have words with him about boundaries." Then I shoved War's chest again. "Or with you! Did you know he was there the whole time?"

War laughed, adding his free hand to his attack on my pussy. "I did. And I liked it."

My eyes rolled back. I couldn't even be mad at him. Not when he was drawing a third orgasm from my body so perfectly it took my breath away. I'd known what we were doing out there. The thought of getting caught had turned me on.

I just hadn't expected Scythe, of all people, to be the one watching.

Vincent might have had a crush on me, but Scythe was incapable of feeling. Vincent had told me as much. And his actions last night had proved it. I could still feel his hand over mine, carving my name in Caleb's skin.

I shuddered.

Scythe did not have a crush on me.

He didn't have a heart to crush with.

My phone rang somewhere amongst our clothes, and I groaned, looking over at my pile of things. I could see it vibrating, but I couldn't see the caller ID. I needed to check it though. I was Verity and Everett's contact should Nichelle be unavailable in an emergency.

"Nuh-uh," War murmured, fingers thrusting in and out of me. "Not 'til you come."

"I already came twice."

"Not enough."

I was right on the verge, and I knew walking away from him now wasn't an option. I'd self-implode. The odds of it being Verity and Everett's school, and Nichelle and my father both being unavailable, were slim.

I gave myself over to the orgasm.

War caught me as my knees gave way, and then he made me come again before the hot water ran cold, forcing us both out.

War wrapped me in a fluffy gray towel and then wrapped another around his waist, tucking the ends in so it stayed up. He padded back into his living area and flopped down on a beaten-up, well-used, brown leather couch.

"So, you're just gonna lie there, like a Greek god, half naked and entirely distracting?" I couldn't keep my eyes off him. His chest and abs were like cut steel, and his towel was low enough to show off the delicious V lines on either side of his hips.

He dropped his head back over the arm of the couch and grinned at me. "Just hoping if I lie here like this long enough, you'll come ride my face." He reached for me, but I danced back out of his grasp.

"I need to check my phone and get dressed. I think I've reached the legal limit of orgasms allowed in one day."

He winked. "I have it on good authority that you aren't even close."

This man would ruin me. There was no doubt about that. When he was done and the way he made me feel went away, I'd mourn it.

The sex.

Him.

I bit my lip and turned away. My clothes were messed up, but I pulled on my underwear and then retrieved my phone from the bathroom floor. The missed call still sat on the screen, the number not one I recognized.

A kernel of worry opened up inside me. Everett and Verity's school had multiple phone lines, and though I had the main one saved to my contacts, they could be calling me on any number of different lines that wouldn't register in my phone.

War peered at me, flipping over onto his stomach so he wasn't looking at me upside down. "Something wrong?"

I shrugged while the call connected. "I don't know. I think it's Verity and Everett's school. Maybe one of them is sick—"

"Providence Police Department. How may I direct your call?"

They knew.

At least that meant Caleb was alive and not dead on the side of the road somewhere. But panic raced through my veins. I didn't have a cover story and I wasn't a liar. Whatever Caleb had told them, I would have to admit to. How long was the jail term for carving your name into someone's chest and then leaving them for dead?

War's warm hand wrapped around my bare thigh and squeezed. "Hey. You okay? Is it the school?"

I blinked and moved the speaker away from my mouth. "It's the cops."

"Hello? Is anyone there?"

I turned away from War's concerned frown and addressed the woman on the phone. "Yes. Sorry. I had a missed call from you. My name is Bethany-Melissa Arthur."

"One moment, please."

The hold music only played for a single heart-stopping moment before she was back on the line. "Ms. Arthur? Yes. We were calling to let you know your brother's body is being released from police custody. We'll need you to organize your funeral home..."

The rush of relief that crashed through me took my legs out with it. I sat heavily on the couch, War moving his feet to one side to give me room. It was about Axel. Not Caleb. I tried to get my heartbeat under control by sucking in a couple of slow breaths. "Have you found his killer then?" My head whirled. It had been weeks since Axel's murder, and I'd been waiting for the gang task force to investigate.

A tapping of keys came down the line. "It says investigations are pending. So which funeral home should we send the body to?"

"They've been pending for weeks! Has any progress been made?"

The woman sighed. "Ma'am. This is a gang-related case. They're very complicated. But I do have some more good news for you. Your brother's house and possessions are also being released. You're free to claim those anytime."

It was the same old bullshit lines I'd been fed for the past month.

The cops weren't doing anything to find Axel's killer. They didn't care. He was just some nameless, faceless man from Saint View who didn't matter.

But he'd mattered to me. He'd mattered to Nash, and

Rebel, and everyone who'd known him. It wasn't enough to just put his murder in the gang-related violence basket and call it done.

He deserved more.

And I was going to get it for him.

## 8

## BLISS

*W*ar dropped me back at Psychos for my evening shift. I wore the same clothes I'd had on all day but freshly washed and dried in the little laundry room in his cabin. I got off the back of his bike, tugging off the helmet he'd loaned me and gave it back to him.

He pushed his helmet over his head, hanging it over his handlebars, then did the same to mine.

I squeezed his arm. "Thanks for the ride. And for today."

"Pleasure was all mine."

I didn't want to let him go. "You sure you don't want to come in for a drink? I know the owner. She'll probably give us a freebie."

He chuckled, wrapping an arm around me and pulling me in. "I gotta get back. The place is still a disaster. Somebody needs to start cleaning it up."

I nodded. "See you soon?"

I hated how hopeful it sounded. My Providence

friend, Sandra, would have told me to play hard to get, but then again, Caleb had said something about Sandra telling everyone I was sleeping with multiple men, and so she wasn't exactly my favorite person right now.

War wrapped his fingers in the front of my shirt and tugged me down so my lips were just over his. "I can't fucking wait until your mouth heals so I can kiss you again. I'll see you really soon, Bliss."

Goosebumps spread across my skin at his promise, and I watched him peel out of the parking lot, already regretting my decision to come to work tonight when I could have just blown it off to hang out with him.

I'd become hooked on whatever drug War was and at risk of becoming codependent. So I turned and walked my ass inside my bar.

Scythe stood in the doorway, guarding the locked door into the side of the club where we held the parties.

I shot him a dirty look.

He frowned. "What?"

"Were you out at War's compound today?"

He rolled his eyes in a very un-Vincent-like way that was really beginning to grate on my nerves. "War is such a tattletale. So a guy jumps a secure fence and watches his boss get her pussy licked by a biker. Is that really such a crime?"

I gaped at him. "You are such a pervert!"

He raised one eyebrow. "I am? Or you are? You were the one writhing around in the dirt, begging him to pound you with his trouser snake."

I shoved two hands against his chest. "I did not beg him to pound me with his trouser snake!"

Scythe laughed, that deep, delicious sound hitting me right between the legs.

I narrowed my eyes. "How exactly do I get Vincent back?"

He shrugged. "He's left the building."

"I wish you'd leave the building."

He sniggered. "Why you gotta be like that, Bliss? I just want to be besties."

I flipped him the bird. "Is it possible to hate someone after only knowing them a few hours? Because I'm pretty sure I hate you."

I stormed past him, my cheeks burning at his teasing over how much I'd been into what War and I had been doing out in the woods. I was oddly hot at the same time though, thinking about the sexy, dangerous man who'd been watching.

Stupid.

I couldn't wait until Vincent was back.

I checked in with the guys working behind the bar, but it was very quiet. Nash and Rebel were both off, so I wandered back to my office, ignoring Scythe's attempts at conversation as I passed him.

I was tired and considered taking out a throw blanket and taking a nap on the little love seat, but that would hardly be setting a good example for the rest of the employees. Even though there wasn't much need to come out here when there wasn't a party on, I was determined to be a good boss. So I pulled out the chair behind my desk, plonked myself down into it, and opened my laptop.

I needed to organize a funeral.

My heart squeezed at the thought.

It had been so easy to block everything out since that

night Nash and I had found Axel's body. Psychos had fallen into my lap. I'd had Caleb to deal with and the overhanging worry of owing money to a man who still hadn't showed up for it. I'd lost my job, met Rebel and War and Vincent. Reconnected with Nash.

I hadn't even had a minute to grieve.

But last night had broken parts of me that would take more than a day of sex with War to repair. The pain of losing Axel wrapped its way around my heart, digging in and breaking it to pieces all over again.

Tears slid down my cheeks, and I wiped them away, but they were instantly replaced with more. So I gave in and let myself cry for the brother I'd lost and for the trauma I'd experienced.

A knock on my office door had me quickly wiping away my tears, though. "Go away, Sc—" I quickly corrected myself, knowing that even as annoying as Scythe was, I couldn't out him. "Vincent! I'm not in the mood."

The door opened anyway, and I shook my head in disbelief. "Are you deaf?"

Nash squinted at me from beneath his tousled brown hair. "Not deaf. Just not Vincent."

I relaxed my shoulders and waved him in. "Sorry."

He froze on the other side of my desk. "Have you been crying?"

"No."

He folded his arms across his chest. "Fine. I'll rephrase. Has water been falling from your eyes?"

The corner of my mouth flickered up. "Maybe. But I'm fine."

"You aren't. You're hurt. I fucking hate myself for

letting you go without me last night. Why the hell is Vincent even still here? He let this happen."

"It wasn't anyone's fault but Caleb's."

His eyes darkened. "You know I'm going to kill him, right?"

If I hadn't already.

Guilt seeped in, even knowing full well that he wouldn't have thought twice about killing me if given the opportunity. I hated that it was there. But I couldn't switch off the fact I was human, and a good person, and that my default nature wasn't murdering other people, even the ones who'd done me wrong.

I wondered what that said about War, Nash, and Scythe...who all seemed to have no problem with the idea of ending a life.

"He's not worth a life sentence. What are you doing here anyway? It's supposed to be your night off."

He shrugged, slumping down into the other seat. "It's probably no surprise, but I don't exactly have much of a life outside this place."

I eyed him. He was so devastatingly attractive. The fact he was fourteen years older than me didn't matter an ounce. Nash's blue eyes pierced right through me every time he looked at me. His brown hair was a little too long and had probably never seen more than a finger-comb. And yet his style was effortlessly hot. I loved how he'd made himself a uniform out of jeans, white T-shirts, and flannel shirts. And how his boots were always done up so loosely that they might fall off at any minute. Yet they never did.

He was tall, and strong, and the smile lines around his eyes only made him hotter.

I smiled at him. "Gonna be a pretty sad little birthday party we're throwing for you if you don't have any friends beside the ones who work here."

He gave me a deadpan look. "Thanks. That's super helpful, Bliss. Way to make me feel better."

I laughed. "You have friends."

He was dead serious when he answered, "I really don't."

I sobered. "People at your gym?"

"Do I seem like the sort of guy who goes to a gym?"

My gaze rolled over his biceps that strained at his shirt, and his flat stomach. His T-shirt did little to disguise the cut of his abs beneath it. "Yes," I replied honestly. "Have you seen yourself in a mirror?"

He looked briefly pleased by my observation, but then the smile disappeared. "I don't want a party."

"Too bad. You're having one. Nobody is turning forty on my watch and not celebrating it."

"I'm too old for this shit, Bliss."

"All the more reason to have one. It might be the last one you get to have before you kick the bucket."

He snorted. "You joke, but honestly, I feel a hundred some days."

I tossed a scrunched-up piece of paper at him, hating that the bar was taking so much out of him. "So change it. Take some time off. Do something wild or crazy or fun. You do remember what that is, right?"

"I don't know. I'm probably old enough to start worrying about Alzheimer's." He leaned across the desk and peered at what was on my laptop screen. "What are you doing anyway?"

"I got a call from the cops today. They're releasing

Axel's body. So we can finally have a funeral." I closed my eyes and scrubbed a hand through my hair. "Shit. I haven't even told my dad."

"Why on earth not?"

"I don't know. Axel went hand in hand with this club, and Saint View, and my mom..."

Nash's mouth pulled into a firm line. "Ah. All the things people don't like. Poverty. Dive bars. Crazy exes. Speaking of which, have you heard from your mom today?"

I shook my head. "No. But she hasn't got my number. I checked in with the bar staff when I got here, but no one had seen her."

Nash's frown deepened. "What are you going to do about her? If I know one thing about your mother, it's that if she even so much as smells a whiff of money, she's going to chase it."

"I don't know. I suppose technically she is entitled to half of Axel's estate."

Nash's frown turned into anger. "Fuck that. That woman did nothing for either you or your brother. Axel didn't want her around here. He flat-out barred her from coming in, not that it stopped her. But he threw her out every time, and I heard him more than once tell her to never come back. He was done with her shit, Bliss. You should be too."

But there was a tiny part of me that wouldn't be silenced on the matter. "I don't know. I feel sorry for her in a way."

Nash pinched the bridge of his nose, like I was giving him a headache. "You're too nice for your own good. You know that, right? Caleb already took advantage of it. I'm not going to let your mother do it as well."

"I think I should go see her."

"Why would you put yourself through that? Honestly, Bliss. I'm beginning to think you like torture. You know she still lives in that trailer on Westmont Street, right? Nothing has changed for her in the twenty years you've been gone. Do you really want to go back there and open up all those old wounds?"

I didn't. But it also didn't feel right to completely ignore her when she'd come searching for me. Things could be different now. I was a grown woman too. I wasn't scared five-year-old who didn't have enough to eat or a safe home. I wasn't a young, impressionable teen. We were on a more even playing field. Seeing her again was long overdue and a skeleton in my closet that needed to be faced. We'd both lost Axel. She had to feel what I felt.

*I* looked at Nash.

He rolled his eyes. "You always were stubborn. When are we going?"

Relief rushed through me. "You're going to come with me?"

"You really think I'd let you face her alone?"

# 9

## NASH

*S*aint View Trailer Park only got more run-down every time I came here. It had been years since my last visit, not since before I'd gone to jail. In that time, kids had grown up, some moving on, some not, but the adults who'd been here back then had stayed. Poverty was a vicious cycle and one that was incredibly hard to get out of once it had grips on you. Many people who lived here would probably be here for life.

Axel had gotten out. So had Bliss. Most people probably assumed I had too. I had a house—admittedly it was in Saint View, but it wasn't deep in the ghetto, like the trailer park was—and I had a job. Food on my table. Clean clothes on my back. All the markings of someone who'd made a success of himself when his humble beginnings had tried to drag him down.

Yet I felt a kinship with this park and the people inside it.

You could take the boy out of the trailer park, but you couldn't take the trailer park out of the boy.

But even if I belonged here, Bliss didn't. She never had. She'd always been too cute, too sweet, too innocent for a life like this. The best thing Axel and I had ever done was getting her out. This life would have eaten her up and swallowed her whole. I couldn't even imagine what would have happened to her if she'd been left to be raised by her mother.

And Jerry.

Instinctively, I picked up Bliss' hand, threading my fingers between hers.

Her head jerked up in surprise. "You're holding my hand," she whispered.

I was and I hated how much I liked it. Especially because I knew exactly how much Axel would have disapproved. He'd always talked about how she'd end up with someone from her side of town. Someone who lived in a big mansion and had enough money to give her whatever she wanted.

Her fingers were soft and warm and fit perfectly between mine. I fought the urge to rub my thumb across her knuckles. As it was, the way I was holding her hand was already overly familiar. I didn't need to make it worse with affectionate touches. "I'm just getting ready to yank you behind me in case of gunfire or crackheads."

Bliss laughed nervously, but she stuck close to my side, probably knowing I wasn't exaggerating for comedic effect. "It's really strange to be back here."

"I told you nothing had changed."

"I know. But I didn't really believe you." She gazed around, taking in the buildings that lined the walkways through the park. Each home was more dilapidated than the last. At best, they needed paint and cleaning and junk removal. At worst they needed gaping holes patched, doors reattached, and reports made to CPS.

The farther into the park we went, the slower Bliss' footsteps got.

"You don't have to do this. You know that, right?"

"I do. I can't keep hiding from her."

"You aren't hiding. You're living your life. A good life. One that you don't need tainted with all of this shit."

"It's still a part of me."

I sighed. Because I knew exactly what she meant. I'd grown up in the trailer on the other side of the park to Axel and Bliss.

"Are you going to visit your parents while we're here?"

I shook my head. "Not a chance in hell. You might be a sucker for punishment, but I'm here only as your body-guard. The quicker we get out of here the better." I could practically feel the pull of this place, drawing me back in, whispering this was really where I belonged. I didn't want to listen. Especially because I knew it was probably true.

"I appreciate it." She squeezed my hand.

I didn't dare look at her for fear my attraction would be written all over my face. I was playing with fire even being this close to her.

We rounded a corner, dodging a boy riding around on a bike he'd probably stolen. Bliss stopped walking.

Her mom's trailer lay dead ahead. And just like so many nights, so long ago, shouts traveled back to us from inside the depths of Bliss' childhood home.

Bliss sucked in a deep breath and stopped walking. "Jerry is here." Her white teeth sank into her bottom lip, drawing it out slowly. "Shit. I just assumed he wouldn't be."

We both stood in silence for a moment, listening to her mom and stepfather scream at each other.

"He won't lay a hand on you."

"I know. Come on. Let's just get this over and done with."

She pulled ahead, and I followed. She didn't let go of my hand, and I sure as hell wasn't letting go of hers. Like she'd made up her mind, she lifted her head and strode the rest of the way.

"Go, little rock star," I murmured, pride filling me at the confidence she'd managed to muster up.

She rapped her knuckles across the door, and the screaming argument from inside cut out instantly.

"What do you want?" Jerry shoved open the trailer's crooked door, letting it swing back and clash against the side. His unsteady gaze wandered over Bliss without recognition. Then it flickered to me, and his grin slowly grew. "Nashy, Nash, Nash. I knew you'd be back. Took your time though." His gaze wandered back to Bliss, and he shoved his meaty hands into the pockets of his stained jeans. "And who have you brought me?"

He leered at her, licking his lips while his gaze raked over her indecently.

I expected her to shudder and move away. Maybe even take a step back and stand behind me. God knows that's exactly where I wanted her. Out from under his filthy gaze and with me between them. But when I tugged on her hand, she stood her ground. Another flash of pride rolled through me. She might have become soft and delicate. But there was still a little of the hood rat inside her who had to be strong, no matter what.

"I want to speak to my mother, please."

Jerry's eyes widened. "Your mother? You got the wrong house, lady."

"No, Jerry. I don't."

Kim appeared in the doorway behind her partner. Her eyes went wide, and she shoved Jerry's arm.

He shoved her right back, sending her crashing into the wall.

It didn't matter that I hated Bliss' mom with everything I had. A growl rolled up my chest and I stepped forward, ready to go eye to eye with Jerry. But Bliss planted herself firmly between us, a silent roadblock in my way. My front touched her back, and she reached a hand back, pressing it against the side of my leg in a gesture meant to calm.

Kim stumbled to the door again. "Bliss?"

"Would you look at that," Jerry drawled, recognition finally dawning. "The prodigal daughter has returned to our humble abode. Fine as fuck and ready to make some money too. Good catch, Nashy boy."

I twisted my fingers into fists that begged to be planted in the older man's face.

Bliss ignored him, though, focusing on her mother.

Kim stared at her like she'd seen a ghost. Her eyes went wide, gaze sweeping over Bliss in a completely different way to how Jerry had just a moment earlier. "Oh, sweetheart." She pushed past Jerry to throw her arms around Bliss' neck. Her dramatic sobs and cries of her baby coming home rang out for the entire trailer park to hear.

Bliss stood stock-still, stiff in her mother's embrace. She didn't try to return the hug.

She didn't stop it either.

Eventually, Jerry yanked Kim off her by the back of her shirt. "Shut up, would you?" He smacked his lips together over Bliss. "Always knew you were going to be a beauty one day. Once you lose some weight, you'll make great money with that pretty face." He chuckled. "You can practice on me in the meantime."

There was no holding me back. I launched myself at Jerry, slamming him up against the side of the trailer, letting his head smack into it in much the same way the door had. "You so much as breathe too close to her, and I'll fucking kill you."

Jerry chuckled, patting my hands that desperately wanted to wrap around his neck. "No you won't."

"Try me, old man. You think I'm still that scrawny twentysomething who couldn't stand up to you? Times have changed."

His rotted canines appeared when his smile widened. "Not that much. I might be older, but I still got people watching out for me. Do you? Axel surely didn't."

The implication I hadn't been there for my best friend sliced right through me. As did the knowledge that he was right. It had always been me and Axel against the world. Now that he was gone, I had no one.

My grip loosened on his shirt, and Bliss took the opportunity to pull me back.

Ignoring Jerry completely, she faced her mother. "Kim, I—"

Kim's face crumpled. "You don't even call me Mom anymore?"

Bliss finally lost her patience. "When were you ever a mom to me? When I was crawling around that trailer floor, hoping you'd dropped a scrap I could eat to ward off the hunger pains? Or when you were leaving me alone for hours or days at a time before I was even old enough to get myself a cup of water?"

"Bliss, I—"

"The only time you were a mom to me was the day you gave me up."

"That was the worst day of my life."

"Well, it was the best day of mine."

Kim's face crumpled. They might have even been real tears this time.

The truth hurt. But I didn't have an ounce of sympathy for the woman. She was a victim of the cycle as much as anyone, but Bliss had always had a way out, and Kim had never tried to get it for her.

A real parent would have done that for their child.

But it was me who'd done that. Me and Axel who had loved her enough to want better for her.

Bliss shook off her mother's pleading. "I came to tell you that Axel's funeral is being held on Thursday morning, at the Saint View Cemetery."

Kim let the theatrics fall. "I'll be there."

Bliss faltered for a second, and I was sure she was seeing what I did. True remorse in Kim's bloodshot eyes.

For Bliss' sake, I hoped she did show up and that Kim was honestly mourning the loss of her son. He never would have wanted her there, but at least a tiny part of Bliss did. Funerals weren't for the dead. They were for those left behind.

Maybe it was that mother-daughter bond because I certainly didn't feel it. Not for Kim. And not for my own mother, who was no better.

Bliss nodded and turned on her heel. I followed close behind.

"What about the money?" Kim called. "Half of that bar is mine."

There it was. The reason I felt no sympathy for her or my own mother. Because every time you tried to give one of them a chance, they threw it back in your face. Rage blew up inside me. I knew Bliss had come here hoping for more. Hoping that maybe, after all these years, she'd changed.

But a leopard couldn't change their spots any better than Kim could care for anyone other than herself.

Bliss just stared, but there was defeat in her face.

"Not one inch of that bar is ever going to be yours, Kim. Axel would be rolling over in his grave if we let it go to you. You want it? Fight us for it in court." I put my arm around Bliss' shoulders and guided her away, hating I'd known this was how it would end.

"Fuck you, Nash. You high-and-mighty asshole."

Something skidded across the dirt just to my left, but I didn't even bother stopping to examine whatever it was she'd thrown at me.

Jerry's amused voice called back to us, "Good to see you, daughter dear. Nash, when you're ready to get back into the game, you know where I am."

"What does he mean by that?" Bliss asked.

"I don't know," I lied.

Even though I knew exactly what he meant.

I just wished like hell I could erase the past so my lie could have been my truth.

## 10

### SCYTHE

*I* got home on Friday night after my shift at Psychos to a quiet house. Bliss was nowhere to be seen, but neither was Little Dog, which made me pretty sure Bliss was indeed home. Otherwise, the overgrown gerbil would have been barking and growling at me, which seemed to be her new favorite pastime.

I shrugged out of the leather jacket I'd found in the back of Vincent's closet that morning and dropped it on the entryway table. "Honey, I'm home!"

There was no human answer, but Little Dog's angry barks led me up the stairs.

I flung Bliss' bedroom door open with a flourish. "What are you guys doing?"

She jumped a mile, then spun around with her hand over her heart, her chest rising and falling rapidly. "Dammit, Scythe! What the hell? Have you heard of knocking?"

I squinted at her. "I have."

"I could have been naked!"

"And I would have been pleased."

She grabbed a pen from the writing desk and threw it at me.

I caught it easily before it could hit me in the head and placed it back in the pen holder. "That wasn't very safe. You could have taken my eye out."

"And I would have been pleased," she mocked sarcastically.

I threw myself across her neatly made bed, ignored her protests about wrinkling the covers, and flopped onto my back. I wriggled a little to get comfortable and propped my hands behind my head on her soft pillows. "This bed is nice. I should sleep in here." I wriggled my eyebrows at her. "Or we could *not* sleep in here, if you know what I mean."

From the foot of the bed, Little Dog growled, and I narrowed my eyes at her. "Dog meat is a delicacy in some countries, you know."

Bliss scooped her up into her arms like I might actually turn Vincent's pet into a stew. "What do you want, Scythe?"

"To hang out. I'm bored."

"Go read a book."

I wrinkled my nose. "That sounds like a Vincent thing."

She smiled sweetly. "Then please bring him back so Vincent can go read a book and you can stop putting your boots on my bed." She shoved my feet to the side so they dangled over the edge, making a spot for her to sit with the shoe muncher.

I toed my boots off and then stuck my feet on her lap.

She glared at me, shoving them off again. "Go play video games then."

"That's for losers who can't get laid."

She raised one eyebrow. "Sounds like you'd fit right in."

"Hey! I could get laid."

Bliss gestured around the bedroom. "And yet here you are, on a Friday night, hanging out at home with me."

I sat up, grinning at her. "And how do you know that sex wasn't exactly what I came in here for?"

She rolled her eyes. "I'm not sleeping with you."

"You slept with War."

"Because I actually *like* him."

I clutched a hand over my chest, like her words had stabbed me right through it. "That hurts, Bliss. That hurts real bad." I nudged at her thigh with my sock-covered foot. "Seriously, though. Why don't you like me? You like Vincent. And War. And Nash. Pretty sure that means you aren't into women."

She scoffed. "So just because I'm straight, you assume I should fall at your feet?"

I shrugged. "Women normally do." I flashed her a smile. "I'm way more charming than Vincent. He's so awkward it makes me want to die."

"What a shame you didn't."

I sniggered. "Come on. Why don't you like me? I've been trying so hard."

She stared at me. "Are you joking?"

"Did you laugh? Because I'm also hilarious. And if I was joking, you'd be in hysterics."

She made a noise of frustration in the back of her

throat. "You forced me to carve my name into a man's body. While he was still alive, mind you!"

I frowned. "Would it have been better for you if he were dead?"

She threw her hands up so suddenly that Little Dog skittered away from her in fright and closer to me.

I took my chance and put a hand out to her, ready to stroke her fur.

She bared her teeth.

Geez. Was every female in this room premenstrual today?

Bliss was still glaring at me.

I sighed. "Okay, fine. What do you want me to say? I'm sorry for the name carving?"

"That would be a start."

"Yeah, well. I could. But I'm not going to."

She shook her head. "Of course not. I don't know why I would have even hoped for something so out there as a simple 'I'm sorry.'" She stood and turned her back on me, storming for the door.

I was on my feet with my fingers around her wrist before she could get a hand to the knob. I yanked her arm just hard enough to stop her, and when she spun back, I was close enough that she hit my chest.

I drank in her gasp of surprise, her soft tits against me. Her free hand rested over my chest, and I was sure I could feel the uneven thumping of her heart.

Electricity crackled in the space between us.

I gazed down at her, her eyes locking with mine.

I grinned. "This would be so much better if we were naked."

Moment over.

She shoved away from me. "Ugh. You're the worst. Get out of my bedroom."

"Not until you admit the real reason you're angry and avoiding me is because you liked what you did to Caleb."

She froze.

Her gaze dropped to the floor, but it wasn't quick enough. I'd hit the nail on the head. I knew it just from her expression.

I put one finger beneath her chin and lifted it so she had no choice but to look me in the eye. "You can say it."

She shook her head.

I chuckled. "Truly, you're in good company. Because I enjoyed it too."

"You're a psychopath though."

I shrugged. "There's a little psychopath in all of us. I wear mine on my sleeve. Most people keep theirs buried. You just let yours out to play for a moment." I grinned at her. "I liked her. Psycho Bliss with blood on her hands was sexy as hell."

But Bliss was done with my teasing. She swallowed thickly; her worry written all over her face. "What if he's dead?"

"Then good riddance."

"Scythe!" she wailed.

With a heavy sigh, I let my hand drop away from her face. I plonked back down on the edge of her bed and started putting my shoes back on.

When she just watched me, I pointed at her bare feet. "Get some shoes on."

"Why?"

"We're gonna go find Caleb."

*I* drove Bliss' car, since mine was probably now at a junkyard, completely written off after Vincent's woeful driving. Dumbass hadn't even wiped the steering wheel down before he'd abandoned it, so it was probably full of our fingerprints. Which wasn't great. They'd have already run those through the system and matched them.

Which meant the cops knew I was still in town.

And so would Tabor, the prison warden whose nose I had escaped out from under.

I laughed thinking about it.

"What?" Bliss asked.

"I'm just thinking about somebody I used to know."

"Are they dead now?"

I shot her a look. "I don't kill everyone I meet, you know."

"Just checking."

Vincent's grip on me when he'd been incarcerated, and in the weeks since, had been weak at best. I'd seen more of his life than I had in years. The way he'd cared and protected for the friends he'd made inside had filtered through so thickly to me, that Mae, Heath, Rowe, and Liam felt as much like my friends as his.

"Where are we going?" Bliss asked. "This isn't the way to the cliffs."

"No. It's not. Because I already know that your worm of an ex won't be up there."

She glanced at me from the passenger seat. "He is if he's dead."

"I'm one-hundred-percent certain the man is not dead."

"You can't know that after what we did."

"You ever had a surgery?"

She crossed her arms beneath her breasts, huddling in on herself. "I broke my arm once when I was a kid and it needed to have screws and plates put in. But what's your point?"

"Did you tell the doctor how to do your surgery?"

"Of course not."

"Then why are you telling the contract killer whether he killed a man or not? Caleb's wounds were barely more than scratches."

"Your definition of scratches and mine are very different."

I spun the wheel, making the turn into Caleb's street, huge houses flashing by outside, not all that different to the one I'd conveniently borrowed from my parents.

With every passing second, Bliss shrank more and more in on herself.

It irked me.

I'd only planned on parking down the road and observing, or maybe sneaking her up to his window for a peep, but the fact she was still scared of the little weasel, even though he'd practically begged for his mommy up on the cliffs, called for more drastic measures.

I jerked the wheel again, parking right in the middle of Caleb's driveway. "Come on. Get out."

She did, and I met her on her side, putting my hand around hers and pulling her toward the door.

Halfway up the drive, she froze. "I don't know about this, Scythe. What are we going to do? Just walk up, knock on the door, and say, 'Oh, hey, just doing a wellness check after we tried to murder you two days ago.'"

We got to the front door, an ugly modern thing with no charm or charisma. "Sounds like a good plan to me. Except the knocking part. I don't knock."

To prove my point, I raised one foot and sent it straight into the wood with a thump.

Bliss squealed, but the door splintered open with a crack, revealing the darkened hallway beyond. An alarm went off, echoing around the too-big house and piercing through my ears.

"What did you do that for?" Bliss hissed, hurrying to the control panel on the wall and tapping at the buttons.

"What's his password?" I watched her fingers dance over the keys. "Your birthday? The day you started dating?"

She hit the enter key, and the noise cut out, blissful silence resuming once more. "You don't even want to know."

We walked through the dark house, glancing into the living room on the right, and then moved into the kitchen on the left. "Actually, I want to know even more now because you're being all secretive about it. His mom's birthday? Your social security number? Surely, he wouldn't be dumb enough to use his own?"

She shook her head, running a hand over the kitchen counter that was littered with half-eaten take-out containers and spoiling milk. "This place is a pigsty. I've never seen it like this."

"He's a slob. But you're avoiding the question. What's his code?"

She tossed me an annoyed glare. "It's the number of women he's slept with."

It took a minute for that to sink in. "Is it zero-zero-zero-two then?" I burst out laughing.

Bliss didn't. "He was a bachelor when he moved in here, okay?"

I tried to shove my laughter down. "He was a fuckboy from day one. He admitted that and you stayed with him?"

She shoved her hands on her hips. "Fuck you, Scythe."

I blinked. "Holy shit. She swears."

She stomped toward the stairs, scowl firmly etched on her face.

I cringed. She actually looked really mad. "Oops. I fucked that up, didn't I?" I murmured to the empty kitchen.

*Royally.*

"How was I supposed to know she was so touchy?"

*Fix it, Scythe!*

I jogged up the stairs behind her, stopping her by putting my hand around her middle and pulling her back tight against my chest.

She let out a surprised "oof" but didn't stop me.

I dropped my head so my face brushed her ear. "Hey. I'm sorry. I took the joke too far."

"I already feel like an idiot. I don't need you making it worse."

My heart picked up its pace at having her so close. Her honeysuckle scent wafted around me, and her soft curves were perfect in every way. I needed to let her go before my dick got hard, and I wanted to do a whole lot more than just stop her from running away.

She ran her hand over the polished wood banister. "He attacked me here, on these steps, right before we broke up." A shiver rolled through her body.

"He's never going to do that again, Bliss. Never."

She nodded.

I released her and followed her up the stairs, presumably to Caleb's room. She paused at the doorway, glaring at me when I lifted my foot to kick it in again.

I dropped it back to the floor obediently and waited for her to open the door the boring way.

Caleb's room was empty.

Bliss turned huge, worried eyes on me. "He's not here. I told you! He's probably dead up on those cliffs and some backpacker is going to stumble across his body when their dog runs off into the bushes and comes back with a severed hand!"

I almost laughed at how ridiculously dramatic she was being. I surely hadn't been this hysterical the first time I'd killed someone. "Hey, if the dumbass severed his own hand after we left, I really can't be held accountable."

"Scythe! Be serious!"

A tiny noise caught my attention. I paused for a moment, listening, then rolled my eyes and took two steps toward the bed. I crouched, peering beneath it.

Caleb's terrified eyes stared back at me.

"Hey, little buddy," I coaxed, like he was a frightened kitten. "You wanna come out and say hello? No one will hurt you." I coughed and murmured, "Much," at the same time, while fighting back my laughter.

The man was fucking pathetic.

"Please don't hurt me," he begged.

I glanced at Bliss. "He sounds pretty alive to me. I think I won the bet. You owe me. I take payments in the three B's. Beer, bowling, or blow jobs."

"We didn't make a bet," Bliss protested while I reached beneath the bed frame and dragged Caleb out by his shirt. "I owe you nothing. Most definitely not a blow job." She wrinkled her nose. "And bowling? What, with the stinky rented shoes? Really?"

Caleb howled and carried on like a cat who'd just been put in a bathtub, but I ignored his trembling and terrified pleas for his life and flipped him onto his back. I knelt across him, my knees either side of his chest, while I pinned his arms. "You look like shit, bro."

His eyes were rimmed with black circles, his cheeks sunken and gaunt. He looked like a man who'd made a very big mistake in attacking a woman in my presence.

I didn't have an ounce of sympathy for him.

He didn't even try to fight back. He knew who the alpha dog was. And it sure as fuck wasn't him. His sobs for mercy echoed around the quiet room.

I glanced at Bliss. "I think we broke him."

There was no sympathy on her face either, and I had a feeling reliving that moment on the stairs had stiffened her spine. She was a different woman now that she'd set eyes on the man she thought she'd killed, and seen that actually, the piece of shit was very much still alive.

Bliss reached between us and yanked his shirt up.

"Aw. He got a Band-Aid!" I crowed.

In fact, the dressing that covered my handiwork on

Caleb's chest was a huge piece of gauze, taped down all around the edges.

I poked at the center experimentally, and Caleb let out another ear-piercing wail.

"My God, you're a little bitch, aren't you?" I poked him a bit more, just for fun. "You can dish it out, but you can't take it. That right?"

I leaned down, getting right in his face, even though it was disgusting, mixed with his tears and snot. "You think this hurts? This is nothing compared to what you did to her. If I'd known exactly how much of a rapey, misogynistic narcissist you were, I never would have gone so easy on you." I looked up at Bliss. "Wanna see your handiwork?"

Something glinted in her eye when she stared down at the man she'd once called her fiancé.

I had no more doubt she was going to be worrying about whether this asshole lived or died.

She ripped the bandage off Caleb's chest. He winced at the ripping noise.

"Oooh." I winced right along with him. "All those chest hairs came right off, huh? Like that tape was a wax strip. Did it hurt?" Then I glanced down at the mess on Caleb's chest. "Oh shit. Probably pales in comparison to that, huh?" I studied our carving. "Probably could have been neater if you hadn't been squirming around so much."

Even so, Bliss' name was spelled out in stitched-up slashes on his chest. They were an angry red and perfectly delightful, if you asked me.

"What did you tell the hospital?" Bliss asked.

"Nothing. Same as what I said to the cops. So please.

Just let me go. I haven't said anything, and I'm not going to."

I glanced up at Bliss. "You believe him?"

She nodded, but her gaze never left his. "You ever so much as think about hurting another woman the way you hurt me, he'll be back. Next time, I won't stop him."

I grinned triumphantly at her making death threats on my behalf.

Sexy.

"I won't. I swear, Bethany-Melissa. Please. I'm sorry. I'm so sorry, baby."

"Does anyone else have vomit in their mouth?" I fake gagged. "Don't call her that. Good grief."

Bliss had clearly had enough. She walked out of the room and down the stairs.

I looked down at Caleb, my gaze narrowing now that Bliss was out of earshot. Something dark swirled inside me. It was the one thing that connected me and Vincent. He always blamed it on my influence, but it wasn't. The darkness had a mind of its own, one neither of us could truly control. Vincent might not enjoy it, but I did. "You're celibate. From now on. Your dick doesn't go near a woman. Bliss is more forgiving than I am, and I don't think for a second that you've learned your lesson from this. But mark my words, Caleb. You touch another woman, whether it be next week, or next decade, I'll know. And in the middle of the night, I'll climb into your bed and carve *my* name in your tiny dick. I'd bet you could bleed out from that and not a soul would miss you. Because you're that fucking pathetic."

I patted his healing chest again, none to softly, then used that spot to get myself up.

Caleb immediately curled into the fetal position, and I walked away without another glance.

———

*B*liss didn't talk on the drive back to my house, and for once, I didn't feel like talking either. For the first time though, the silence felt companionable, rather than awkward or fearful.

In my driveway, she pulled herself slowly from the car. I matched her pace, not wanting to leave her alone outside. At the top of the stairs, I unlocked the door and pushed it open, holding it for her so she could go ahead.

She stopped and raised her head. My gaze met hers, but I kept control of my impulsive tongue and remained silent. Not dominating the conversation. Not teasing. I just shut up and let her lead.

She lifted up on her toes and grazed her lips over my cheek.

Without a word, she walked inside and up to her bedroom, scooping up a yipping Little Dog as she passed.

I just stood there, the feel of her lips against my cheek lingering.

Eventually, I sank down onto the steps, breathing in the cool night air, and contemplated why a tiny brush of Bliss' lips had such a devastating effect on my body. Everything inside me was quiet. All the conflict and struggle Vincent and I constantly fought went away.

It was odd and unsettling. But also kind of nice. It was the same silence I felt after I drew a knife blade across someone's throat, only nobody had had to die to calm the storm inside me.

"What are you doing sitting out here on the step in the middle of the night?"

I glanced up to find my mother in front of me, her car keys and phone clutched in one hand, and a plastic supermarket bag in the other.

I hadn't even heard her pull up. "Hello to you too, Mother. I'm out here contemplating why you haven't dug out that freaking ugly rose bush." I squinted at it, just to my mother's left. "Didn't we discuss this years ago when we all lived in this house?" I dragged my gaze back to her. "Honestly. The neighbors are going to think I have no class."

She dropped the shopping bag at the exact same moment she dropped her jaw to stare at me bug-eyed. "No...Scythe?"

"The one and only."

She gave a tiny yip of joy and bent down to throw her arms around my neck. She squeezed me hard and planted a hundred little kisses all over the top of my head, while I laughed and batted her off. "So does that mean you're pleased to see me?"

She sat beside me with a wide smile on her aging face. "You have no idea. Oh, this is so wonderful! And changes everything. Do you know what Vincent was planning?"

"I have some idea."

She went on like I hadn't spoken. "Marriage! And children! He even started working a job. Can you imagine?"

"The daycare was okay," I murmured, though it was lost to her excited chatter.

"But none of that matters anymore. Because you're

here." She stood and crossed the yard to the trash can. There, she lifted the lid and dumped the plastic shopping bag inside.

"What was in the bag?"

She waved her hand around like it was unimportant. "Chocolate ice cream."

I gaped at her. "Why would you throw out perfectly good chocolate ice cream? Damn, Mother. Who hurt you? Because only a monster would do such a thing."

She raised an eyebrow. "It's so strange to hear humor come out of your mouth."

"Yeah, well. Vincent can't help that he's as funny as a lobotomy."

"You know he wants to get out of the business altogether."

My fingers twitched, and I suddenly wished I had a knife blade to play with. "No more slitty, stabby, knife life? What will he even do in his spare time? That would be a sad little existence."

"Wouldn't it! I'm so glad we're in agreement. So there'll be none of that. I'll get you a job bag ASAP because you must be itching."

I didn't tell her about running my blade into Caleb's skin. Besides, it had barely taken the edge off. "Definitely. Bring me something to do."

She slapped her hand down on my leg. "Excellent! So that just leaves one thing to discuss."

"What's that?"

"He wants to marry the fat girl."

I blinked. "Excuse me?"

"The one who's been hanging around. Come on,

Scythe. You know the one. It's not like you have more than one woman living here."

I didn't like the sneer in her tone. "Bliss. Her name is Bliss."

"That's right. Ridiculous, stupid name. Anyway. Obviously, that can't happen. She's not one of us."

"She makes him happy." The argument was out of my mouth before I'd even truly considered it.

I never argued with Mother. I had no reason to. She brought me jobs I would enjoy. I did said jobs. She paid me money. Everybody lived happily ever after.

Except for the guy I whacked.

I knew it wasn't such smooth sailing for Vincent. I could only be glad I hadn't seen the conversation where he'd told her he wanted to quit to get married and have kids.

That would not have gone down well.

"Yes, well, that's even more dangerous, isn't it? If she likes him too, there's only one thing for it."

"Mmm? What's that?"

Her profile was obscured by shadows. "We have to get you married to someone else before Vincent returns."

## 11

# WAR

*T*he walkie-talkie on my nightstand blasted a static-laced chirp that was about the worst possible way to wake up. It set my teeth on edge, as did Fang's voice coming out of the speaker, calling my name. "Prez. The new bodyguard from Psychos is here. Says he has a meeting with you."

Ugh. It was too early in the morning for this bullshit.

I scrubbed a hand across my face, trying to wake up, and reached out a hand for the walkie-talkie so I could respond. "Tell him to fuck off and come back at a reasonable hour. Only birds get up this early."

There was a pause, and then, "He said to tell you that while you were sleeping, he found forty-seven issues with our security, breached the fence multiple times, and that your cabin is so lacking he knows you sleep naked." There was another pause, and then Fang's voice came through again, clearly holding back laughter. "He's saying you have a nice dick."

I glanced down at myself, as naked as the day I'd been

born. Then over at my door. Sure enough, it was open a crack. I knew for a fact I'd closed it last night.

Well, fuck.

At least he liked my dick.

"Fine. Send him into the clubhouse and I'll meet him there."

I tossed the walkie-talkie onto the bed and then rolled myself out of it. In my chest of drawers, I found a clean pair of jeans and a long-sleeved black T-shirt. There was no need to do my hair if I wore a baseball cap, so I found a black one and shoved it on my head. Clean socks, my favorite pair of boots, and I was on my way to the clubhouse with a rumbling stomach, hoping like hell somebody else was awake to make some food.

No one was hanging around out in front of the clubhouse, probably because it was cold as the Arctic this morning. So I went straight in through the side door. Despite the early hour, people were awake. Queenie sat at the bar, bleary-eyed and sipping a steaming cup of coffee. Siren sat by her side with a full face of makeup and not enough clothes on for how chilly it was.

"Hey, baby," she murmured in my direction. "Daddy's making bacon and egg sandwiches for breakfast. You want one?"

I ignored her, still pissed over the bullshit she'd pulled in my cabin with Bliss. "What's different in here?" I wrinkled my nose. "It smells weird."

Gus stuck his head out of the kitchen doorway on the left. "I had a cleaner come out. That thing you can smell? It's called disinfectant. This place was disgusting."

I couldn't deny that was true. Our cleaning routine was nonexistent at the best of times, normally piling up until somebody had had enough of it. But with so many extra people here for my dad's funeral, it had gotten out of control. Calling people to come in and take care of it had been on my list of things to do, I just hadn't gotten there yet. As much as I didn't like Gus, or the fact he was still here, hanging around, I appreciated it.

I nodded at him.

He wiped his hands on an apron he had tied around his trim waist. "I restocked the refrigerator too. Got enough food to make everyone breakfast today and some stuff for a cookout."

Ice glanced over from where he was sprawled across one of the couches. "He got us beer and bourbon too. Your old man is a good one, Siren. Looking after us."

Siren beamed at Ice and then at her dad. "He's the best."

Gus shook his head. "Now, now. I'm just trying to help War get back on his feet. I know he would have done all these things for y'all but he's got a lot on his mind right now, what with Fancy still being in the hospital, and taking on the president's patch." He eyed me. "Your cut still says VP, son. You're gonna need to change that."

"I'm on it."

I was uncomfortable with everything Gus had done. He'd done a really good job of getting everyone on side and acting like he was just trying to be a friend. Yet something told me not to trust him.

I couldn't very well say that while everyone else was gazing at him with love hearts in their eyes 'cause he'd sprayed around a bit of lemon-scented water and made them some bacon.

"Has anyone seen Vincent? Bodyguard from Psychos? Tall. Dark. Not wearing an MC cut?"

Ice flicked his head toward a doorway. "Fang sent him to church since that's the only place around here where you can have a quiet conversation."

I nodded my thanks at him and told Gus to bring us in a couple of sandwiches when they were ready.

Our church was nothing holy. There was no pretty stained-glass windows or crucifixes. It was just the term we, and every other, MC used for the room where meetings took place. It wasn't often we had someone in here who wasn't a patched-in member of the club, but Vincent sat at the head of the table, his feet crossed and propped up on the tabletop. He reclined in his chair with his hands behind his head, eyes closed.

My gaze flickered to his biceps for half a second before traveling over his relaxed face and lower. His T-shirt clung like a second skin to his pecs and abs.

"You just gonna stand there fucking me with your eyes or are you gonna buy me dinner first?"

My gaze slammed into his.

He smirked.

I probably should have been embarrassed, but the fact was, I had been checking him out. "You're in my seat."

"I know."

He made no attempt to move.

I chuckled and took the seat to his left. It was the one I'd always sat in as VP so I was more comfortable in it anyway. "Wouldn't have picked you as the type who likes to be wined and dined."

"Maybe less on the wine and dine and more on the

beer and blow jobs." He leaned forward. "Hey, do you like bowling? I mentioned it to Bliss last night, and she thought it was gross."

I shrugged. "Beer, bowling, and blow jobs are three of my favorite things."

He slammed his hand down on the tabletop. "See! That's what I was saying. She didn't see the appeal."

I snorted. "Well, she wouldn't, would she? She hasn't got a dick. Speaking of, do you want to maybe try closing my door the next time you sneak into my cabin to check out my cock? There was a cold breeze that killed my morning erection dead."

"Looked fine to me."

I raised an eyebrow. "You flirting with me, Vincent?"

He shrugged, resting his elbows on the tabletop. "Your security is truly awful. You do realize that, don't you? Your mountain man on the gate is suitably terrifying, but you have approximately seven billion miles of fence line, none of it is particularly strong, and your cameras are intermittent at best. Honestly. A zombie horde would take you guys out in a heartbeat. And then what would you do?"

"Be zombie chow, I guess."

Vincent frowned. "You guys have clearly pissed someone off if your old man's accident is anything to go by. Bliss hangs out here. I need her to be safe. She doesn't seem to like it when I follow her around and watch the two of you having sex, so I'm really gonna need you to step up your security game."

I sobered, knowing he was right. It wasn't just Bliss' safety I needed to worry about. There were all my guys, their wives, and some even had kids living here on the compound, either in cabins like mine or in their rooms at the main clubhouse. It was something I hadn't really put much thought into before my old man had been murdered, but now, with my mom still in the hospital, it was something that had fallen on me.

We weren't safe. Not out on the road. Not here. Someone had it out for us. I had no idea why, but my father's death hadn't been an accident.

"So we replace the fences. Upgrade the security cameras. What else?"

"I'd get a dog or two. Couldn't hurt to have some of them roaming around and barking their heads off every time someone gets too close. I have one you could take."

"Yeah?" I asked. "What breed?"

"Jack Russel."

I let out a laugh. "You want me to take your Jack Russel as a guard dog?"

Vincent grinned, and fuck if it didn't make the asshole even more attractive. "Look. You can take it and feed it to your Dobermans or Rottweilers, okay?"

"Not sure how I feel about that."

He rolled his eyes. "Ugh. Dog lovers. You're as bad as Bliss. Probably for the best though. She's been sleeping with it in her bed. And for once, she isn't mad at me. I'd like to keep it that way for at least a day."

"She's a pussycat."

"With claws."

I nodded. "It's kinda what I like about her. She's soft and sweet until you find a spot that's hard and sharp. She surprises me." I rested back against my chair, thinking about the woman who'd been sadly missing from my bed last night.

"Are you making her your girlfriend?" Vincent asked quietly. "She's been through some shit. She doesn't deserve more. If you're fucking that woman from the clubhouse..."

I had no intention of doing her wrong. "She doesn't want to be exclusive." I eyed him. "Pretty sure she's interested in someone else."

"Nash?"

"Maybe. You, definitely."

He shook his head, but his smile told me exactly how pleased he was by that. "So, what? Assuming that's true, we just...share her? You get Monday through Wednesday. I get Thursday through Sunday?"

"I ain't giving you the entire weekend."

He laughed, but then his smile fell. "My family is expecting me to marry someone else. And soon."

"Join the club." I sighed. "Family sucks."

"Yeah, it does sometimes. Bliss' does too."

"Three peas in a pod then, huh?"

Vincent raised an eyebrow. "That a come-on?"

I sat back and folded my arms across my chest. "If I was gonna ask you for a threesome, I'd just come right out and say it, Vincent."

He eyed me, his gaze tracing my face so long that heat built inside me. He pushed to his feet. "Then why haven't you?" He leaned down, getting in my face. "Because we both know you were watching me while you fucked Bliss the other day. I got you just as hard as she did."

The door swung open, and I jerked back.

Gus stood there, with a tray full of delicious-smelling bacon and egg sandwiches. His gaze darted between me and Vincent, who was way too slow to get out of my personal space.

Gus' confusion turned to one of awkward understanding. "Uh, I'll just leave these here for you." He put the tray down on the edge of the table and slid it across to us. "Sorry for interrupting."

"You weren't," I said quickly.

Vincent walked around the table and grabbed a sandwich. "I was leaving anyway. See you at Psychos, War?"

I nodded.

Vincent left with his sandwich, leaving me and Gus alone again.

Gus eyed me carefully.

I narrowed my eyes at him. "Whatever it is you're thinking, just spit it out."

He shook his head. "Not my place to say. I don't judge you at all, of course. And maybe none of your guys here will either. But out there, beyond these walls, the rest of the chapters might. Not all of them take well to faggots in their ranks. Especially not in their presidents."

I ground my teeth. "This a reminder that I'm bound and gagged to marry your daughter one day?"

Gus shrugged. "It's just a friendly piece of advice from someone who cares about you and doesn't want to see you hurt."

The underlying threat was there. What this club and its members were capable of when someone did something they didn't like. Even if that person was the prez. Gus wasn't wrong. I'd heard more than one story of the way the club dealt with men who liked men.

We had not moved with the times at all.

It didn't matter. Whatever that had been with me and

Vincent wasn't a big deal. I didn't even know where it had come from. He'd been like a completely different person lately.

I couldn't deny that I liked it though. And that later on, when I put my hand around my erection, Bliss wasn't the only one I was thinking of.

## 12

## CALEB

*I* lay on my bedroom floor for almost a whole day, not daring to move because even breathing hurt the gashes on my chest and the myriad of other injuries I'd sustained. I was fairly sure one of my ribs was cracked, and the slashes in my skin had reopened to ooze around the stitches. I'd downed a handful of painkillers I'd nabbed from my bedside table sometime after Bethany-Melissa had left, but they did nothing to numb the pain.

All the time on the floor gave me a lot of time to think. With every passing moment, the fear, anger, and violence grew within me. I could practically hear the laughter of my colleagues in my ear, each of them staring and pointing, shaking their heads at what a sad, pathetic waste of space I was.

They all had wives who worshipped them. Women who stayed home and made sure their every need was met at the end of the day. They had clean houses, dinner on the table, warm pussies to fuck whenever they wanted it, and if they wanted a woman who wasn't their wife, they took her. Their wives didn't dare comment because they knew how good they had it.

My colleagues commanded power and respect from other men and were cutthroat in their business dealings.

Then there was me. So weak I couldn't even get off the floor because the pain was unbearable. So pathetic that a fat fucking bitch like Bethany-Melissa didn't want me.

My anger boiled.

Over my dead body was she doing this to me again.

I'd chosen her specifically because I knew she couldn't do better. I wasn't going to accept another beautiful, tanned, toned woman whose eyes strayed more often than they didn't. I'd been there, done that, and I'd lost. Sandra had married Frederick, and I'd been left with the consolation prize of Bethany-Melissa, a DUFF if ever I'd met one. She was Sandra's designated ugly fat friend, in every sense of the phrase.

But she came from a good family, one whose connections I could use, and she'd stared at me with those starstruck eyes, like she was shocked I'd even looked twice at her. Her pussy was as good to pound as any, but she wouldn't dare cheat because she could do no better.

She wasn't leaving. I wouldn't be shamed twice.

And that asshole she was following around like the slut she was? He would pay.

I let out an agonizing scream of pain when I eventually dragged myself off the floor. I reeked of piss and sweat, but I couldn't get changed. Blackness was already flickering at the edges of my vision, threatening to drag me under. I stumbled down the stairs, clutching the railing desperately for support, and picked up my keys from the kitchen countertop.

Behind the wheel of my car, I grit my teeth and drove to the police station. My head hurt, and my vision kept blurring. More than once a horn blared, but I kept going until I reached my destination. I parked the car, breathing hard, like I'd run here instead of driven.

With a groan, I hauled myself out of the car and staggered inside.

Fuck Bethany-Melissa. And fuck that guy. Scythe, she'd called him. Fuck them both. I'd promised not to tattle on them to the police, but lying on that floor, I'd realized that was a little bitch move. Scythe had threatened and attacked me. I wasn't going to be a victim, crying on the floor, and looking over my shoulder wherever I went. That wasn't the sort of man I was going to be.

He'd be found and charged. And when I hired the very best lawyer, he'd spend the rest of his life in jail.

Bethany-Melissa would come crawling back to me without his money and protection. She had to. She had nothing else.

I bypassed the line of waiting people in the police station and went straight to the counter, leaning heavily on it. "I need to make a report." My voice was hoarse from screaming.

The woman behind the counter and plexiglass glanced up at me and balked. Her gaze traveled over my face, and then lower, fixating on the wounds across my chest that spelled out Bethany-Melissa's cheap nickname.

"Sir, do you require medical assistance?"

"No," I snapped, no patience left for women and their stupid questions. "I need to make a report."

"There's a line," somebody grumbled behind me.

I whipped around and silenced them with a glare. The middle-aged man dropped his gaze to the floor, just like I knew he would. Pussy.

"Sir. You don't seem well. Have you taken something?"

I slammed a fist down on the countertop. "No, dammit! I just need to make a report. My fiancée has been taken by a psychopath. He did this to me. He carved letters into my skin and then left me for dead. His name is Scythe."

The woman stared at me with huge eyes.

"Fucking hell, is there not one of your sex with even an ounce of intelligence? Get me a man to talk to, lady!"

She calmly picked up the phone, her eyes blazing at me. "Security?"

A man in a different uniform took the phone from her hand and put it back down in its cradle. "Excuse me. Did you say the man with your fiancée is named Scythe?"

"Yes!"

The woman turned to him. "That mean something to you, Tabor?"

Tabor shook his head. "No. no. I must have misheard him. But don't worry about getting security up here. I'll deal with it."

He pressed a button on his side of the plexiglass which popped open a door. He strode through it and over to my side, leading me away.

"Where are we going?" I demanded, peering at the badge on his shirt but unable to make out anything other than the brown of his uniform. Fucking pills were doing a number on my vision.

"I'm Steven Tabor. I'm the warden of Saint View Prison."

I yanked my arm out of his grasp. "I don't need a warden. I need an officer to make a report to. My name is Caleb Black. I own Onyx Business Consulting. I'm the one paying your pitiful salaries, and I will not be brushed aside."

Tabor took my arm again, his fingers pressing into my flesh. "That may be true, Caleb Black, well-respected businessman. But right now, you look like a homeless junkie, high as a kite, and hallucinating. Nobody is going to take you seriously when you've got no shirt, no shoes, and you reek of piss." He dragged me outside, moving so quickly I stumbled trying to keep up.

Out of sight of the cops, he yanked my arm sharply. "Nobody is going to listen to you except for me. Tell me everything you know about Scythe."

## 13

### BLISS

*B*y the end of the weekend, the swelling in my face had gone down, and by Tuesday, the bruises had faded enough that it felt safe to go back to my own house.

Only, I found I didn't want to.

Scythe and I had been like ships in the night since I'd kissed him on the cheek after our little proof-of-life trip to Caleb's house. My lips still tingled, thinking about brushing over the light stubble on his cheek. But the real change in my feelings toward him came from the way he'd protected me.

I'd heard every word he'd said to Caleb after I'd left. I'd been standing on the stairway the entire time, and though his threats on Caleb's manhood had been barbaric, they'd settled the frightened part of me that was scared he might try to hurt me again.

But I missed my siblings, and though Scythe had done a good job of packing me everything I needed—

vibrator included—I wanted to restock with fresh under-wear and some clean clothes.

Verity and Everett climbed all over me for a good thirty minutes when I arrived, until I thought to ask them who was at home with them. "Where's your mom?"

Verity shrugged, brushing back her long blond hair off her shoulder. "Don't know. She went out somewhere after Dad's visitor was here. Then Dad got a migraine and went upstairs. It's fine, though. I'm big enough to take care of Everett."

"I'm big enough to take care of myself." The little boy scowled at his big sister.

She glared right back at him.

"Okay, okay," I interrupted before it turned into a bloodbath. "You're both very big. Why don't you go play, and I'm going to go check on Dad and make sure he's okay? Then I gotta go to work. I'll see you guys later."

The two of them scampered off, and I jogged up the stairs to Dad and Nichelle's bedroom, rapping my knuckles lightly on the door.

There was no answer, but I was concerned enough that I pushed the door open anyway and peeked through, praying that what Scythe had said about my father sleeping naked didn't apply to migraine-induced lie-downs, too. "Dad? Are you okay?"

He sat up suddenly at my voice, and I winced at how much that would have hurt

"Bethany-Melissa? What are you doing here? I thought you were staying with a friend for a while?"

"I am. But I just dropped by to say hello to the kids, and they said you weren't feeling well. I have to go to work, but is there anything I can do for you before I leave?"

"No. No. But please, come sit for a moment. I was going to find you as soon as my headache went away. I have some upsetting news."

I swallowed thickly. "Is it Nichelle? Is that why she isn't here?"

"No, no. Well, maybe. Your mother was here earlier."

That was the last thing I expected him to say. "What did she want?"

"To see you. I told her you were staying with a friend."

"Thank you. Sorry she came by. I don't know why she would have. I hate that Nichelle got upset over it." She always did. Nichelle hated any reminder that my father had once slept with other women besides her. The last time that had happened, she'd stormed off and run up Dad's credit card. Which was very likely what she was doing now. Retail therapy was all the therapy Nichelle seemed to need after dealing with my mother.

I wished that was all the counselling I needed, but I figured my mother-child bond was probably so fractured a therapist—a real, medically certified one—would have a field day with it.

My father peered at me through the dim light. "Bethany-Melissa, she told me Axel died. Is that true? I wasn't sure if it was just a way for her to try to get me to give her money again..."

I'd never been the sort of kid who got in trouble. Axel's instructions to me had rung in my head for years. Behave. Don't give them any reason to send you back. So I really wasn't used to the disappointed look on my father's face right now.

"It's true," I murmured.

"Why didn't you tell me?"

"You don't talk about them. Mom and Axel. And it makes Nichelle upset. I didn't want to burden you all."

He put a weathered hand on my thigh. "But he was your brother. It must have been terribly upsetting for you. I would have supported you, no matter what."

I felt even worse, seeing the sincere sympathy in his eyes. I'd hurt him by not letting him in. "I'm sorry." It was all I could seem to say. But I wanted to make it up to him. "We're having a funeral on Thursday since his body was only just released from police custody. Would you come? Nichelle and the kids too, if you think it's appropriate."

He squeezed my leg supportively. "Of course we'll be there. We'll be standing right behind you the entire time."

I nodded and went to stand. "I appreciate it. I'll make sure I stand far away from Mom then, so Nichelle doesn't have to run off and rack up another credit card bill."

My father chuckled. "She's not going to get far with it, I'm afraid."

"Things still aren't good at work?"

His mouth pulled into a grim line. "Unfortunately, no. I haven't seen Caleb lately either, so I'm not sure how much longer it will be before the merger goes ahead. I don't know how long we can hold out until we buckle altogether."

Guilt swamped me. There was so much I hadn't told my father about. "Dad, I—"

He squeezed his eyes shut. "It's okay. I know about your breakup. You might have given me the heads-up though, so I wasn't surprised when I heard it at the country club."

I cringed. "I'm so sorry. I just couldn't stay with him. He's...not a good man, Dad. I don't think you should get involved with him."

He sighed. "Men like Caleb, and myself, are hard to love. Business comes before all else, and it takes a certain type of woman to handle that. You and your mother...you aren't those women."

I wasn't sure if he meant it as a jab, but it wasn't one. Nichelle didn't truly love my father. She enjoyed the lifestyle he gave her, and I was sure he enjoyed having a pretty young woman on his arm, but there was no real affection between them.

Not being that sort of woman wasn't anything to be upset about. I didn't want their relationship.

Between War, Scythe, Vincent, and Nash, I was all sorts of confused about what I wanted. But the one thing I did know for sure was Caleb was not even in the running.

"Anything else I need to know?" Dad asked, his voice patient.

"I work at a bar now. Not in a daycare center."

He paused. "Well, it's your life. And why you've been working at night makes a lot more sense now."

"It's in Saint View."

He frowned. "Really, Bethany-Melissa? I could easily get you a job at the club if you want me to put in a good word for you."

I shook my head. "I like it where I am."

"What's the bar called? Maybe Nichelle and I could come for a drink there sometime."

The thought of my father sitting at the bar at Psychos, with its sticky floor, and mostly MC clientele was preposterous.

I laughed and leaned in to kiss his cheek. "I appreciate the support, but it's most definitely not your scene. And speaking of, if I haven't just added to your headache, I need to get going. You're all right to watch the kids, aren't you?"

He shooed me off without questioning me more about the name of the bar, which was a relief because I really didn't want to tell him. If he looked it up or asked around about it, there was every chance someone might have heard of the place, and I most definitely did not want my father knowing what we were doing there to bring in some extra cash. There were some things a father just didn't need to know about his daughter.

he bar was quiet when I got there, but being a Tuesday, that didn't surprise me. It didn't even matter that we were in for a quiet night. It felt good to have seen my brother and sister and to have unloaded some of my secrets onto my father. There was a lightness that came from confessing the things I'd kept hidden from them.

I dumped my bag behind the bar and leaned across it, planting a kiss on War's lips, which tasted of popcorn salt and beer. Scythe, or Vincent, as I was going to have to remember to call him all night, at least out loud, was sitting next to him, tossing popcorn into the air and catching it in his mouth.

I glanced between the two of them looking all buddy-buddy, and then down at the beer in front of Scythe. "Drinking on the job?"

"It's my night off."

"It's your night off, but you came to work anyway?"

He shrugged, tossing another piece of popcorn up into the air. "War said he likes beer. So do I."

I glanced at War with a questioning eyebrow.

He shrugged. "We found something in common. Beer and bowling, and—"

I held a hand up. "Blow jobs. Yeah, I heard all about every man's three favorite B's from Vincent."

War caught my fingers and brought them to his mouth. He placed a kiss on my knuckles. "Actually, I was going to say Bliss." He winked. "But I like blow jobs too. Just for the record."

"What's this about blow jobs?" Nash asked, finishing off a customer's drink order and wiping his hands on his jeans.

"We like 'em," War filled him in.

Nash groaned, leaning heavily on the bar top, turning our little threesome into a foursome. His biceps bulged beneath his T-shirt, and my gaze rolled down his corded forearms. Oh boy. I had to drag my attention away. The forearm porn was too much.

Nash didn't seem to notice. "It's been way too long since I had really good head. Or any sort of sex actually. Fucking hell, I'm probably going to find a new V-card in my mailbox if this keeps up."

Nash seemed kind of tortured by the apparently long-ago memory of his last sexual encounter.

I had to bite my lip to stop myself from offering to

help him out. I hadn't forgotten what Rebel had said about his ten-inch cock. I was still so incredibly curious about whether the rumor was true.

Scythe glanced over at Nash, his face dead serious. "You're nearly forty. Can you even still get hard?"

War spit out a mouthful of beer on a laugh, and I jumped out of the way of the spray, frowning at him. He went wide-eyed, and reached across the counter, grabbing a cloth and cleaning up. "Sorry, babe."

"You should be. That was gross." I eyed Nash though. Having all three guys here had put me in an oddly good mood, and there was no way I wasn't going to get in a little teasing of my own. "So, can you get it up, Nash?"

He gave me a death stare.

I didn't turn away, and the look drew out, morphing into something different. Something hotter, that held promises he refused to make out loud.

War leaned over to Scythe and stage-whispered, "You think he's staring at her like that, just willing it to bone up?"

Scythe pushed himself forward to peer over the bar top at Nash's junk. "Still looks pretty soft to me. There's pills for that, you know, Nash. No shame in admitting you need help as you approach middle age."

It broke whatever was going on between me and Nash, and I turned away, heat prickling my cheeks.

Nash recovered quicker than I did. Or perhaps I'd imagined the heat in his eyes. But while I busied myself wiping over the beer taps with a damp cloth, he went back to defending his manhood. "My dick works fine. Thank you both for being so interested."

War washed his popcorn down with a swig of beer.

"We'll see next week at your party, huh? I assume you'll be participating. You can't work when the party is in your honor. And everybody should get blow jobs on their birthday."

I scrubbed at a spot on the tap harder, heat flushing my cheeks.

Nash didn't seem to notice. "I don't know. Depends who's there, I guess."

Was that his gaze I could feel? I didn't dare glance up for fear the images in my head might be somehow also displayed on my face. My core tingled at the thought of watching Nash get his dick sucked in the middle of Psychos' main floor.

But it clenched, moaned, and begged to be the woman on her knees in front of him.

"Are you going to do anything else?" I asked, desperate to change the subject. "For your birthday, I mean? Buy yourself a midlife-crisis car, maybe?"

"You should definitely do something crazy," War mused. "Skydiving?"

"Or swim with sharks," Scythe supplied. "If one eats you, I call dibs on your Jeep, since I'm currently still carless."

Nash glared at him but folded his arms, considering our suggestions. "They're all terrible ideas, but yeah. Somebody accused me recently of not knowing how to have fun. So maybe I will do something I've never done before."

I smiled softly to myself, knowing that somebody was me.

"Even if you don't, we're gonna have the biggest, best

ever birthday party for you," I assured him. "Rebel and I have been planning it."

"Complete with sex swings and toy shows," Rebel added, drifting by with her empty drink tray. She patted Nash on the back. "You're gonna love it, Boss Man. You'll be the center of attention, and every woman there will be ready to please the birthday boy."

I gaped at her, trying not to choke. Sex swings and toy shows? We had most definitely not discussed either of those. I was suddenly questioning my decision to put Rebel in charge of entertainment.

War chuckled. "You okay there, Bliss?"

Rebel glanced at me. "Uh-oh. We've embarrassed her delicate Providence sensibilities, boys. Was it the sex swing or the toy show that did you in?"

It was too hot in here, and there was too much attention on me. I snuck a glance at Nash and found him watching me with an amused grin.

He put his hand on my shoulder as he walked past on his way to the refrigerator and spoke low into my ear. "Sorry to throw you under the bus, Blissy-girl. Better the attention be on you than me though."

His breath tickled my neck, and I found my eyes wanting to flutter closed, and my head wanting to tilt to give him better access.

He had no idea that the heat coursing through my body right now had little to do with Rebel's teasing and everything to do with the fantasies in my head, each one starring him and me. Everything felt tight inside me, and I needed a moment to get myself under control. "I'm going to the ladies' room."

I left them to their ribbing and made my escape,

striding down the hall to the women's bathroom. It was as dingy as the rest of the bar and nothing like the nice ones that had been installed out in back where we held parties. But the best thing about these bathrooms were how quiet and clean they always were. Men outnumbered women ten to one on a regular bar night at Psychos, and so the women's room tended to be perpetually empty and clean.

I used the facilities quickly and then splashed some water on my face, trying to calm down. It did little good. When I looked in the mirror, my eyes were too wide, and my chest rose and fell too rapidly.

The door opened, and War stuck his head in, cheeky grin firmly in place. "Need some assistance?"

I shook my head quickly. "Nope. I'm fine."

He slipped through the doorway anyway, locking it behind him. He smirked at me. "No you're not. What was that back there?"

"What?" I asked, feigning ignorance and avoiding making eye contact.

He moved in to lean on the bathroom vanity and put a finger beneath my chin, forcing me to face him. "You getting all hot and bothered over Nash."

"I wasn't." It was a lie. My core throbbed at the things I'd been thinking about. But I wasn't going to admit that to War.

"Yeah, baby girl. You were. It was written all over your face. I could practically see you ignite when Rebel mentioned there being plenty of women ready to satisfy his every need. You were jealous. Or you were thinking about being one of them."

I brushed his hand away, busying myself by turning

back to the mirror, though I could still see everything he did in the reflection. "Stop it."

He cocked his head to one side. "Tell me what you were thinking."

"I wasn't thinking anything."

"Liar, liar, panties on fire. Why do you think I followed you in here? I thought you might need a hand." He chuckled. "Or a couple of fingers."

I let out a long sigh, giving in. "Was I really that obvious?"

"Yes."

"It's so embarrassing. I don't know why I keep doing that. He's made it very clear he doesn't want me in that way."

War pressed in closer, his hands coming to rest on my hips and twisting me so my back was to the mirror and I had nowhere to look but up into his cat-green eyes. "He wants you, Bliss. Why the hell do you think he hasn't had sex in so long? He's looking at every woman in the bar, at the parties, on the street, and comparing every single one of them to you." He pressed a kiss to my lips. "Not one of them does."

"You don't know that," I whispered.

His lips trailed down my neck, sucking and kissing a path of heat that did nothing to help the tingling between my thighs. His fingers hooked in the sides of my skirt, pulling it down, taking my panties with it.

I didn't stop him because I needed it. Whatever he was going to do, I needed it so bad.

"I do. Because it's exactly the same way I feel every time Siren or Kiki or any of the other women throw themselves at me. They aren't you. So I don't want it."

His hands tightened around my waist and then hoisted me up so my behind landed on the vanity. "Nash is caught up in his loyalty to Axel, and probably his own savior complex."

The vanity was cold on my ass, but the heat from inside me chased it away. "He still sees me as a little girl."

"Then open your legs and let me get my tongue between them so we can show him that you're actually all woman."

He spread my knees wide.

I leaned back on my hands, giving myself over to his persuasion. I was so wet and needy, there was no way I was going back out there and working an entire shift without doing something about it first.

I'd probably come the moment I saw Nash, and that would be hard to hide and completely mortifying.

War was all too willing to take advantage of the state I'd worked myself into. His tongue moved through my slick folds. "He wants to lick you like this, Bliss. I promise you that. He wants his tongue buried in your pussy, tasting your sweet arousal."

I gasped, the pictures in my head all too vibrant with War's encouragement.

He groaned against my clit, and the vibration had me shoving my fingers into his hair to stop him from moving away.

"He's thinking about his party and how much he wants to use toys on you. He's thinking about how pretty your cunt would be, wrapped around a vibrator set on high. He's thinking about your pussy swallowing down one that only he has the control to. He's thinking about clamping your nipples and working your sweet ass to take a plug."

I bit my lip, trying to fight the cry building in the back of my throat. But then War gave me two fingers, sliding them deep inside my pussy, and all inhibitions left the building.

He pumped his fingers in and out, setting the perfect pace, torturing me with all the dirty things he—or Nash —could do to me.

I soaked up every word, starved for more, and gushed when he gave it to me. I dripped on his hand, and he lapped it up like it was honey, tonguing me fiercely, deter- minedly working me toward orgasm in between talk so dirty I couldn't imagine anyone ever doing it better.

"Come, baby girl. Come so I can taste it."

He didn't need to give me permission twice. He covered my clit with his mouth and drove a third finger up inside me. I brought my feet up, digging my heels into the countertop so I was fully on display for him and bouncing against his fingers. "Oh!" I screamed, unable to keep it quiet. "Oh. Oh. Oh!"

"Think of him when you come," War demanded. "Say his name."

The orgasm barreled down on me so hard it was blinding.

And for a second, I could believe it was Nash there, sucking and licking and pleasuring me so perfectly. "Nash! Oh my God, Nash!"

I gave myself up to the fantasy, my internal walls clamping down hard. I writhed and groaned, and War rode out my orgasm relentlessly, drawing it out until I was practically whimpering.

My mind cleared, and one thought slammed into my head like a freight train.

I sat bolt upright, shoving War away.

He stumbled back with a smirk that was so painfully sexy I could die, licking my cum off his lips.

"I just shouted Nash's name."

"Several times, I believe."

My eyes widened in horror. "What if he heard?"

"He didn't. The bar is noisy enough even on a quiet night. He would have had to be standing right on the other side of the door."

He was right. I got down off the vanity and retrieved my skirt and panties from where they'd fallen. "Come on. We need to get back out there. We've been in here for ages. Everybody is going to know what we're doing."

War didn't argue. He just washed his hands and followed me to the door. I checked my skirt and panties were back in place, flicked off the lock, and pulled on the handle.

On the other side of the door, crammed into the tiniest of corridors, stood Vincent, Rebel, and worst of all…Nash.

War snorted on a laugh. "Oh, shit. Would you look at that. Nash was on the other side of the door."

I turned in horror to War. "Did you know?"

He laughed and leaned in to kiss my cheek. "I didn't, but you know I like an audience. No biggie."

I couldn't face Nash. "Rebel! You too?"

She cracked up laughing. "Hey, I just came to check you were okay and found these two pervs standing outside. They started it."

Scythe was no less repentant. "I need a cigarette and a cold shower. That was hot."

Like that was an excuse.

I finally dared to take a peek at Nash.

His gaze burned, filled with fire, jealousy, and lust.

I blinked, not expecting to see any of those things.

He cleared his throat. "We should get back to work."

Rebel booed as he turned stiffly and walked away.

I didn't say a word. I just watched him leave, wondering how the hell I could get him to look at me like that all the time.

*ash was quiet for the rest of the night. The hours dragged on, and I busied myself with cleaning, since there weren't enough customers for me, Rebel, and Nash to wait on. War and Scythe left sometime around eleven, claiming we were boring. I didn't ask where they were going. I was too paranoid about Nash and what he'd heard.

At midnight, I told Rebel to go home, even though we didn't close 'til one. We didn't have a single customer left in the bar, and I couldn't handle the tension between me and Nash for a moment longer. Closing an hour early wouldn't kill anyone.

Rebel grabbed her bag, hoisting the strap over her shoulder, and gave me a hug. "Sorry."

"Not your fault. You weren't the one calling out his name while you..." I dropped my face into my hands. "This is mortifying."

She pulled my hands away and squeezed them. "He's

not angry. He's just turned about. And jealous. Maybe confused. Actually, I'm confused. Why were you screaming his name when it was War making you come?"

I shook my head. "War has a very descriptive way with words."

"I can imagine. But, Disney," she laughed, using the nickname she'd given me on the very first night we'd met when I'd wandered into Psychos wearing a ballgown. "If Nash gets you so hot you can forget who you're actually with, why aren't you doing something about it?"

Wasn't that the million-dollar question.

I pushed her gently toward the door. "Go. I'm gonna close up and leave too."

She flounced out, still as full of energy as if she'd just gotten out of bed rather than been on her feet all night.

I found Nash in his office, buried beneath a pile of paperwork. "I sent Rebel home. I think we should close early. There's no one here."

He didn't lift his head. "Okay, you go on. I'll see you tomorrow."

"You're staying?"

He was steadfastly refusing to look at me. "Lots to be done."

"It's past midnight. It can wait, Nash. You're always here."

He finally raised his gaze to meet mine. "Where else would I go?"

"Home? To bed maybe?"

He turned back to his paperwork. "I prefer being here."

I sighed. I hated how awkward we were being. "Nash, I'm really sorry about before. About what you heard..."

"It's fine."

Just like when women said they were fine, it was very clear to me that when Nash said he was fine, he wasn't. "No, you're not. You can barely even look at me."

"I said it was fine."

"But it's not! You're making it weird!"

Nash shot to his feet, papers tipping off the edge of his messy desk and floating to the floor. "Dammit, Bliss. Just leave it alone!"

I blinked. "I didn't mean to embarrass you. War and I were just..." I had no idea how to finish that sentence.

Nash moved around the desk so he stood in front of me. "Is that what you think the problem is here, Bliss? That you embarrassed me?"

I dug my teeth into my bottom lip and nodded. "I'm mortified, and I owe you an apology—"

He held up a hand. "Dammit, Bliss. Just stop. I'm not embarrassed." He inched closer. "Or fuck, maybe I am, but not because of you."

I craned my head up so our gazes met. "Then why?"

He brought one hand up, like he was going to stroke it down the side of my face. But then thought better of it and stiffly closed his fingers into a fist, which he dropped back to his side. His gaze turned tortured. "Because I liked the way my name sounded on your lips."

I sucked in a breath, my head spinning. "Nash, I—"

He closed his eyes, like me saying his name was torture.

I stepped in closer, putting my hand on his chest. "Nash. Look at me."

He shook his head. "I can't, Bliss. Fucking hell. If I look at you, I'm going to want to kiss you."

"Look at me," I repeated.

He groaned but slowly opened his eyes. "We can't do this." His head lowered so his lips were mere inches from mine. "Fuck, I want to kiss you so bad I can't breathe."

I wanted it too, but I didn't want to be the one to take it.

I didn't want to be one more thing on his list of regrets.

But he was so close to me. My eyes closed, and I silently begged for him to go further.

"Will you come somewhere with me?"

His warm breath disappeared, and he took a step back. A scream of frustration rose inside me.

I fought to get control of myself and nodded. "Anywhere."

# 14

## SCYTHE

*W*ar and I stumbled out into the Psychos' parking lot and toward the row of bikes parked by the side of the building.

I nudged him with my elbow. "Which one's yours?"

He squinted at them all. "Ah, third from the end. Harley. Not that I'm gonna be riding it anywhere tonight. How much did we drink in there?"

My head was feeling it too. It had been a long time since I'd had anything to drink, because Vincent didn't. "I lost count. Pretty sure some of those last few were doubles."

"No driving for you then either."

"Wrote my car off anyway. Gonna have to steal another sometime soon."

War glanced at me and laughed. "Can I help?"

"Steal a car?" I shrugged. "Sure."

"Fuck, man. I haven't done that since I was fifteen." He clapped me on the shoulder. "Good fucking fun if you can get the cops to chase you."

"Too drunk tonight though."

"Me, too. But it's early, and Bliss doesn't get off 'til one. Wanna go bowling?"

Excitement lit me up. "Yeah? You want to?"

War nodded. "The alley isn't that far. We can walk."

We set off, wandering along the cracked sidewalk at a casual pace, neither of us in a hurry. The night air was cool and crisp. Neither of us had worn a jacket, though thanks to the alcohol, I wasn't really feeling it.

"Did you get those security cameras fixed?" I asked.

War shoved his hands in his pockets. "Yeah. And the fences. Had a couple guys on it since you were out." He grinned over at me. "Bliss allowed to come visit me now, Dad?"

"It's Daddy to you."

War snorted. "It's always the quiet ones. Here I am, just thinking you're a regular, introverted sorta guy, and then you go telling me to call you Daddy."

I joined in the laughter because it seemed hilariously funny. "If you ever really called me that I'd laugh so fucking hard."

"Ditto. Wouldn't mind if Bliss did though." He pulled a pack of cigarettes from his back pocket and flipped the lid on them. Inside sat a little red lighter that he pulled out and lit up.

I watched the flame with interest, but it had never really done anything for me. I knew some guys who got off on fire, but for me, I only ever got that feeling when I had a blade in my hand.

"Fuck, she does it for me," he continued. "I can't get enough of her." War touched his smoke to the flame and inhaled, letting the lighter go out once his cigarette was lit. "How's your quest to get back in her good books?"

He offered the pack to me, and I nodded, taking a cigarette. I hadn't smoked since high school because Vincent was a pansy and probably worried about lung cancer or some bullshit, but I hadn't forgotten how good they could be, especially after a couple of drinks.

"I think she hates me a little less." I lit it and inhaled, sucking in the smoke like it was a long-lost friend. Fucking perfect.

"She forgive you for whatever it was you did? How'd you manage that? She seemed pretty mad."

My boots crunched over some dried autumn leaves that nobody had bothered to rake from the sidewalk. "Might have been when I threatened to gut her worthless ex. I think she liked it? Honestly not entirely sure." I grinned at him. "She kissed me though."

He looked interested in that. "Yeah? Is this where I punch you for kissing my girl?"

"She ain't your girl any more than she's mine. Fuck. Tonight she was Nash's girl, even if it was you making her moan."

"That bother you?"

I thought it over and found it didn't. "As long as she doesn't suddenly want to include that fucking dickhead, Caleb. Nash is all right."

We reached the entrance of the bowling alley, but War paused with his hand on the door. "And we already know you have a thing for watching me fuck her, so we're all good on that front."

Asshole.

I couldn't resist giving him some of it back. "You talk a

lot of talk, but how are you gonna take it when the shoe is on the other foot?"

He laughed. "What, when it's you fucking her and me watching?"

I nodded. "Or Nash."

He shoved me through the door, his laughter following. "I don't have much to worry about there, do I? Neither of you have any game. And speaking of..." He rested his elbows on the counter and smiled at the pimple-faced teenager working on the other side. "Can we get a couple of games, please?"

The teen nodded. "Closing at midnight though. Shoes and balls are over there."

War and I pulled some bills from our wallets and paid the kid. At the shoe rack, we both went for the same size and swapped our boots for the clown shoes with the slippery bottoms.

I picked up a ball and then found our designated lane, with War right behind me. We both sank down, side by side, and waited for our names to come up on the screen.

War pointed to it. "I'm up first." He stood and walked backward to where his ball sat waiting. "Watch and learn, brother."

He poked his fingers in the holes and then made his way to the top of the lane. He eyed it for a moment, swung his arm back, then forward, and let the ball loose.

I craned my head to one side, watching it roll down the highly polished lane.

Eight of the ten pins fell.

"I'm rusty," he complained. "It's been forever since I

played." When his ball returned, he picked it up and hurled it down the lane once more.

It knocked both pins down for a spare.

He was grinning when he sank back down in the seat next to me.

"Nice start. You know how to play."

He shrugged. "Played a bit with my dad when I was a kid. Not for a while now, though."

"How come?"

"Life. He was always busy with club stuff. I was busy with the same, or my own shit. We stopped making time for each other." He sighed. "And then he went and got himself killed, so that's all the time we're ever gonna get."

War leaned back and crossed his arms over his chest. "You ever hear any of the guys at the bar go by the nickname Scythe?"

I froze. "Why?"

He watched a teenage girl in the next lane throw her ball, which almost immediately went straight down the gutter. "Had a source tell me he's the one who killed my old man."

I forced a neutral expression onto my face but also quietly patted my pocket, checking my knife was still there.

It was.

"Who's the source? He reputable? You check into it?"

He lifted a shoulder in a shrug. "Local banger from a rival club. Had plenty of scuffles with 'em over the years. Would be a pretty huge get for them to be able to take out the prez though. Didn't think they had the balls, to be honest with you."

"So maybe your source was wrong."

He shook his head. "Scythe has a reputation. He's not part of the club. He's more like a hit-for-hire sorta guy."

I shook my head slowly. "Never heard of him."

War nodded. "If you do..."

"Yeah, of course. First thing I do will be to let you know." I forced a grin I didn't feel. "I'm always down for a good old-fashioned witch hunt.

I got up to take my turn, putting my fingers in the holes.

"Make it good!" War yelled.

I glanced back at him.

His green-eyed gaze caught and held mine. It was like a punch in the stomach, looking at him now, when I'd stared into the eyes of his father, right as I'd pulled the trigger.

They were the same. The same shape. Same color.

Same fucking everything.

I couldn't even remember his old man's name, but I remembered his eyes.

Fucking great.

I needed to disappear. I needed to leave right now, get on a bus, or steal a car and go somewhere far away, where people hadn't heard of me. It was time anyway, what with the police probably finding my fingerprints in that car. It wouldn't be that long before they found more.

Instead, I picked the ball up and hurled it down the alleyway. It slid along and smashed right into the center pin with a crack.

War was on his feet when I turned around.

He threw his arms around me in a drunken hug and thumped me on the back. "Look at you, V! A strike on your very first ball. Well fucking done!"

I'd killed his father. Or Vincent had. I didn't really even fucking know, the line between us was never blurred more than when there was a blade in my hand. Vincent always blamed the killing on me. But it wasn't that cut and dried. It was some dark part we shared and the thing that connected us. It urged me on the same way it urged him.

It didn't matter. To the rest of the world, Vincent and I weren't two different people. So it didn't matter whether it had been him or me or some third personality neither of us could control.

The gun that killed War's dad had been fired by my hand.

Now I had to look War in the eye and lie to him.

*Or you could tell him the truth...*

Vincent might have. But Vincent had friends. People who cared about him. Loved him.

I didn't.

This thing with War and me felt like the beginnings of something I'd never had but desperately wanted.

Friendship.

I didn't want it to go away.

And I didn't want to leave.

Not him. Not Bliss. Not Nash, or Rebel, or the bar.

I had never had anything to lose before. But suddenly having something made me realize exactly why Vincent was so easy to manipulate.

Because losing people you cared about felt unimaginable.

And if I told War the truth, that would be it.

So I shut my mouth and gave him a hug back. One that lingered longer than it should have, and one we'd probably both deny in the morning, passing it off as being too drunk to remember.

But I'd remember. I'd remember the way his body felt pressed against mine, strong and hard in all the same places I was, and a complete contrast to Bliss' soft curves. I'd remember his tobacco and leather scent, filling my nose, and the rasp of his stubble when he pulled back to give me the hugest grin.

I'd remember the way his eyes changed when they locked with mine, and both of us realized we maybe weren't as drunk as we were making out.

I swallowed thickly. This didn't feel like friendship.

This felt like attraction.

My gaze flickered to his lips, and I had the same urge to draw him in and kiss him that I had when I looked at Bliss.

I blinked, turning away and running my hand through my hair. I wasn't going to ruin this. I needed a friend more than I needed a fuck, even if the thought of being with War did get me hard.

"Your turn," I told him and moved stiffly back to my seat.

The game went on, the two of us neck and neck the entire way. He was good, getting strikes and spares on most rounds, and our scores rose as quickly as the heat between us.

There were four seats we could have taken, all allocated to our lane. And yet we both kept returning to the same two, sitting side by side so our arms and thighs couldn't help but brush.

The alley emptied out, the families all finishing their late-night games and taking tired kids home, the teenagers and league players all losing interest or calling it a night.

Going home was the last thing I wanted to do. I would have stayed here for hours more, just soaking in the feel of hanging out with another guy who I actually had something in common with.

"Excuse me? We're closing." The pimple-faced teenager was back, this time pushing a broom around the floor.

War flashed him a smile. "No problem, kid. Vinnie here is on his last ball, and he's gonna roll it straight down the gutter anyway."

I scoffed. "You think I'm gonna let you win?"

War eyed me. "You better fucking not."

"Challenge accepted," I muttered.

There was no way I was throwing a game for him, no matter what. But I needed a strike to beat him. I picked up my ball and moved to the top of the lane.

War followed, standing just to my left.

I glanced over at him. "You seriously gonna stand right there while I throw this?"

He nodded, his mouth turned up in a smirk. "Yep. Gonna make sure you don't step one toe over that black line."

"I don't need to cheat to win." I grinned back at him. "I'm just better than you."

I eyed the little arrows painted on the lane, took a deep breath, and swung my arm back.

"You ever thought about being with a guy?"

My entire body locked up, stopping my arm mid-swing. It jerked painfully, but I managed to hold on to the ball. I turned to face War. "What the fuck?"

War snorted. "Look, you may not need to cheat, but I do."

I shook my head, turning back. "Shut up and let me concentrate."

I drew my arm back again.

"I reckon I'd be good at blow jobs. I've practiced on bananas."

There was no holding on to the ball this time. I dropped it onto the lane as I cracked up laughing. We both watched my ball creep down the lane with zero pace and eventually roll into the gutter.

"I hate you." I wandered back to the ball return. "I haven't gotten a gutter ball since I was about ten."

War was practically hysterical with laughter as he sat back down. "It's not my fault you're easily distracted by me."

I bit my lip, letting my gaze rake over him. Then shook my head, getting it back on straight. I had one more ball to win it.

I picked it up and threw it quickly before War could say another word.

It was a terrible throw. The worst one I'd thrown all night.

War cheered when it dropped into the gutter once more.

His hand landed on the back of my neck. "Good game, my friend. Good fucking game. Let's do it again soon, yeah? I forgot how good something so simple can be."

"You play dirty," I complained, slipping off my shoes and swapping them out for my boots.

War did the same, tying his shoelaces together and

slinging the bowling shoes over his shoulder as he stood. "I'm surprised you don't."

"I'm a man of honor."

Neither of us could keep a straight face over that.

"Yeah, a man of honor who discussed stealing a car with me earlier tonight. So very honorable."

"At least I didn't cheat by offering a blow job."

The teenager behind the counter looked up, his eyes huge as they darted between me and War. Oops. Probably said that a little loud. I pushed the shoes over to him. "Thanks."

War did the same, and the teenager took the shoes, putting them away on a rack behind him. War and I turned for the doors and let ourselves out into the night air once more.

It was dark outside, storm clouds moving in on a brisk wind. The parking lot was empty, only the lights from inside spilling out and providing any relief from the darkness. War stopped, pulling out his cigarettes and lighting one for each of us before passing mine over.

Our fingers brushed, and I cracked my neck, trying to ignore the tension between us. But it was fucking impossible with him right next to me, standing so close our arms touched. Neither of us made a move to step aside.

War blew out a trail of smoke rings. "Penny for your thoughts. You still pissed I cheated?"

"No. I am wondering if you were serious about the banana though." I glanced over at him and grinned. "You swallow too?"

He glanced at me, putting his cigarette to his lips again. "What do you think?"

He blew the smoke out slowly, letting it curl toward me in the darkness.

I leaned in, so my lips were less than an inch from his, and inhaled.

His gaze locked with mine, something hot and heavy and barely concealed while I breathed in his air.

The lights went out behind us.

War's mouth was on mine in a second. He pushed me until my back hit the wall, our cigarettes dropped in the need to get hands on each other. His fist curled into the front of my shirt, his other coming up to the side of my face, holding me tight.

He kissed me hard, tongue insistent, taking what he wanted.

And fuck if I wasn't willing to give it to him.

I opened my mouth, groaning at the taste of him. My dick went hard, with him pressed against me, his erection straining at his jeans. I trailed off his lips, burying my face in his neck and sucking and licking his stubbled jaw.

"Fuck," War groaned, searching for my mouth with his.

On instinct, I went for his belt, yanking at it to get it undone while I kissed him back. His hands slipped beneath my shirt, running up my abs and then back down to the button on my jeans.

"I want more," War said in my ear. "Been thinking about your cock since I watched you jerking off outside my cabin."

His fingers worked my button and zipper quicker than I could get his belt undone, which was a good thing, because I was ready to explode just from his lips at my ear. He licked my neck and dragged my zipper down, searching for my erection hidden behind it.

The door to the alley opened with a loud squeak of hinges.

All three of us froze. Me. War. The kid who just wanted to lock up for the night.

War's fingers were an inch from my exposed cock, that I really fucking desperately wanted him to touch.

He moved slightly, turning his back on the guy and shielding us both in the process. Very slowly, he pulled my zipper up.

I groaned my disappointment, and War turned to the younger man.

The employee spoke up before War could get a word in edgewise. "Don't stop on my behalf. I'm gay too. I get it."

He locked the front door and walked to the only remaining car left in the parking lot, his keys jingling as he went.

"I'm not gay," War and I both said in unison.

The young guy stopped when he reached his car, a badly concealed snort echoing in the silent night. "Keep telling yourself that while you feel each other up, boys. Enjoy the closet."

He opened his car door and disappeared inside.

War and I both stared at each other.

The sudden urge to laugh came over me. "Not gay, but you've been thinking about my dick, huh?"

War grinned, walking backward in the darkness. "Can't a man just appreciate another man's cock?"

I did up the button on my jeans, following him back toward Psychos. "You were thinking about sucking it. You were so ready to get on your knees right now and show me exactly how good you can swallow."

He sniggered and turned around to walk beside me. "I'm into chicks." He glanced over at me. "But yeah, I probably would have," he admitted.

I groaned. "I'm into women too. But I probably would have enjoyed it."

War palmed the back of his neck, his leather jacket gaping. "Well. This is new."

I shrugged. "You gonna go all weird now?"

He shook his head. "You?"

"No."

"Good. 'Cause I don't mind you, Vincent." He sighed. "Gonna have to go home and jerk off now though. First Bliss. Then you. My dick has been up and down more tonight than a flag on a pole."

Neither of us suggested picking up where we'd left off. The moment had passed. But every time I looked at him, I hoped there'd be another.

# 15

---

## BLISS

*N*ash drove me into the center of Saint View, where the main strip ran through the town. Most of the little shopfronts were dark and closed for the night. But two remained open, light spilling from windows and beneath doors.

"So are we stuffing dollar bills in G-strings at the strip club or are we getting tattoos?" I asked, peering out my window at the two establishments.

"Neither." Nash got out of his Jeep, and I did the same, slamming the door closed behind me. He jogged around, meeting me on the sidewalk. "The tattooist also does piercings. Come on."

He grabbed my hand, and I jumped at the jolt of electricity that shot up my arm from his touch. I closed my fingers around his, loving the feel of his hand in mine, and followed him past the couple of people hanging around out in front.

Nash pushing open the door triggered a little bell, and a young guy with a tattoo that crept up the side of his face poked his head out of a back room. Recognition dawned in his eyes, and he grinned. "Nash! Long time no see."

Nash tugged me toward the guy and shook his hand. "Dax. This is Bliss."

I waved hello across a wooden counter painted in colorful swirling tattoo art. It was intricate and detailed and had so many things going on that I wanted to stop and run my fingers over each picture, making sense of how they all combined together.

Dax said hello but then turned back to Nash. "So what's it been? A month?"

"Six weeks maybe, I think."

The guy lifted Nash's shirt sleeve and peered at what had to have been his handiwork on Nash's skin. "Healed up nice. I love that piece. You wanna add to it? You've got maybe three inches of space left on this arm before I get my gun on your other."

Nash chuckled. "Yeah, we'll see about that. But no. No tats tonight. Thought I might get a piercing."

Dax raised his own pierced eyebrow. "Wouldn't have picked you for a piercing sorta guy. You got any others?"

I was interested to know the answer to that myself.

Nash shook his head. "None."

Dax grinned at him. "Fresh meat, huh? Word of warning, they're like tats. Once you get one, it's hard to stop there."

Nash laughed. "Sounds like you're just trying to get me to spend even more of my hard-earned paycheck in your store." He glanced over at me. "Dax owns the place. His brother and a couple other guys work here too."

Dax picked up a bottle of hand sanitizer and squirted

it all over his palms. "They aren't as good as me though. Nash knows who to come to." He rubbed his hands together, smearing the sanitizer around. "Of course, I'm only brave enough to say that because none of them are here right now."

I laughed. "Don't worry, I can keep a secret."

Dax snapped on a pair of gloves and then he turned to Nash. "Okay, my friend. Where are we getting this piercing? Ear? Eyebrow?"

"You'd look good with an eyebrow ring," I mused. "Sexy."

Nash's gaze met mine for a moment, but then he shook his head. "I'm celebrating a sort of big birthday this week."

"He's forty," I interrupted.

He shot me a glare. "Thanks, Bliss. I hadn't forgotten."

I giggled.

"Anyway. Some people pointed out that I needed to do something wild and crazy..."

Dax nodded in understanding. "Ah. Got it. Earring probably isn't gonna cut it then, huh?"

"Probably not."

I wandered away, drawn to all the tattoo examples on the walls. The talent of the men who worked here was next level. There were so many different types of design, from black-and-gray portraits to brightly colored cartoon styles. All of it was extremely high quality and not at all what I would have expected from a tattoo shop in the middle of Saint View.

"How brave you feeling?" Dax asked Nash. "Could pierce your cock?"

I smothered a laugh, glad it was hidden by having my back to the men. Nash would never.

He paused for a moment. "Yeah, okay. Do it."

I choked, spinning around with big eyes to stare at the two men. "Excuse me, what?"

They both stared at me, Dax with a grin of amusement. "Uh-oh, you didn't tell your girl? You know you're gonna be out of commission in the bedroom for a couple weeks, right?"

"I'm not his girl," I said at the same time Nash said, "She's got that covered elsewhere."

I was sure he was remembering me shouting out his name while War made me come. Heat rushed through me. "Are you seriously going to do this?"

"It's not like I'm having sex anyway. And you were right. I have to do something to mark the milestone. I don't mind a bit of pain."

"These piercings are super popular lately," Dax piped up. "I've got one. Tattoos hurt more, and ladies love them." He pointed to a privacy screen. "Go on around the back there, and we'll get started. Bliss, if you want to go with him, there's room. He might need a hand to hold. Men are known to be big crybabies when the needle is coming straight for their junk. Nash can handle a tattoo okay, but I ain't ever tried putting one on his dick."

I glanced at Nash.

He was fighting back laughter, probably because of the horrified expression on my face.

"Are you really doing this?" I asked again.

He nodded. "Yep."

Dax pulled out some sort of barbaric-looking piercing instrument that had my stomach rolling. "Oh Jesus."

Nash paled. "Fuck me, man. Is that what you do it with?"

Dax chuckled. "You'll be fine."

Nash suddenly didn't look so fine. A clammy sweat broke out across his forehead. But he moved for the partitioned-off privacy screen.

I wanted to be a good friend. "Do you want me to come?"

He shrugged, playing it cool. "I'll be fine."

Dax laughed. "He's shitting himself. Come hold his hand." He gave me a little shove, and when Nash nodded, I rounded the privacy screen with the two guys in tow.

Nash passed me his wallet and keys, and Dax pushed me over a little stool to sit on. I took it, putting it in position by the top of the bed. I sat, then realized I was now exactly at Nash's dick height and he was about to take his pants off.

Heat flooded me. "I'm just gonna..." I twirled my finger in a whirlwind motion and spun the stool so I was facing the wall.

Behind me, Dax chattered over the top of the sounds of Nash's fly lowering and his clothes being removed.

All I could think about was the rumored ten-inch, porn-star-wannabe-sized cock.

There was a rustle as Dax laid a large plastic sheet over the bed, and Nash got up on it.

I didn't dare move.

"You can turn around, Bliss." Nash poked me in the side with his outstretched hand.

I swiveled back carefully, making sure I didn't spin so far that I would cop a glimpse of everything he had going on down there.

God, it was hard to keep my eyes on his face.

He had one hand behind his head, and I held out my hand for his other one.

He put it in mine. "You okay?"

"Fine," I babbled. "Just fine. I mean, you've got your infamous dick out, and Dax is about to shove a needle through it, which sounds like torture, and I'm really sorry I ever said you should do something crazy for your birthday, because I did not mean mutilate your dick, but if you like it you absolutely should get it. But if this has anything to do with our teasing you at the bar tonight—"

"My infamous dick?"

I blew out a long breath. "Seriously? In everything I just word vomited, that's what you're gonna pick up on?"

"Why is my dick infamous?"

Oh Lord. Me and my big mouth. "Rebel told me a rumor about it. That's all?"

Dax snorted. "Well, shit. That can't be good."

Nash nodded. "Exactly. Keep talking, Bliss. What exactly did Rebel say?"

I sighed. "She said it's massive. Ten inches at least."

Nash glanced at Dax. "Do your work colleagues talk about your dick too?"

Dax sniggered. "Probably. But I mean, bro. She's not wrong. You're...blessed."

Nash groaned, and Dax laughed.

I was dying to take a peek.

Nash rolled his eyes. "Just look, Bliss. It's only a dick."

I looked.

Really quickly.

I spun back to Nash with a hand clapped over my mouth, trying to stifle my embarrassed laughter.

He raised an eyebrow. "Well?"

"I'll report back to Rebel that the rumors are true."

Nash just shook his head.

"All right, if the dick measuring has finished, let's put a bar through it. Okay, so this might bleed. Some people only bleed a bit, others bleed a lot, and it's not uncommon to last a few days. If you're team less blood, a bandage should be fine. But if you're team bleeds like a vampire bit your jugular, then you might want to think about an adult diaper."

Nash sat up. "Wait, what?"

"Also, no jerking the salami for a month."

"A month!"

"Be careful when you urinate. This piercing goes right through your urethra, so some guys find that your piss goes in every which direction for a while, until you get used to it. Might want to sit to piss."

I patted his arm. "Considering I just cleaned the bathrooms at Psychos, I'd really appreciate that."

Nash's eyes were wide. "Shit, Dax. Anything else?"

He shrugged. "Just all the regular stuff. You have an increased risk of infection both at the site of the piercing and urinary tract infections."

I winced. "They hurt."

Nash gaped at me. "No shit!"

Dax continued on like we hadn't said anything. "They can rip condoms, so you're more likely to pick up an STD if you don't notice when you put it on or if it happens during sex. I mean, and of course, there's a really slim chance I might hit the wrong spot and you'll just never be able to have sex again..."

Nash yanked his shirt up. "So, a nipple piercing then, yeah?"

I bit back laughter.

Fifteen minutes later, Nash walked out with a bar through his left nipple and his ginormous dick still one-hundred-percent intact.

## 16

---

## BLISS

*T*he rain was a surprise when Nash and I got out of the tattoo parlor. He drove me back to my car with it splashing on the windshield the entire way. The wipers moved swiftly across the glass, and I focused on the back-and-forth movement, trying to ignore the slow panic settling over me.

I'd never had a problem with storms before. But the weather outside was all too similar to the night Caleb had attacked me up on the bluffs.

Nash stopped in front of my car that we'd left in Psychos' parking lot, and I forced a smile at him. "I hope the piercing doesn't hurt too much."

"I'll be fine. Are you okay, though? You went all quiet."

I didn't want to tell him what the problem really was, so I turned it into a joke. "Was just reflecting on the fact I saw your extremely large penis tonight."

"Lucky you, huh? Fuck, I don't know what I was

thinking even considering that piercing. I'm cringing just thinking about it."

The rain picked up even harder, and I peered out into the night. "I should go. It's late. Or rather, early."

"I don't like you driving in this. Leave your car here. I'll drop you home."

I shook my head. "Then I won't have a way of getting to work tomorrow. I'll be fine. I'll take it slow and easy."

Nash didn't seem happy. "Text me when you get there so I know you made it safely."

I nodded. "Okay."

My gaze lingered on his, and for a moment, I thought he was going to say something more. But then he pressed his lips together, clearly not ready to put it out there.

I was too distracted by the storm to try to decipher him again.

I pushed open the door and jumped down from his Jeep, squealing as the cold rain poured down around me. "Oh my God!" I ran for my car, hitting the button on the key fob to unlock the doors.

I slid in behind the steering wheel, water running down my neck and beneath my clothes, and sticking the fabric to my skin. "Holy shit, that was intense."

"So's the level of your voice."

The scream I let out was blood-curdling. I spun to peer into the back seat and found Scythe sprawled out across it.

At least as much as a six-foot-something man could sprawl in the back of a hatchback.

My heart raced, thumping too hard and too fast. I slapped his arm. "Don't do that! What the hell are you doing back there anyway? How did you even get in? Jesus Christ, Scythe. I nearly peed myself!"

He clambered between the two front seats, plonking himself down in the passenger side. "Please refrain from urinating while I'm in the car. That's truly disgusting."

I glared at him. "So are you, and yet I don't seem to be able to get rid of you."

He flashed a smile. "You'd miss me if you did. Can we go home?"

I ignored the little kernel of warmth that leapt to light at the idea of him and me sharing a home and reminded myself it was temporary.

Except I'd gone back to my parents' place that night, so I really had no reason to continue staying with Scythe.

Other than the fact I'd come to like it.

If I told him that, his head would likely explode though. And since he didn't seem in a rush to get rid of me, I let the thought go.

I drove us back to his place carefully, peering through the rain sheets and driving with my high beams on where I could. He tossed his jacket at me as we turned into the driveway, and I pulled it over my head, using it as an umbrella to get me to the front door without getting soaked again.

We both ran for it, Scythe drenched in the heavy downpour in just the few seconds it took to get from the car to the undercover front steps. I shook out his jacket and passed it back to him. "Thank you. Who knew you had manner—"

I flinched at the lightning that lit the sky, quickly followed by the loudest crack of thunder I'd ever heard in my life.

Scythe put his hands on my arms. "Hey. Steady."

But my heart wasn't listening. It thumped unevenly, and my breath came in too-sharp pants.

Scythe frowned, but I moved away, letting myself into the house and passing Little Dog, asleep on her doggy bed. She'd taken to sleeping with me in the absence of Vincent, but when I hadn't come home on time, she'd clearly given up waiting.

Scythe frowned at her, too. "Do you think she's deaf? Or dead?"

I was kind of wondering the same thing. That thunder had been so loud it seemed impossible it wouldn't have woken her. But her little chest rose and fell, her breaths regular. "Let's just leave her. It's late. I'll see you in the morning."

Scythe nodded, and I left him to go to my room. Inside the house was warm and dry. Safe. Especially with the psychopath with a penchant for murder sleeping in the room across the hall. Yet every step I took in the dark, while thunder cracked and lightning flashed outside, I grew more and more uneasy. My palms went clammy, and my heart pounded so hard it was almost painful.

In my room, I stripped off my clothes, throwing on an old T-shirt over my panties, and buried myself in a pile of blankets and pillows in the hopes of driving out the sounds of the storm.

It didn't help. The rain hitting the roof sounded too similar to the rain hitting my car that night. The lightning outside was too similar to the strike that had lit up Caleb's dark eyes, staring at me from beneath a hoodie.

I'd thought I was over this.

I'd thought seeing him alive and curled up in the fetal position, terrified for his life, would help.

But it didn't. I still saw him attacking me on the stairs, ripping my clothes off my body and taking me roughly. He was still there in my head, threatening me for being a slut and a whore. I heard myself calling out for Vincent to help me while Caleb stood there behind me with his hands on my body, touching me in places I didn't want him to.

The thunder cracked once more, and a whimper left my body.

I squeezed my eyes shut and tried to sleep, but the storm had other ideas. It raged outside, the wind howling and battering at the windows until the glass shook. The thunder carried on for an hour, relentless in its booming. But it was the lightning that brought the flashbacks, each one more vivid than the last, until my chest was so tight I couldn't breathe.

I wasn't safe. Not here, alone in the dark. I was too far gone to the panic attack, and no amount of rational thinking was going to change that.

But I knew something that would.

As the storm reached its highest point, I slid out of bed and walked across the hall, quietly turning the door-knob and letting myself in.

Scythe slept with his back to me, blankets pulled up over his waist, but his chest and arms bare. The lightning show outside flashed over him, illuminating his tawny skin.

"If that's anyone other than Bliss, just know I sleep with a knife under my pillow."

I breathed out slowly, just the sound of his voice a

comfort in the darkness. I moved to the side of his bed. "Do you really?"

He flipped over to face me and reached one hand beneath his pillow, producing a wicked-looking blade with a solid-stone handle.

"That's a safety hazard," I whispered.

"It's the only way I sleep at all. What are you doing in here?"

"I couldn't sleep."

"I gave you the most comfortable bed in the house."

It was. But the problem was, he wasn't in it. "I didn't want to be alone."

His gaze pierced through me in the darkness. Then slowly, he put his knife down on his bedside table and lifted the covers.

An invitation I shouldn't want to take. Not with everything I knew about him.

He could just as easily kill me, the way he had so many others. He could pick up that knife at any time during the night and draw it across my throat. I wouldn't even be able to scream.

Another crack of thunder had me diving beneath his blankets.

He dropped them down around me, and we lay face-to-face, watching each other in the darkness. Our breaths mingled, mine coming too fast, and not helped by the sudden rush of attraction I felt for the man. His dark-brown gaze raked over me so intensely I couldn't breathe.

I couldn't stand it. I flipped over so my back was to him. "Thank you," I whispered.

"Your breathing is too fast. Come here."

"I'll be okay."

He sighed. "You're clearly not."

He shuffled over, the bed dipping with his weight as he tucked himself in behind me and draped an arm across my middle.

I closed my eyes when his warmth invaded me. His arm around me, locking me in place, was heavy and comforting, and my heartrate instantly slowed to a more normal pace.

Every muscle in my body relaxed, inch by inch, sinking into his comfy bed and the security of his embrace.

Until I realized something I really should have considered earlier. "Are you naked?"

"Very."

I rammed my elbow back into his stomach. "Scythe! You could have told me."

His only response was to hold me tighter. "Shh." He mumbled, "Go to sleep."

I relaxed again, closing my eyes.

But it wouldn't come. The storm outside dulled, the thunder and lightning moving on, and the rain flattening out to the more gentle, soothing sound of rain on the roof. Yet sleep refused to take me.

My body was tense for an entirely different reason now.

One that had nothing to do with Mother Nature, and everything to do with the very naked man behind me.

He moved so his entire body was spooned around mine. His chest molded to my back, legs tucked up behind my knees, and dick pressed against my butt. His breath was the even, slow, rhythmical breathing of sleep, but all I could think about was the low heat that bubbled inside me, growing hotter with every minute that passed.

"Are you sleeping?" I whispered so softly, even I barely heard it over the rain.

He didn't answer. I bit my lip, wondering how I'd created this situation that I both didn't want to leave, and yet it was torturing me at the same time. I wriggled a little, trying to ease the prickly heat spreading over my body.

Scythe's hand moving across my belly and up to my hip stopped me.

My breath hitched as he smoothed his palm down along my thigh, to the hem of the oversized T-shirt I'd thrown on over my panties. His fingertips brushed my leg, and I let out a tiny gasp when his skin connected with mine.

That was no accidental touch.

He was clearly as awake as I was.

His fingers stroked over my skin, tentatively at first, featherlight touches to my mid-thigh. But when I didn't stop him—when I in fact wriggled a little closer back— he grew more brazen.

His fingers flattened out against my skin and ran up my leg, over my hip and stomach, back to where he'd started. Only this time, his hand was beneath my shirt, the material all rucked up around my waist.

I held my breath, desperately hoping he'd go farther.

He ran his hands higher, taking the shirt with him until his fingertips brushed the underside of my breast.

I closed my eyes and pressed back, silently encouraging him.

He cupped my breast and ground his hips against my

ass. His dick grew hard, prodding me deliciously, the size of him promising a good time.

I let out a little moan, welcoming his touch, and that was all the permission he seemed to need.

He pushed my shirt higher, lifting it right over my head, and I helped him along, so that all that was between us was my panties. His hand immediately went back to my breast, but with more authority this time, cupping me and pinching my nipple between his thumb and finger.

I reached back for him, finding his hip and holding him tight while he ground on me.

His lips pressed to the back of my neck, and then the side, and I lifted my chin, giving him better access.

"I'm not a gentleman," he warned me, licking his way along my skin to my shoulder. "I'm not Vincent."

"I know," I whispered.

Vincent couldn't have given me what I needed in that moment.

But Scythe could.

He growled in my ear, taking my panties off in one quick tug, and then reached his hand between my thighs. He cupped my mound and then found my clit, starting up a slow, torturous roll that had sparks lighting up inside me.

"Oh," I moaned.

He pulled my leg up and back over his, getting himself in a better position, his dick now rubbing at my core instead of my butt and lower back. He teased me, his thick length running through my arousal and up over my clit, coating himself and turning me on with every touch.

"You're so wet," he murmured against my skin. "That for me?"

"Yes," I groaned.

Because it was.

I hadn't thought of Nash or War for a second. Or even Vincent. It was Scythe whose body I needed. Whose strong reassurance and confidence had turned my trembles of fear into shivers of pleasure.

"You're such a good girl." His teeth bit down onto my shoulder, the slight pain just enough to make me gasp. "Gonna take you now. Your pussy is so wet, I can't wait any longer."

His fingers worked harder on my clit and the thick, blunt head of him found my entrance. He didn't wait. His cock was slick with my arousal, and he'd done all the asking for permission that he was going to do.

I wanted it. I was so ready to give myself up to him. I needed it as bad as he did.

He pushed inside me, invading my space and stretching me so deliciously my head spun. I gripped his hip, digging my fingernails into his muscled thigh to hold on while he thrust into me again.

Each thrust was slow and deliberate. An agonizing pull from my body before drawing him back in. He never let up on my clit, rubbing slow motions over it that matched the tempo he fucked me with.

"Scythe," I groaned.

"Fuck, I love hearing that name on your lips, Bliss. I've heard you yell War's and Nash's. And now mine."

The beginnings of an orgasm lit up inside me.

I craned my neck back, desperate to kiss him.

His lips found mine instantly.

It was nothing like the sweet brush of lips I'd shared with Vincent. Scythe kissed with confidence and need, plunging his tongue into my mouth in a deep, dirty kiss that matched the way he fucked me. He was sensual and strong, and in his arms, all my worries and doubts disappeared.

All that mattered was him.

He picked up the pace, his hips slapping against my ass, the pressure inside me building and mounting behind my clit and deep inside me, too much to contain.

"I can't wait to feel your pussy clamp down on my cock, Bliss," he murmured in my ear. "I can feel how close you are. Come."

It wasn't just cheap words. There was a growl in his voice that vibrated through his chest and into my back. His hips moved faster, jacking himself into me, while he pinched my clit.

I wanted to come for him, with him buried deep inside me, darkness surrounding us, and the rain falling outside. I gave in and let myself feel every movement, every muscle-relaxing thrust that brought my orgasm to the surface.

I shut my brain off and just let myself feel.

He claimed my mouth once more, kissing me deeply as the orgasm took hold.

"Oh!" I yelled, my shout of ecstasy muffled by his lips. Everything inside me lit up, pleasure shooting from the place we were joined. "Oh my God."

He came with a groan, buried deep inside me. "Fuck, Bliss. You're so tight."

He drove home several more times, and we both

moaned with every movement, all of it so good it verged on too much.

He held me tighter, his movements slowing, and my orgasm glow faded.

The minute it disappeared; common sense flooded back in.

I needed to leave.

The storm had made me lose my mind. Vincent, I was interested in. But Scythe terrified me. He was a cold-blooded killer who freely admitted it.

Except he didn't feel like one when we were both naked and wrapped in each other's arms, our bodies slick with sweat from great sex.

He mumbled into my shoulder, "I know what you're thinking. And you're not leaving while I'm still inside you, Bliss. Shut your brain off for a minute and just let me hold you."

My resistance melted. It was a very Vincent thing to say, and if he hadn't worded it so casually, I might have asked if he'd slipped through Scythe's defenses.

But I didn't. I fell asleep in the arms of a psychopath.

I had never felt safer or more content in my life.

## 17

## WAR

*I* got to the hospital at nine, right at the start of visiting hours, and made a desperate beeline for the coffee machine. It was terrible, of course, but even bad coffee was better than no coffee when you'd barely slept and had a mild hangover to boot.

I sipped the dark liquid carefully as I walked up to my mom's room, lifting a hand in greeting to the nursing staff at the desk, who I was beginning to know by name after weeks of coming here every day. "How is she?"

"No change, I'm afraid. Sorry, War." Louise was probably around the same age as me and had worked here since she'd left college. She'd kept me entertained one day with mildly flirtatious stories that heavily featured her ex, each one accentuating the fact she was single.

She was pretty, and probably had a bangin' body beneath her scrubs, and pre-Bliss, I probably would have gone there. But despite Bliss and me making nothing between us official, I'd just completely lost interest in other women.

Apparently, the same could not be said for men, however.

I shoved my free hand in my pocket, the back of my neck heating when I thought about how I'd pushed Vincent up against the side of the bowling alley and kissed him until all I could think about was taking it a whole lot further.

I had no doubt in my mind that if the guy working there hadn't walked out and busted us, I would have been down on my knees, learning how to give a blow job.

Or vice versa.

He'd seemed just as eager.

I blew softly over the top of my coffee and forced another sip of the barely drinkable sludge down my throat.

Fancy seemed tinier and frailer by the day. Every time I came in here, I was floored by the way the larger-than-life woman could suddenly look so helpless. I could still hear her big voice shouting for all the guys at the club to sit down and shut the fuck up.

Every single one of them had listened. Because Fancy knew her place, and she demanded the respect it brought.

She was queen to my old man's king.

The king I'd probably never be, even though the crown had been placed firmly on my head.

I slumped down on the hard plastic seat by her bed and picked up her hand. It was cool and clammy, and much too lifeless for my liking. "Hey, Mom. How are you doing today? Any chance you might want to wake up? Would be good to see your eyes and hear your voice."

I did this every day. But I'd stopped hoping for a

response. The doctors kept saying there was a chance she could wake up, but the longer this dragged out, the more I doubted their assurances.

I wasn't sure the Mom I knew was still in there, fighting to get back to me.

I had a feeling she knew about my dad and just didn't want to do life without him.

I couldn't even blame her. I barely knew Bliss, and yet, the thought of not seeing her for a day had me sweating.

It was just sex. Really fucking good sex with a woman I couldn't get enough of and had no plans on giving up anytime soon. Nothing more.

Even as I thought it, I knew it wasn't true. There'd been plenty of other women in my life. None had made me want to call them twenty-four seven. None had made me want to give up other women. None had held my interest for more than a night, and yet I'd been chasing Bliss around for weeks.

I needed more coffee. I was too in my own head today.

My phone buzzed in my back pocket, and I leaned forward to pull it out, pausing when I saw who the text was from.

**Vincent:** How much do you remember from last night?

I had no chill. Or any desire to lie.

**War:** All of it. What are you doing?

**Vincent:** Lying in bed with Bliss.

I scoffed.

**War:** In your dreams.

A photo popped up a moment later, and my jaw dropped open. Bliss had her head on his chest, her auburn hair splayed over his arm that held his phone for the selfie. Her shoulders were bare, a sheet pulled up over her breasts. Vincent smirked at me from the photo, the middle finger on his free hand extended to flip me off.

I shook my head, a grin growing.

**War:** You dirty, dirty dog.

**Vincent:** It isn't like that.

**War:** I'm jealous.

**Vincent:** Come over.

"Fuck," I muttered. Because there was literally nothing more I wanted than to walk out of this hospital and go join them. My dick started getting hard over the thought of it.

**War:** Can't right now. Visiting my mom at the hospital. Rain check though, yeah?

**Vincent:** You can bet on it.

I groaned, trying to get myself under control because now wasn't the time nor the place.

My phone buzzed again, though.

**Vincent:** Bliss is awake. She wants to know if you can get her drugs?

"Shit."

**War:** For personal use? Or for Psychos?"

**Vincent:** Psychos. She hasn't heard from her contact, and we've got Nash's party on the weekend.

**War:** Drugs aren't really my game. Doubtful I could get her that much that quickly.

**Vincent:** Roger that. We'll work something out. Say hi to your mom for me.

I looked over at Fancy. "My friend Vincent says hi."

There was no response. Not that I'd really expected one. But the nurses kept telling me that there was a chance Fancy could hear me. So I talked anyway. "I really need you to wake up. I met someone I want you to meet..."

I paused, on the verge of saying something more, maybe about Vincent and how kissing him had woken up something inside me that had been lying dormant for a really long time.

I couldn't.

Fancy and my dad had once sat me down on one of our kitchen chairs in the cabin I'd grown up in, not all that far from the one I lived in now. Dad had pressed his mouth into a grim line and crossed his arms over his chest, glaring at me, while Fancy had gazed at me over his shoulder, concern etched into her frown.

"Do you and Hawk have something to tell us?" she'd asked.

My dad had stared intently at my fifteen-year-old self and waited for a reply.

I'd nearly shit myself. At that age, the man was still a few inches taller and had at least fifty pounds on me. He was stern and gruff and war-ruined. He took no shit; not from me or from any of his guys. And when he called you out, isolating you for one of his 'talks,' you knew you'd fucked up royally.

But I honestly had no idea what Hawk and I had done. "No, sir."

Dad had sighed. "One of the guys heard you tell him to suck your cock the other day."

I'd burst into laughter. "So? We were just screwing around. I didn't mean for him to actually do it."

My father had relaxed visibly. "So there's nothing more than that going on between the two of you?"

"Fuck no." And I hadn't been lying. Hawk was my best

friend. There was nothing sexual between him and me. We gave each other shit constantly, but it wasn't laced with some sort of hidden meaning.

Fancy had nodded and glared at my father. "You set those men straight. They aren't going to be walking around this compound, spreading rumors that my son is some closeted fag. They're just boys being boys and running their mouths."

I'd sat by and said nothing.

Dad had eyed me though, watching me for the next few days like he didn't quite believe me.

That weekend, I'd found myself in a room with one of the club girls, who'd been only too happy to break in the prez's son.

I hadn't minded either. She'd had big tits and a rounded ass that was perfect for hanging on to.

I liked women.

I'd just never told anyone that sometimes I liked men too.

---

*A*fter an hour of sitting by Fancy's bedside, talking shit and reading half the newspaper to her, I was sick of my own voice. I rode back to the clubhouse, ready for a beer, even though it was barely eleven.

Ice was behind the bar, where he often could be found. The kid liked mixing drinks it seemed, and I was more than happy to take them out of his hands.

"Nothing fancy for me this morning, kid. Just need a beer to knock this hangover on its head and remove the taste of hospital air from my mouth."

Ice jumped at my voice, shoving some papers beneath the bar and spinning around to face me. "Shit. Prez. Didn't even see you there. Hang on a sec, I'll grab you one."

He looked distinctly guilty. I'd one hundred percent sprung him doing something he wasn't supposed to be. "What's with the papers?"

He shook his head too quickly. "Nothing. Just some junk mail. Nothing important."

I took the beer from his outstretched hand and peered at him curiously. "Why are you lying to me all of a sudden? Not a good look for a new member, Ice. You're shit at it anyway. What's on the papers?"

He dug his teeth into his bottom lip. "We all had mail today. Fang brought it up from the mailbox and handed it out. All the envelopes were identical."

I shrugged. "Okay. Did I get one too?"

Ice closed his eyes for a second and took a deep breath.

I sniggered. "Could you be any more dramatic, kid? Just fucking tell me what it was, or hand mine over so I can see for myself."

He sighed. "I dunno if you have one, but here's what was in mine." He pulled the papers from where he'd stashed them and grudgingly handed them over.

I squinted at the black-and-white papers, trying to make sense of them.

Realization hit me in the gut.

They were surveillance-style photos, grainy and weird-colored, obviously not taken on a regular camera.

Because they'd been taken in the middle of the night. In the almost pure darkness.

Two men kissing outside a bowling alley when they'd thought no one was around.

I jerked my head up sharply.

Ice held his hands up. "Please don't shoot the messenger. I swear, I had nothing to do with it. I literally just opened an envelope with my name on it."

I looked down at the rest of the photos, leafing through the images, one after another, each one more incriminating than the next. My face. Vincent's. Our hands on each other's belts, flies open.

I ground my molars together. "Has everyone seen these?"

A muscle ticked in Ice's jaw. "I don't know."

I slammed a hand down on the bar. "Fuck." I stormed for the door, needing some air.

"For what it's worth, Prez?" Ice called. "It doesn't matter to me."

I didn't stop. I stormed right out of the clubhouse toward my cabin, pulling my phone out and calling Hawk's number. With each step, I crunched drying autumn leaves beneath my boots until I was in the clearing by my cabin.

Hawk hadn't picked up. It had gone to his voicemail twice.

I couldn't remember a time where I'd ever heard his voicemail message. The man always picked up when I called.

Dread pooled in my stomach. I'd been warned about being with a man. I'd put it down to my parents' old-fashioned values, but already, there was a different feel in the air.

One that didn't sit well with me.

I stopped at the bottom of my stairs, photos crumpling in my hand.

"You've seen then." Gus stood from the wooden porch swing and leaned on the banister, staring down at the papers.

"Where did they come from?"

The older man shook his head. "No idea. But, War. Fuck. I know your dad warned you about this..."

"I'm not gay."

"Those photos say otherwise."

I groaned and scrubbed a hand through my hair. I took the steps two at a time and slumped onto the swing. "There was no one fucking there, Gus. It was the middle of the night."

He came and sat next to me, perching on the edge, rocking us slightly. "Then someone is following you. Or him. Probably you though, since the photos were sent here."

"Just fucking great. What the hell did I do?"

"Besides make out with another guy?" Gus chuckled. "Look, son, I'm on your side. I don't give a fuck who you wanna make out with. We all know you're gonna end up with Siren anyway. That's been done since birth. Sow your wild oats with whoever the fuck you want. But the other guys might not be as comfortable with it."

"Hawk isn't answering his phone."

"Might be a few others who don't answer theirs either."

"How am I supposed to run a club if none of them will even talk to me? We're supposed to go on a run next week."

Gus clapped a fatherly hand on my shoulder. "It'll

blow over. Get a woman bouncing on your cock in the middle of the clubhouse, and everyone will be reassured that you aren't suddenly gonna start asking to suck their cocks. I think you've got bigger problems though, don't you? Someone is targeting your family, War. First your dad and Fancy. Now you. Maybe that's what you should be focusing on instead of making out with random guys outside of bowling alleys." He screwed his face up. "Honestly, War. What are you? Sixteen? Get a fucking room next time."

# 18

## BLISS

*I* yanked a brush through my hair, wincing as it caught on a tangle. Trying again, I pulled it through more slowly, gently detangling the knot before twisting my hair up off my neck into a ponytail and then wrapping it into a neat and tidy bun.

I sighed, staring at my reflection in the dressing room table mirror. I'd stayed at my dad's place the night before, knowing we had the funeral first thing in the morning. We were all going. Dad, Nichelle, Me, Everett, and Verity. They were all off in their own rooms hopefully getting ready, too, and we'd planned to all drive together.

A united family. Mourning the loss of a brother only I accepted.

My father was going to come face-to-face with my mother, and I battled back the nerves butterflying around my stomach over the showdown I was sure would follow their reunion. I felt ill thinking about it.

I picked up my makeup bag, rummaging around

inside it for my mascara and eyeliner, and groaned when I came up empty. "Dammit."

I knew exactly where they both were. Sitting on the vanity in my bathroom at Scythe's place. Which was a bit of a disaster because I did not have time to run over there and retrieve them, nor did I have time to run to the store and grab a replacement.

I did have a stepmother who loved makeup. So I ran lightly down the hall to the room she shared with my father and rapped my knuckles across the door.

"Yes," Nichelle called from inside.

"It's me. Can I come in?"

The doorknob turned, and Nichelle's perfect blond head poked through. "Hey." Real concern was etched into her expression. "How are you?"

I nodded. "Good. Just about ready. I've left my eyeliner and mascara at a friend's place, though. Could I borrow yours?"

Nichelle widened the door, nodding and ushering me inside. "Of course. My makeup is all in the bathroom cabinet. Go on through. I'm just getting dressed, and your father is already downstairs waiting with the kids. Use whatever you want."

Well, this was new. Nichelle actually being pleasant and letting me borrow her things with no restrictions or reminders about how I'd have to pay for it if I broke it. Apparently, all it took for her to be polite was your brother dying.

I just thanked her politely and left her to *um* and *ah* over which dress she wore, while I went into her bathroom in search of something to make my eyes pretty. It was probably a pointless task. The minute I started crying, I'd wash it all off, but I wanted to at least start the day looking semi-respectable.

Their bathroom had two sinks, side by side, beneath a wide mirror. My father's side of the bathroom held only his toothbrush and toothpaste. While Nichelle's was a disaster zone of makeup, bottles of lotion and perfume, and an array of sponges, brushes, and hair styling products. I poked through the things on the vanity, not finding what I was after, so moved on to rifling through her drawers, knowing for sure that there had to be mascara in here somewhere.

"Ah! Success," I murmured, finding what I needed in her top drawer. I plucked the little tube from its hiding spot, my fingers brushing over something black and silky tucked into the back of the drawer.

I froze, catching a glimpse of the logo embroidered into the material.

And then squeezed my eyes shut tight.

I did not just see a Psychos' sex club mask in my stepmother's drawer.

Ew. Ew. Double ick ew.

Images of her and my father wandering around my club in their underwear, or less, tried to invade my brain, and I shook my head hard not to let them in.

I had definitely not seen them at the party I'd thrown, where we'd pulled the masks out. So this had to be from a previous party under Axel's management. Gag. Hopefully whatever kinky thing they'd been trying on was over and they'd never go back there. But I wasn't risking it. I closed the drawer quickly, clutching my fingers around the mascara. "Nichelle?"

She came out from her walk-in wardrobe, smoothing

out a black dress that clung to her toned, trim body. "Did you find it? What do you think of this dress? Is it okay? Should I wear heels? They'll probably sink into the ground at the cemetery."

"You look great," I said honestly. "You know how I told you I was working at a bar?"

She wrinkled her cute nose. "Yes, and I still haven't told your father if that's what you're worried about. But also, it's still a yuck from me."

Nichelle would turn her nose up at any job I had. I had a feeling it was the working part that she was most opposed to.

"Did I ever tell you the name of the place? It's really funny."

Nichelle crouched to grab a pair of shoes, sorting through the copious amount she owned. "No. I don't think so."

"It's called Psychos."

Her head snapped up, her horrified, wide-eyed gaze meeting mine.

Red tinged her cheeks, which had to have been burning bright to be noticeable beneath her makeup.

She forced a fake laugh. "Oh. That is an odd name. Sounds like a scary place. Probably not one your father and I would ever go to..."

The 'again' was silent, but we both knew it was there.

I nodded. "Probably for the best."

I turned around and squeezed my eyes shut, dying of secondhand embarrassment. I ran back to my room, thankful at least that we'd had this conversation.

Because it would have been a whole lot worse to have

it if I'd stumbled across them having sex in the middle of Psychos' main floor.

---

$\mathcal{T}$he grounds at the cemetery were still soggy from all the rain, and I was glad I'd opted for flats, when Nichelle's heels got stuck in the ground with every step. But to her credit, she struggled along, clutching my father's arm and not uttering a word of complaint about her ruined and impractical shoes.

Everett and Verity wandered along in front of us, quiet for once, like they instinctively knew the occasion called for it. Or perhaps my father had given them a strongly worded lecture in the kitchen while Nichelle and I had still been upstairs, *not* talking about the horrific fact I now knew they'd been hanging out at sex clubs.

Shudder.

We were a little early, but a small crowd was already gathering, milling around the outdoor area I'd opted for instead of having the service inside the church. Axel hadn't been a religious man, and half the people likely to show up here today would probably perish as they passed beneath the entrance anyway.

I greeted a few people I knew from the bar, and Rebel rushed over to hug me, her big eyes already filled with tears.

"Are you okay?" I whispered, hugging her back.

She nodded quickly, swiping beneath her eyes at the welling moisture. "I'm fine. I just miss him."

I did too. But I'd been missing him for a lot longer than Rebel had been, and I was well practiced with the hole that left inside me. He'd been an everyday part of her life. That hadn't been the case for me.

There was something more troubling plaguing me today.

If Axel's murderer was somebody he knew, they might be here right now.

The thought churned my stomach.

"Bliss."

I turned at the deep voice behind me and was immediately slapped in the face with a scene right out of a movie.

Nash, War, and Scythe stood there, shoulder to shoulder, dressed in suits.

I was pretty sure my jaw was on the ground, my tongue hanging out like a panting dog.

"Holy fucking shitballs, Dis," Rebel muttered. "Good luck choosing just one." She waved to the guys, then went back to stand with Fang and Queenie and some of the others from War's MC.

Speaking of War... I'd never seen him out of blue jeans, plain-colored T-shirts, and scuffed-up leather jackets. Even the day of his father's funeral, he hadn't strayed from that.

"You own a suit?" I asked.

He chuckled and shook his head. "No. But Vincent has a bunch. Borrowed one of his. Bit tight, of course, because he needs to go to the gym more, but it'll do."

Scythe rolled his eyes. "Buy your own next time then. And quit acting like you're the first prize winner in the guns show."

He barbed with War, but his gaze rolled over my body.

I turned away quickly. His expression had too much heat behind it, like he was remembering exactly what I looked like naked.

I was doing the same to him, so I couldn't even be mad.

But Scythe in a suit was straight out of every woman's fantasies. He'd opted out of a tie and had left the top few buttons on his shirt undone, showing off the bronzed skin of his chest. He stood casually, with his hands in his pockets, his attention all on me.

We'd barely spoken since we'd woken up together the day before. I'd been avoiding him, awkward because crawling into his bed and then having sex with him was not what he and I did. We bickered and he teased, while I waited for Vincent to return.

We did not have mind-blowing sex that I couldn't stop thinking about.

I was supposed to be scared of Scythe, and yet, I wasn't.

I was anything but scared, and even less so now that I knew what he could do to my body while we were naked and horizontal.

Scythe smirked like he knew exactly what I was thinking.

I turned to Nash before I could truly register how much I liked his face when he did that. "Did you borrow one of Vincent's suits too?"

"Nah. This one is mine."

The black slacks fit his trim hips perfectly. He'd gone for a classic white, button-down shirt, with the sleeves rolled, and a black tie that he wore a little loose, like it had already tried to choke him.

"It looks good on you."

His eyes flared, and I realized that I'd probably said too much, even with that one simple compliment. So then I attempted to turn it into a joke. "Maybe this should be the new dress code at the bar?"

He leaned in, his mouth close to my ear so only I would hear. "I like it a whole lot better when your dress code is lingerie."

He was referring to what I'd worn to the last Psychos party.

My gaze snapped to meet his, surprise punching through me. He opened his mouth like he was going to say something more, but then his gaze diverted, and a frown formed between his eyebrows.

I followed his line of sight, stiffening when it led directly to my mother. Like Nichelle, she'd worn an unfortunate pair of high heels, so was struggling on the soggy grass. Unlike my father and Nichelle, Jerry didn't hold my mother's arm, carefully helping her navigate the puddles and mud.

Jerry gripped her arm viciously, his fingers digging in so hard it caused her pain. It was clear from her pinched expression. He half dragged her along, arguing with her about something we were too far away to hear.

Warm fingers found the back of my neck and squeezed gently.

I didn't even know which of the guys it was, but it didn't matter. All three of them stood behind me, watching. Their support unspoken but still felt.

The priest cleared his throat, ready to begin the ceremony.

I knew I needed to go take my place at the front. The

priest was waiting for me, and eyes turned in my direction, but I suddenly couldn't move.

Two men wheeled Axel's casket out from the church, carefully placing it to the priest's left. I swallowed a lump in my throat, knowing my brother's body was inside. The casket was closed, of course. After the way Axel had been murdered, we couldn't have had an open casket. But it didn't matter. My brain did an outstanding job of painting a mental image for me, one that hurt like a hot knife to my chest.

My heart cracked wide open, and all the grief I'd been holding in came flooding to the surface. It was rough and raw and like sandpaper scratching and tearing at my throat. "I can't," I whispered.

Nash's hand slipped into mine. "Yeah, you can, Blissy girl. Come on. I got you."

With a gentle tug, he guided me to my spot, at the front of the group, between my father and his family, and my mother and hers.

Nash was right where he was supposed to be. He'd always been more of a brother to Axel than a best friend.

The priest got the funeral underway, his sermon floating in the air around me. They were nice words, meant to soothe and calm, and spouted hopeful statements about eternal life.

But none of them were right. They were generic, nothing words from a man who hadn't known my brother.

"Nash," I whispered.

He had his head lowered but swiveled it slightly in my direction.

"Could you say something? You were the closest to

him. I'm sorry, I should have asked before, I just didn't even think of getting someone to do a eulogy."

He squinted at me. "Shit, Bliss. Could have given a guy some warning."

I cringed. "I'm sorry."

But he sighed and stepped forward anyway, cutting the priest off. "Sorry. Sorry. Can I say something before we move on, please?"

The priest stepped to the side. "Of course."

Nash cleared his throat and looked out over the crowd, who were all silently waiting for him. "Fuck. There's a lot of you."

There was a titter of laughter, while Nash tugged at his shirt uncomfortably. "Bliss made me do this, but she's right. Somebody did need to stand up here and say something."

I smiled and nodded encouragement at him.

"Axel was my best friend. My brother. We grew up together in a trailer park where nobody gave a shit what we did, if we ate that night, or even if we were still alive."

I darted a glance at my mother and Jerry. Jerry had a scowl on his face, but my mother stared at the ground.

I wondered if she agreed with Nash's assessment.

"So Axel and I started watching out for each other. And then later on, we watched out for Bliss too." Nash's gaze met mine. "Axel loved his little sister, and everything he did was with her best interests in mind. Leaving school to get a job was because Bliss needed food. Finding her old man and giving her up to him was one of the hardest things I'd ever seen him go through, and yet he did it because he knew she needed a better life." Nash looked at my dad. "I don't know if he ever got the chance to thank you for the life you gave her, but I'll thank you on his behalf."

I glanced over at my father, who nodded respectfully at Nash and smiled. I wanted my family to know him. He was as much a brother to me as Axel had been.

Well, that wasn't exactly true. I'd had very unbrotherly thoughts about Nash.

Nash turned toward the casket, and I wondered if his brain was conjuring up images he didn't want to see as well. "Axel was always the one who made things happen. First with Bliss. Then the bar. Axel was the one who brought all good things into my life." Nash turned back, his eyes meeting mine, and his voice softened. "Even after his death, he's still bringing me good things."

My heart swelled at the honest and open confession of feeling. I didn't know if Nash and I would ever be what I wanted us to be, but there in that moment, whatever he felt was enough. There was a love in his words that I couldn't get from anyone but him. He knew who I'd been, and he knew who I was now.

"Axel was good. Kind. He put everyone else before himself. He loved hard..." He grinned ruefully. "Fell in love often. Nightly some might say."

There was laughter around us, and I smiled around the lump in my throat.

He lowered his head, staring at the ground. "I don't know what to do without you, buddy. I don't know what you got involved with, or who did this." He raised his eyes slowly, looking out around the crowd, his blue eyes piercing. "But somebody stole a life before it was even half over. It's a pain I'm going to have to live with every day, as will everyone who loved him. Somebody here knows something. Maybe somebody even knows who killed him." Nash's fingers clenched into fists. "If that someone is you, come forward now. Say something. Because we won't stop hunting you. We won't forget or brush this under the carpet." He swallowed like the emotion was getting to him. "This is Saint View, and this crime won't go unpunished."

There was a ripple of uncomfortable comments as Nash stepped back to stand beside me once more.

Nash's words had stirred up suspicion, and now I wasn't the only one standing here, casting a dubious eye over every man and woman in attendance.

War and Scythe, their expressions stoic.

Nichelle and my dad, shooting sympathetic looks in my direction.

My mom, refusing to meet anyone's eyes.

Jerry, full of confidence, gazing around at everybody else like he was better than them.

All the guys from War's MC were there, too. Hawk, Aloha, Ice, Gunner, Fang, Queenie. Siren standing with her father, Gus. Rebel's little pixie face blazed, her big eyes filled with tears.

In the back, I noticed Dax from the tattoo parlor, standing with three other guys.

Interspersed all around were faces I didn't recognize. People I didn't know but who had known Axel. Women who could have been jilted lovers out for revenge. Men who could have been his dealer, a man who'd already shown his violent streak.

I reeled, wondering if his killer stood here right now, with fake tears in their eyes, and a cold, vicious heart capable of taking another life.

# 19

## BLISS

*A*xel's casket was lowered into the ground while his favorite song played over a portable speaker. Nash had chosen it, and as soon as the opening riffs started up, the lump in my throat became unbearable. My tears burned the backs of my eyes, but the first clump of dirt that was thrown onto his casket was what finished me.

It was done. It was final. Life would go on now, and gradually, people would stop talking about him.

But there'd always be a part of me missing. And I'd have to live my life with the regrets of all the things I hadn't said. The things I hadn't done. The time we'd missed because I'd let him push me away.

War engulfed me in a bear hug as soon as the priest concluded the ceremony, and I pressed my face into his neck, breathing in his familiar scent. Eventually, I stepped back and put some space between us. "First round of drinks at Psychos is on me, okay? Spread the word."

I left before anybody else could stop me, hurrying away from the crowd and out to the parking lot where I could be alone.

I just needed a minute. Each step I moved away from the congregation was freeing. When they all disappeared from view, hidden behind trees, cars, and tombstones, I finally felt like I could release the breath I'd been holding the entire time.

The tears came with it, rolling down my cheeks thick and fast, a constant stream of sadness and grief and fear and hurt. It all came flooding out as I threw my purse onto the passenger seat and slumped behind the wheel of my car.

Cold, hard metal pressed to the back of my skull. "Drive."

I opened my mouth, but the man in the back seat cut me off.

"Scream or turn around and you're as dead as your brother is. Now start the car and drive."

I twisted the key with trembling fingers and pulled out of the parking lot, glancing in the rearview mirror.

All I caught was a glimpse of a black hoodie before he shoved the gun harder against my head. "Watch yourself. I don't think your family and friends back there would want to find you with your brains smeared all over the windshield, do you? Wouldn't want to make it two funerals in a week."

Everett and Verity were back there. I put my foot down on the accelerator, trying to put as much distance between us as possible.

If he did kill me, I wouldn't let it be where they could see it.

I didn't know where I was going. I drove blindly, waiting for his instructions, until he barked at me to turn left.

My heart sank as I turned off the main road and onto one that led into the woods. I wasn't entirely sure where we were. I thought War's MC compound wasn't far, but I didn't think you could get to it from this side. There wasn't much point going there looking for help anyway, when they were all back at the funeral. The road was dirt and narrow, and the trees grew tall on either side, providing enough shade to dapple the midday light.

With every passing mile, every turn of the wheels that took us deeper into the woods, my dread grew. "Please don't do this," I whispered.

The man didn't answer, which only made it worse.

"Pull over here. This is far enough."

I stopped the car, but my fingers remained clenched on the steering wheel. I racked my brain, trying to determine whether I knew his voice. He spoke low, and his words were muffled, like he had his hoodie up over his mouth or he spoke into his arm.

"I need my money, bitch."

The most insane sense of relief washed over me, even though I all too clearly remembered the threats this man had made on my body when he'd come into my bedroom in the middle of the night.

I knew what this was now.

It was a business deal.

One I'd been waiting for. One I needed, if I was going to continue running Psychos parties.

Maybe it was because we'd just been at his funeral, and thoughts of my brother were fresh in my mind. But I could practically hear his voice in my ear. Nash's words about how Axel had been the one to make things happen echoed in my head along with them.

I wasn't going to let him down. Not either of them. Nash, Rebel, Scythe—all their jobs depended on me keeping this bar and the parties running. The money the parties brought in was what would get my family out of debt.

Maybe this money could even help my mother. Because no matter how much I hated her for everything she'd done and everything she let happen, she was still my mother. Watching Jerry manhandle her, and the way she was stuck in a vicious cycle of poverty and neglect fired me up. She was never going to get away from him if someone didn't help her.

All of it rested on my shoulders. And on my ability to hold my own in a world I didn't belong in.

I stiffened my spine. "Put the gun down."

The man in the back seat laughed. "Excuse me?"

"I said, put the gun down. You aren't going to kill me. Because then how are you going to get your money?"

He pressed it harder into my skull. "There's always a next in line."

"Except there's not. You kill me, the bar goes to my mom. You've probably met her? Coked-up prostitute who lives in the trailer park?"

"Your old man has money. Can always get it out of him, sweetheart."

I laughed. "You clearly haven't done your research. My father is about as broke as they come. I mean, you could probably try selling their silverware, but I'm quite sure that's not really how you roll. So, I'm quite sure that

I, sir, am the one you want to do business with. So like I said, put the gun down."

Ever so slowly, he lowered the gun.

I smiled smugly to myself, pride rolling through me over not being a doormat.

But then his dark laughter started up from the back seat. "You want to play with the big kids, sweetheart? Okay. I'll play. But just remember, there's other ways of making you comply."

He leaned in close so his breath tickled the back of my neck. "I still haven't forgotten what you looked like, all wrapped up in that sexy lingerie, ripe and ready for the taking."

My spine stiffened as fear clawed its way back up my throat.

No man was ever going to lay his hands on me like that again.

I'd rather die.

So I filled my voice with a confidence I didn't feel. "Your money is in my purse. I've been carrying it around, waiting for you to show."

"All of it?"

"Every penny." I reached across to my purse and tossed it back to him.

While he was distracted, I glanced in the rearview mirror again, but he was smarter than that and had slumped low enough that I couldn't see him at all.

"You did good, pretty girl," he eventually said. "Not gonna lie, I didn't think you had the smarts to come up with the cash." He tossed the purse back onto the front seat, along with a plastic baggie of pills and powder. "See you next month."

The back door opened.

"Wait! I need more."

He paused. "How much more?"

"Three times."

He let out a low whistle. "That's a lot of product for me to trust you with."

"I'm good for it."

He paused for a long moment, and I had the creeping suspicion his gaze was crawling all over me, even though I couldn't see it. He was analyzing me, and I refused to bend under his scrutiny.

Bliss was strong. She had a backbone, and she was going to run this business in the same way Axel had.

I was going to provide for my family and for my friends.

But most of all, I was going to provide for myself.

"Fine," the man agreed. "Three times the product."

"I need it by tomorrow."

"Planning an overdose?"

"Planning an empire."

He chuckled. "I'll send a delivery boy. You'll have it by close of business." He paused. "Don't make me regret this, pretty girl. Pay on time, and you and I can be best friends."

"And if I don't?"

He laughed. "I'll be your worst fucking enemy."

---

*I* drove back to Psycho's completely nauseated. The dealer had slammed my car door, and the minute it had closed, I'd pushed my foot on the accelerator and gotten the hell out of there. In my rearview mirror, I'd watched him disappear into the woods, tucking his bag full of cash into the inside of his hoodie.

By the time I pulled into the parking lot of my bar, it was full of cars and bikes, and loud music thumped.

I got out and wandered inside, each step dissolving away the stress and fear as I enveloped myself in the now familiar surroundings. I breathed in deep, counting the familiar faces, reassuring myself that everyone was here, and safe.

All except one.

I grabbed Rebel's arm when she passed on her way to the bathroom. "Have you seen Nash?"

She glanced around her, frowning at the rowdy crowd who had gathered to celebrate Axel's life rather than mourn it. "He came in with Vincent and War, but they're over there, and Nash isn't, so I don't know." She squeezed my arm. "I really gotta pee, but if I see him on the way to the bathroom, I'll let him know you're looking for him."

I thanked her and moved on, smiling when Everett and Verity zoomed past me, playing some sort of chasing game. I caught them and pulled them both into a hug, needing their skinny little arms squeezing me tight. "I'm so glad you guys are here," I murmured into their hair.

My dad and Nichelle watched them from the edge of the room, out of place and uncomfortable, but it warmed my heart anyway. It was my two worlds combining, and though I knew it wouldn't last, for a moment it was lovely.

I released my squirming siblings and made my way over to War and Scythe.

They stopped their conversation when I approached. War gave me a lazy grin. "Hey, baby girl." He glanced in my father's direction. "Am I allowed to kiss you in front of the parentals, or do they still think you're a virgin?"

He was exactly what I needed right now after my encounter in the car. "You can kiss me."

War didn't hesitate. He tugged me into his arms, dropping his mouth down on mine.

When we pulled apart, Scythe's gaze was full of amusement. "What about me?"

"What about you?" I shot back.

"Do I get to kiss you here too? Or do I have to wait for another thunderstorm?"

His smirk was infuriating.

"I think you'll have to wait until Hell freezes over, actually," I said sweetly. "I'll see you later. I need to find Nash."

"I saw him disappear through the party room doors just a few minutes ago."

I thanked him and moved in that direction, pushing through the crowd to the not particularly well-hidden door, and slipped through it.

A big hand grabbed the door, stopping me from closing it, and I spun around, ready to tell whoever it was that this part of the club was off-limits today.

I came face-to-face with Scythe's broad chest, and the words died in my throat as he slipped in behind me. He shut the door, which did little to muffle the sounds of crowd in the bar but everything to speed up my heart.

"You're off duty today," I told him. "You don't have to follow me around. Go have fun."

He grinned at me in the dim light of the windowless coatroom. "I will. But Hell froze over." His hand came around the back of my neck, fingers flexing in my hair and tugging on it gently, forcing my face up to his. "So I came for my kiss."

Before I could protest, his lips claimed mine.

Instantly, all protests flew out of my head.

Scythe kissed me slow and hot. Deep and steady. His tongue pressed past my lips to move with mine, and I dug my fingers into his biceps, holding on to him while he took control of what he wanted.

Despite my sass earlier, it was exactly what I wanted too.

The other night hadn't been a mistake. It hadn't just been me seeking comfort in a moment of terror.

It had been something deep inside me that craved this man. Every part of him.

Including his darkness.

He seemed to know it. "I'm only gonna sneak around with you so long, Bliss. It's fun, for now. But one day soon, I'm going to kiss you in front of everyone. Including War, and your dad, and all your friends." His lips trailed along my jawline. "You can pretend you hate me. But I know how you moan when my cock is buried in your pussy. And I know how you're gonna scream when I do it again."

He placed an open-mouthed kiss to my neck, sucking hard and grazing my skin with his teeth.

It would leave a mark, and I didn't even care. My knees went weak, and his arms tightened, keeping me upright.

Scythe let out a low growl that was practically a purr. "I'd do it right now if Nash didn't need you more."

He released me and then gave a flick of his head. "Go. He wasn't in a good way on the drive over."

I nodded, and when he left through the door that led

back to the club, I went in the opposite direction, into the party room.

It was empty, of course, and dark, but light spilled from beneath my office door. I headed in that direction, not surprised when I found it unlocked and Nash lying across my couch, staring at the ceiling.

He didn't even glance in my direction. "Sorry," he said quietly. "I needed a minute, and my office is right in the thick of things out there."

I perched on the edge of the couch, and he shifted his feet over, making more room for me. But that was the only movement he made. He didn't glance in my direction.

"Are you okay?" I whispered. "Scy—Vincent said you weren't."

"I'm fine."

He wasn't.

"You're a bad liar."

"Just add that to the list of my shitty qualities. Bad liar. Bad friend—"

"Hey. You are not a bad friend." I peered at him, guilt seeping in. "I'm sorry about springing the eulogy on you. But you did so well. Don't beat yourself up about it."

He gave a bitter laugh as he sat up and finally looked at me. "Is that seriously what you think I'm in here hating myself over?"

I stared at him. "I should have given you time to prepare..."

"Fuck the eulogy. You think Axel would have cared that I can barely string a couple of sentences together? You think I care about what anybody else out there thinks of me? I don't. But he was my best fucking friend,

Bliss. My brother. He was the one there when Dad pummeled the shit out of me, and then again when my dad left me with my mother, who wasn't any better. Axel was the one fighting for me when I went to jail. He always had my back. So no, Bliss. I'm not in here beating myself up over a fucking eulogy." His gaze locked with mine. "I'm in here beating myself up because even when I was up there talking about him, I was thinking about you."

I froze, not entirely letting myself believe what I'd heard.

He brushed a lock of stray hair behind my ear, his gaze dipping to my mouth. "I'm always thinking about you, Bliss. Every fucking night when we're together in this bar. Every day, when I'm lying in my bed alone, wishing you were with me. You haunt my fucking dreams, and then you walk into work and smile at me like you have no idea how fucking beautiful you are."

"Nash, I—"

He groaned. "Don't. Don't look at me like that."

"Like what?"

"Like if I leaned in and kissed you right now, you'd let me."

Heat rolled through me. God, he was so sexy with his expression full of anguish and his collared shirt half undone. His eyes were wide, his hair mussed up like he'd been running his hands through it. He was gorgeous. But he was also my hero. My protector.

"Kiss me," I murmured so softly I wasn't even sure he'd heard me until his eyes flared.

"Bliss. I can't. Besides the fact you're his sister, you're twenty-fucking-five."

The agony on his face was clear. I'd seen it before. In all the times he'd held himself back from touching me.

I'd been patient. I'd waited for him to say the things I desperately wanted him to say. For him to touch me the way I craved.

I was done waiting.

I straddled his lap, putting my weight in my knees, either side of his thighs. "Then I will."

But I was all talk. I was freaking out on the inside now that I was here, paralyzed with how badly I wanted this, and desperately not wanting him to reject me. I gazed down at him, our breaths mingling.

Indecision warred within me, and suddenly, it was Caleb's voice in my head, reminding me I was too fat. Too ugly. Behind him were the boys from high school who had pretended to date me only to make fun of me behind my back or win a bet.

Nash said all the right things, but his actions didn't match. Axel was gone, and my age was an excuse I had never cared about. So why did he? My brain whirred, working overtime, filling me with doubts until I was hot and clammy and crawling off his lap, embarrassed I'd thought for half a second I could be someone I wasn't.

He caught my wrists.

My gaze locked on to his.

And then his mouth slammed down on mine. He pulled me over his lap, dragging me down so I was firmly seated, his hands tight on my back, holding me in place. He groaned into my mouth, snaking one hand up to the back of my head like he was worried I might try to run away again.

I wasn't going anywhere.

All doubts flew out of my head at the way he held and kissed me, all with his thickening erection beneath me.

It smashed through Caleb's voice, so ingrained in my head. His kiss obliterated all my doubts and woke my body up to the possibilities of what his could do.

He was hard and strong and safe. His kiss was the same, dominating and controlling but somehow sweet at the same time. His tongue moved with mine, and a fire erupted within me, one I knew for a fact he had the experience to quench.

"Nash," I gasped, drawing away from his mouth as need mounted within me.

His lips traveled down my neck, sucking and kissing a trail across my skin then back up to claim my mouth once more like he couldn't get enough of it.

I mewled with need, wanting his mouth, but more too. Unconsciously, I rocked on his lap, trying to find some relief for the feelings he was evoking deep inside me that desperately needed tending to.

His hands gripped my hips, encouraging me to move until I was grinding on his lap and kissing him so deeply it spun my head. I was insatiable for his taste, his touch. I wanted it all because this felt right. For all his reasons it was wrong, it wasn't. I didn't care about his age or what we'd been to each other in the past or what I was to Axel. All that mattered was how Nash made me feel.

His teeth grazed my earlobe. "I've been thinking about doing this since the moment you walked back into my life."

"Only this?" I murmured.

He groaned. "You want more?"

I kissed him again, plunging my fingers into his hair

and pulling lightly on it until he was clutching me like he needed my body to breathe. "I want everything."

"You don't know what you're asking."

It didn't matter. "I trust you."

It was true. All doubts had been put to bed, and all that was left was a deep affection and an intense longing for the man who spent a lifetime looking after other people. My heart swelled with too much feeling, too much emotion to pour out right now, but it was there, on the tip of my tongue.

I could fall in love with Nash Sorensen. In fact, I was pretty sure I was already halfway gone.

Shouting erupted in the bar, and we both stopped, swiveling our heads toward the door.

"Do we need to go out there?" I whispered.

He turned back, guiding my head down until his lips brushed mine. "I've got a hard-on that's gonna give away exactly what we were doing back here. Probably better that we don't. Vincent and War are out there. They can handle it."

I grinned, rocking over him some more while he groaned and claimed my mouth again.

A woman's blood-curdling scream had us changing our minds.

We both jumped up and sprinted for the door.

Chaos met us on the other side, and in the middle of it were my mother and father as well as Jerry and Nichelle.

Scythe stood in the middle, separating the two parties, his expression like thunder.

"Oh, sweet baby Jesus," I muttered, shouldering

through the crowd, Nash right behind me. "I knew this would happen eventually."

"What the hell is going on?" Nash roared through the din.

Nobody paid him any attention.

"Did you seriously just proposition my husband for sex, Kim?" Nichelle yelled, her insults directed squarely at my mother, her eyes blazing with anger. "What in your coked-up brain made you think he would ever want that?"

Mom's eyes were trained on the floor. She took Nichelle's wrath without arguing back.

Jerry sniggered, his beer gut jiggling. "He wanted her plenty once upon a time, lady. Paid through the nose for it too. How do you think Bliss happened?"

Nichelle turned an unhealthy shade of crimson, her gaze darting between my mother and father. "That isn't true. They were in a relationship."

Jerry raised an eyebrow in Dad's direction. "Oops. Did I just let the cat out of the bag? About how you had to pay for sex back in the day? Your pretty little wife probably wasn't even born then, huh? She probably has no idea how you were one of my regulars, back before she came along."

My father narrowed his eyes. "It wasn't like that, and you know it, you asshole."

I blinked. I didn't think I'd ever heard him swear.

I pushed my way over to my mother, standing in front of her. "Did you?"

She lifted her eyes to meet mine. They were bloodshot and unfocussed, but there was a sadness in them that hit me deep in the gut. "He made me."

"Shut up, Kim," Jerry growled.

I spun and glared at him. "No, you shut up. I asked her a question. Not you."

"Fucking mouthy bitch, just like your mama, ain't you?" He took a step toward me, his arm rising almost in slow motion.

I'd been on the receiving end of Jerry's backhands a hundred times before I'd gone to live with my father. Once upon a time, he'd terrified me.

Now, I didn't even flinch.

Nash, Scythe, and War were on him before his hand even came close.

They dragged him back, slamming him into a seat so hard the wood cracked. Scythe looked to me, his eyes wild, barely in control, just begging me to give him permission to go further.

God, it was tempting. For everything Jerry had done to me, and to my mother, he deserved whatever punishment Scythe was in the mood to dish out.

My mother gaped at the three guys, who I'd known would have my back. Her panicked gaze darted between them in terror, and she backed away, stumbling when she ran into a table.

I couldn't blame her. Scythe was terrifying when he was like this. I'd seen it before, that night up at the bluffs. I hadn't forgotten what he'd done to Caleb.

But War and Nash were not exactly puppies either. They each had a punishing grip on Jerry's arms, tight enough that he howled his complaints.

"They won't hurt you," I assured my mother.

She shook her head, grabbing at my hand. "They will. You need to run, Bliss. Don't make the same mistakes I did. They'll hurt you too." A tear ran down her face as she stared at me. "They'll hurt your babies."

The guilt and pain in her eyes cut through me, burying deep inside. It didn't mend the parts of me she'd broken with her weak will and lack of care. But this was the first time I realized she even cared about what had happened to me at all.

"They aren't like that," I said quietly. "They'd never."

She shook her head, her dirty hair, the same color as mine but dull and ratty, falling around her shoulders. "You don't know that. They all start out nice. But the good ones..." She peeked at my father. "They leave."

He turned away, refusing to meet her gaze any longer.

Mom looked down at her hands once more. "And when they leave, all you have left is the ones who hurt you." She glanced at Jerry. "The ones who force you to do things you never wanted to do. The ones who keep you pinned down with threats and violence." Her voice grew with every sentence until she was shouting. "The ones who hurt your babies and leave you helpless to do anything about it. Until finally, all you want to do is die. But they won't even let you do that, will you, Jerry?" She pushed past me and slapped a hand across his meaty face. "Just fucking let me die, why don't you? Let me go!"

A hush fell over the bar.

All eyes were trained on my mother as she fell apart, sobbing in the middle of my brother's wake, without a single soul to comfort her.

Verity pushed her way forward from behind Nichelle's legs. "Ma'am. Are you okay?" She held up a little package of tissues. "Would you like one?"

My heart swelled with pride at my little sister's

compassion, and though I knew my mother maybe didn't deserve it, it triggered me to search deeper and find some within myself as well.

Mom put a tentative hand toward Verity, then stopped as she took in the little girl's face. Her gaze bounced between me and my sister. "She's just like you, Bliss. Except for the hair color, of course."

I nodded. My father had said the same thing more than once, and even I could see that, although I got my hair color from my mom, I was more like my dad. Verity was cut from the same cloth.

"Would ya look at that," Jerry drawled from across the room. "She's even prettier than Bliss was, but Bliss was too young. This one..." His filthy gaze crawled over my sister's body. "She's almost ripe for the taking."

My father's roar of outrage was drowned out by Scythe's and the crunch of Jerry's nose as Nash threw his fist into it.

The calm in the storm was over.

"Get the kids out of here," I yelled to Nichelle, herding Verity in her direction. I grabbed my father's arm. "Go. Nash has got this. Get your wife and children out of here."

He looked ready to argue, but then he thought better of it. He squeezed my arm. "Are you going to be okay?"

I glanced over to my guys.

*My* guys.

"They won't let anything happen to me. We'll take care of it. I'll come back to the house as soon as I can."

He leaned in and kissed my cheek and then let me go to follow his wife and kids to their car.

Bringing them here had been a mistake.

Hoping the two sides of my life could combine seamlessly had been foolish. Maybe I could walk both paths, but my father, Nichelle, Verity, and Everett could not. They needed protecting from this life. In the same way I once had.

In the same way my mother still did.

She watched my guys lay their fists into her good-for-nothing partner and pimp. And she did it with a complete hate and loathing in her eyes that chilled me to the bone.

I hated Jerry. But my mother's hate ran so deep and hot that I doubted it could be matched. Unless there was another woman who bore the daily brunt of his vicious moods and cruel treatment.

I took her hand and led her away, into the quiet of Nash's office. I pulled the chair out from behind his desk and dragged it around so it was on the same side as the spare chair. Mom sank down into it, her fingers trembling.

For a long time, I just stared at her, taking in the woman who'd once seemed much bigger than the frail, middle-aged lady who sat before me now. She was so very broken, in so many ways, and I found my heart breaking for her. For the woman she'd maybe once been. Surely, she'd once had hopes and dreams?

Nobody aspired to be a drug-addicted prostitute with a pimp boyfriend who beat and raped them.

Yet that was somehow the life she'd ended up with.

It was the cards she'd been dealt.

It all too easily could have been me.

"What do you want?" I asked her finally.

She looked up slowly, her gaze focusing on mine. "To die."

I swallowed down the lump in my throat. "I can't let you do that."

"You have to, Bliss. I can't do this anymore. It's too much. Axel is gone. You hate me. You're never going to forgive me. I have nothing left to live for."

I dragged the words up from my feet with great difficulty, and even as they sat on my tongue, I wasn't sure that when I said them, I would mean it. "I don't hate you."

A flicker of hope flashed in her eyes.

That was enough for me to want to try. To try to forgive and to try to find her something more than what she had right now.

"You need to leave him."

"He'll find me, no matter where I go."

"Then you'll stay here. There's a ton of empty rooms out in back. They won't be pretty. They don't even have a window. But they'll be safe. There's almost always someone here, and I'll get the security system upgraded for when there's not."

She blinked at me. "I can pay."

I shook my head. "The prostitution stops. No more."

She bit her lip. "It's all I know, Bliss. I never finished school. No one is gonna hire me now."

"I will. You'll work for your room and board and a small weekly wage. That you will not spend on drugs. You hear me?"

She nodded eagerly. "Okay."

"You'll see a drug-addiction counsellor. And if they tell you to go to rehab, you'll go."

She nodded again. "Whatever you want."

I grabbed her arms. "No. This has to be what you want. It won't work otherwise. I run a club, Mom. There are drugs here, so the temptation will be in your face. You've gotta want it more than that. I'm giving you a helping hand, because you're my mother, and because I know nobody else ever has. But it's one strike and you're out with me."

Her eyes welled with tears that then rolled down her cheeks. "Thank you," she whispered. "I promise, Bliss. I won't let you down."

I stood stiffly, knowing there was about a three percent chance that she wouldn't be back out on the streets, sleeping with men for money, and filling her veins with drugs in under a week.

When I had to kick her out, it was going to break my heart.

She wrung her hands. "Those men..."

I waited for her to continue.

"They care about you?"

I nodded. "You'll see, Mom. They're good guys."

Good guys who might very well be killing a man out in the middle of my bar.

But if they were, I couldn't bring myself to care.

## 20

## SCYTHE

I stood back and put my hands on my hips, surveying Jerry's beaten-up, close-to-lifeless body that we'd dumped on the steps of his trailer. "You sure Bliss would kill us if we kill him?"

War pondered the question, then sighed heavily. "Yeah. She's good at her core. Even though he's a piece of scum, who doesn't deserve to breathe, pretty sure she wouldn't condone murder. Plus, can you really be bothered getting rid of a body right now? Because I can't. He might still die anyway."

"He's a cockroach. He'll outlive us all."

War nodded and wiped the blood off his hands on the back of his suit pants.

I frowned at him. "You better dry clean those before you return them. That's disgusting."

"Says the man with blood all over his jacket."

I glanced down at myself. "Shit." He was right. Jerry's blood had stained my shirt a lovely shade of crimson, and there were smears all over my jacket too. "That's not gonna come out. Gonna send that asshole the bill to replace it. Come on, let's go."

Thankfully, night had fallen and the streets were empty. It was only a couple of blocks, and now we made the return trip to Psychos, grateful the darkness hid our crime.

Not that anyone would have stopped to question the two big guys with split knuckles and blood on their suits. I almost laughed at the thought.

Saint View knew better than to ask questions.

But out in front of the bar, I looked War over, and he did the same to me, and both of us came to the same conclusion.

"We can't go in there like this, can we?" War asked.

I might have, if it hadn't been for the fact I knew Bliss was struggling with some PTSD. "Bliss crawled into my bed the other night. She's not having a good time with her memories."

"Caleb?"

"Yeah."

"That fucking prick."

I nodded. "I don't want to trigger her again. I'm wearing a lot of blood right now. Can you drive me home?"

War pulled his keys from his pocket. "Yeah, come on. You can ride bitch on the back of my bike."

I scowled at him. "Don't act like you don't just want me to put my arms around you."

He sniggered, throwing his leg over and turning the bike on. I followed suit, holding on to the bars behind me for balance.

Even still, my thighs brushed his, and the temptation

to slide down the seat, wrap my arms around him, and feel up his abs was strong.

I liked War. More than I should have. I wasn't going to fucking lie to myself and pretend like I didn't.

I'd liked the kiss. And if that kid hadn't walked out of the bowling alley, I probably wouldn't have stopped where we had.

My dick threatened to get hard at the thought, and wouldn't that have just been the highlight of War's day? Me boning up when my dick was pressed against his back.

No fucking way was I giving him that satisfaction. I closed my eyes and thought of my mom.

She was a buzzkill every time.

Concentrating on her face did the job, and my dick was still perfectly soft when we arrived back at my place. I got off and passed him back the helmet I'd borrowed. "You wanna come in? I've got a refrigerator full of beer, and I don't want to drink it alone."

War grinned, turning off his bike, and pushing the kickstand down. "Thought you'd never ask, Vinnie boy. Let's do it."

I hated he was still calling me that. Not because I hated the nickname, like Vincent did. But I just hated that he wasn't calling me Scythe.

He could never find out though. I was gonna have to get used to Vinnie boy, because if War ever found out I was Scythe, not only would this friendship end, but so would my life.

I wasn't an idiot.

I knew who War was. I knew what his club did. They were hardly saints.

He'd think nothing of killing me.

And when it came down to it, I'd defend myself.

I wasn't sure what would be worse. Him killing me. Or me having to live with the knowledge I'd killed the only friend I'd ever had.

Both could be avoided if nobody told him. It was only me and Bliss who knew. I was planning on keeping it that way.

We went inside, and I pointed to the refrigerator on my way up the stairs. "Beer's in there. Help yourself. I'll be back in a minute."

I took the stairs two at a time, unbuttoning my shirt and shrugging it off as I shouldered my way into the bathroom. I kicked the door shut behind me and dropped the ruined shirt on the tiles before I caught sight of my reflection in the mirror.

"Fuck," I muttered. "Could have told me, dickhead."

I had a blood spray right across my face, likely from when I'd thrown a punch straight into Jerry's nose. My shirt and pants had protected my body, but my face hadn't been so lucky. I suspected it was in my hair too, though it was too dark to see for sure. I needed a shower.

I undid my belt and pulled it from my pant loops, then undid the button and fly. With quick movements, I dragged my pants down my legs, taking my underwear with them.

The door swung open. "Hey, you got a change of pants? I don't want to sit on your white couch with these..." War froze in the doorway, his gaze dropping from my face, down my chest and abs, and unashamedly lingering on my cock.

"Take a photo, it'll last longer," I said dryly. "You ever heard of knocking?"

"Wasn't expecting you to be standing there naked."

"And yet, I am. You wanna shut the door?"

He took a step closer and shut the door behind him. He grinned at me as he leaned back on it, taking a sip of his beer. "It's closed."

I'd meant for him to step out and shut the door. But clearly that wasn't the game we were playing. "How drunk are you right now?"

"I just drove us home. I'm not drunk at all." He tilted the beer bottle in my direction, a questioning expression on his face. "Do *you* need to be drunk right now?"

"No."

He pushed off the wall and came to stand in front of me. He eliminated almost all the space between us and pressed the beer bottle to one side of my neck while his mouth came to the other. "Good. Because I've been thinking about your cock since the other night. So stop me now if you don't want this."

I didn't say a word. My dick got hard at the unsaid promises hanging in the air.

Cold liquid spilled across my shoulder, and I flinched in surprise. But then War's mouth was there, tongue rasping over my shoulder and along the skin protected from blood by my clothing.

I groaned at the sensation of hot and cold and his wet mouth.

He pulled back, eyeing me carefully, and then very deliberately, dragged the bottle across my chest, letting beer drip over my pecs and slide down my abs.

I reached back and braced myself on the bathroom

sink, watching the liquid roll over the ridges of my stomach.

War watched me, chasing each little river with his tongue.

He licked off every drop, then kept going, kissing and sucking and nipping at my chest and abs until my dick was hard and straining for his touch.

His mouth covered my nipple, and I speared my fingers into his short hair on instinct, lighting up inside at the touch of him there.

But he pulled back, taking a swig of beer. "I want to lick this off your dick. I just want to be sure you aren't going to suddenly freak out on me and start throwing punches. I watched what you did to Jerry. I'm too fucking pretty to have my face smashed in like that."

I grabbed the beer out of his hand, took a swig while the two of us stared at each other, and then poured the rest of the bottle over my erection.

It was cold, but I was so fucking hot for him I was surprised it didn't sizzle.

War dropped to his knees on the plush bathmat and, with his eyes on me the entire time, fit his mouth over the end of my cock.

I groaned at the feel of him and instantly wanted more. It had been so freaking long since I'd had a blow job, and the urge to fuck his mouth hard and fast and come down his throat stole over me in a blast of heat.

War didn't disappoint. He took me deeper into his mouth, and then when he withdrew, he used his tongue to lick the rest of the beer off, each stroke getting me harder and harder until he returned to swallow me down once more.

"Fuck," I groaned, gritting my teeth as the first urge to come bored down on me.

"Good?" War asked between suck and pulls.

"You have no idea."

He chuckled. "I have some idea."

Which meant he also probably knew exactly how much I wanted to completely let go and fuck his mouth with abandon. I eyed him, the unspoken question hanging in the air between us.

War's voice went husky. "You keep looking at me like that and I'm gonna have to jack off while I do this."

"Fuck. Do it. I want to watch."

War groaned, but he didn't say no.

I grabbed at the back of his shirt, and he struggled out of it with my help, seams protesting because it really was half a size too small for him. He leaned back on his knees to get his pants open and then shoved them and his underwear down his thighs, just enough to free his heavy erection.

Precum leaked from my tip at the sight of his fingers wrapped around his cock. He stroked himself with one hand, while the other returned to me. He stared up at me, our eyes locking.

"Do it," he groaned.

And there was the advantage of us both being men.

He knew exactly what would make this better.

I let go of the bathroom sink and grabbed the back of his head instead. I jerked my hips, letting my dick sink deep into War's mouth.

He closed his eyes, moaning his encouragement. I did it again, driving into the hot cave of his mouth, feeling the tension he created when I pulled out, only to do it again.

Each stroke grew more confident, both of us testing the other, seeing how far we could push it.

War's pace on his own dick picked up, until I was fucking his mouth and he was fucking his hand in the same tempo, both of us groaning at the sensation and the sight.

"I'm gonna come," he bit out.

"Look at me."

His green-eyed gaze trained on my face, and I pounded into his mouth a few more times.

His hand moved between my legs, cupping my balls, and it was all over. I came in his mouth, spilling myself into his throat. He swallowed me down like his mouth had been made for me.

His thick, white cum spilled over his hand and onto the bathroom mat while he jerked himself, both of us making sounds so loud and indecent I was sure the neighbors would file complaints.

Completely spent, I dropped back against the vanity. He slumped his ass onto the mat, chest rising and falling like he'd been running a marathon.

Both of us were too blissed out to make it weird or uncomfortable.

War looked down at himself and the mess we'd made. "Well. That was new."

"Did you like it? Sucking my cock, I mean."

He grinned at me. "Why? You want me to do it again?"

"Fuck yes."

He sniggered. "When you can get it up again, maybe I will." He reached a hand in my direction, and I took it, hauling him to his feet, so we were chest to chest.

His gaze flickered to my lips. "You're like some sort of warrior with blood all over your face."

"That turn you on?"

"Obviously. Nothing like a little violence to get the blood pumping."

I knew exactly what he meant. "You need a shower."

"Joining me?"

"Can you get it up again?" I eyed his cock.

"You doubt my ability to go twice in a row?"

I shrugged with a grin. "Let's see, shall we?"

# 21

## BLISS

*I* tucked my mother into bed on the couch in my office, pulling a throw blanket off the back to cover her thin frame.

She rested her head on one of the decorative cushions and stared at me with big eyes.

I suddenly felt like I was the mother and she was the child.

Not that I ever remembered her tucking me into bed.

"I'll leave the door open for you. There's a bathroom just down the hall on the right. And if you want something to eat, help yourself to anything in the kitchen behind the bar."

"Thank you," she murmured. "I know you didn't have to do this."

I already knew I'd regret it. And that in the morning, she'd be gone with probably half my bar tucked into her purse.

She'd go back to Jerry and beg his forgiveness, and he'd beat the shit out of her again, just like he always did.

She knew no different.

But for one night, I could at least feel like I'd tried to break the cycle. I'd tried to help the woman I couldn't help but love even though she didn't deserve it.

I double-checked the safes were locked though, and all cash put away for the night, before I turned out the lights and met Nash in the entranceway.

He shook his head. "This won't end well, Bliss. I know she's your mom..."

I put a hand on his arm. "I know. But I need to sleep at night. I'll be able to do that, knowing I tried."

He put an arm around my neck, drawing me in and pressing his lips to my hair. He inhaled softly. "You're a better person than me."

I sold drugs in this club because I wanted to make money. Which made me little better than Jerry, even if I did have better reasons for doing it. I was definitely not a better person than Nash.

But for a moment, I let myself pretend I was.

I pulled away, glancing at the clock on the wall above the door, only then realizing it was nearly one in the morning. "Oh hey. It's past midnight. Happy birthday."

He groaned. "Can we pretend today isn't happening?"

I grinned up at him. "Nope. You've got a party to go to tonight."

"Maybe we should just cancel it. Without the drugs, it'll probably cost more than we bring in."

"Nope. Not getting out of it that easily. Got enough for tomorrow night, and there's three times the amount on its way. We're partying every weekend at Psychos this month." I grinned at him, pushing aside the knowledge that what I was doing wasn't aboveboard. This was how

Saint View rolled. And this was who I was now. "We're gonna make a mint."

"What? The guy finally showed up? There were no problems?"

I didn't want to tell Nash that I'd nearly wet my pants at first, before I'd found my lady balls and negotiated a deal. "No problems at all. It was very businesslike."

If businesslike meant having a gun held to your head and threats of violence made against you. But I wasn't in Providence anymore. Although I didn't have much experience, in the scheme of things that happened here, me negotiating a drug deal was pretty small potatoes.

But Nash's forehead lined in a frown.

I reached up and prodded it with my finger. "You're forty now. You're going to need Botox if you keep scowling like that."

He caught my finger and pulled it away, his blue eyes serious. "You're getting in over your head."

I understood his worry, but there was nothing else I could do. I had people I needed to provide for. He was one of them. "Nothing has changed. The parties will be epic. Everyone will have a great time, and we'll have more requests for invites than ever before. I'll pay our suppliers on time, and our bank accounts will stay nicely fat." I smiled up at him, patting his chest. "All you need to worry about is having a good time."

He still looked doubtful as we locked the club and he walked me to the car.

"I'm a grown woman, Nash."

"I know," he murmured into the darkness of the night and drew me in. "Trust me, Bliss. I fucking know."

He tilted my head up and brushed his lips across mine. "Go home. It's late. I'll see you in a few hours."

I nodded, wishing I was brave enough to ask him to come home with me, but also knowing we'd jumped a huge hurdle tonight, and that if I tried to push it any further, we might just fall flat on our faces before we'd even had the chance to run.

So I watched him walk across the darkened parking lot to his Jeep. We both pulled out of the parking lot together, him turning left to go to his home in Saint View. Me turning right to head back to Scythe's place in Providence.

Nash's kiss played over in my mind as I took each turn. I was so off with my head in the clouds, lost in memories of his touch, that I almost didn't see War's bike sitting in the driveway until I was right on top of it.

I parked to the left and trailed my fingers across the leather seat on my way to the front door.

Little Dog waited for me on the other side, looking all too adorable with her pink cast still firmly immobilizing her leg. I scooped her up, dropping a kiss on her furry head, and wandered through the dark rooms, not bothering to turn a light on because I needed to go to bed.

I'd expected the two guys to be hanging out downstairs, watching a movie or playing video games, but there was no one around. "Guess they went to bed, huh?" I scratched Little Dog behind the ears, and she nuzzled into my hand, begging for more. "You like that?"

I reached my bedroom door and pushed it open.

I stopped on the other side.

"Hey, baby girl," War said from his spot sprawled on my bed. "You're home."

I dropped my purse on the floor and glanced at him. And then at Scythe, laid out next to him. He just smirked in my direction.

That TikTok song that said something like, "I can take your man if I want to," started playing over in my head. "What are you two doing in here?"

"It's storming outside." Scythe propped himself up on one arm. "Thought you might want to snuggle."

I narrowed my eyes at him. "There's not a cloud in the sky out there. Pretty sure I can see every star in the Milky Way."

He laughed. "We can pretend."

"I really hate you sometimes."

He got off the bed, his bigger frame towering over mine. "You don't even hate me a little bit and you know it." He reached past me to grab a beer from the little bar fridge in my bedroom, and I tried really hard not to breathe in the fresh, clean scent of him. He'd clearly gotten out of the shower not all that long ago. He dove over War's legs, claiming his spot on the other side once more before he uncapped his beer.

War held a hand out to me. "I was waiting up for you. I put a movie on and—"

"It just happens to be my favorite, so I wasn't missing out." Scythe took another swig of his drink then patted the spot between them. "We saved you a spot."

"Is there a spot that's not next to you?" I asked sweetly.

He grinned back. "Nope. You need to be right here so I can tell you every time the book was different than the movie."

"He's been doing it the entire time. It's the most

annoying thing ever, and I'm ready to poke his eye out with the remote," War groaned, pulling me down and stealing a kiss. "Mmm. Hi."

I smiled at him. "Hi, yourself."

He moved me to sit on his lap, and by now, I knew better than to protest that I was too heavy. His hand dove into the back of my hair, while he kissed me deeply, and then he playfully tossed me into the middle of the bed, taking the spot Scythe had made for me.

I bounced on the mattress and yanked my favorite pillow out from beneath Scythe's head, fully satisfied when his head thunked down onto the mattress. "So what are we watching?"

"*Little Women*," Scythe announced.

I glanced sharply at the screen to find we were indeed watching the most recent version of the classic story. "Seriously? This is your favorite?"

"Does that surprise you?"

"Uh, yes."

He found a couple of the decorative cushions and shoved them beneath his head. "What were you expecting?"

"I don't know," I admitted. "*Deadpool*?" I glanced at War. "Porn?"

War sniggered and pulled me in for another kiss. "I prefer the sort of porn where you're the star. Got any of that?"

Scythe rolled his eyes. "Bliss would never."

I narrowed mine. "Excuse me?"

He twisted onto his side. "What? You wouldn't."

I had no idea why I was arguing with him. Because he was right, but it was just the fact he was calling me out.

There was something about Scythe that just made me want to argue with him. He thought he knew me so well, and it irked me that more often than not, he actually did. I wasn't entirely sure that he and Vincent stayed as compartmentalized as they said they did. "Says who?"

He let out a long-suffering sigh. "So you're telling me you'd let War film the two of you?"

I swallowed thickly, butterflies taking flight in my stomach at the mere idea.

"Leave her alone." War put an arm around me, dragging me closer to him. "I like her sweet little vanilla heart."

I slapped his chest. "I am not vanilla!"

He stifled a laugh. "Right. Of course not. You're strawberry."

I smacked him again. "At the very least, I'm Neapolitan. We had sex at Psychos."

"Behind a door," Scythe scoffed.

"It had a peephole!"

Scythe rolled his eyes. "Whoop-de-do. One random person copped an eyeful. That doth not maketh a porn star, my friend."

"You were watching when we had sex outside his cabin," I protested.

"You didn't even know I was there."

I shoved him so hard he toppled off the edge of the bed and landed on my hardwood floor with a thump.

War burst into laughter and pulled me down again to lie with him. "He's trying to rile you up. Just ignore him and come kiss me. I happen to like Neapolitan."

I groaned, ignoring his request for kissing. "Am I really that straight?"

"Like a ruler," Scythe mumbled, picking himself up off the floor.

I glared at him. "Why are you still here?"

"You never told me to get out."

"Get out."

"Nah."

I threw my hands up, but then a slightly evil idea crept into my head. "War, get your phone out. We're recording it."

His eyes went wide, and he sat up abruptly. "Seriously?"

I stared him dead in the eye. "Seriously."

He looked at Scythe. "Sorry, bro. Get out."

"The movie isn't finished!"

"She said I could film her. Like I give a shit about your movie. Get out."

I grinned triumphantly at Scythe. "Maybe if you're lucky, we'll even send you a copy."

Heat flared in his eyes, and in a second, he was on top of me, pinning me to the bed with his hands wrapped around my wrists.

I gasped, his face a mere inch from mine, his body strong and dominant to the point where I was completely helpless.

I wasn't scared of him. I knew what he was capable of, but I also knew what it felt like to be in his arms and to feel him move inside me.

His nose ran up the side of my neck, until his lips brushed my ear. "I hope you do, Bliss. Because there's nothing better than watching you come."

He pushed off the bed, releasing my wrists and standing, backing away toward the door, his gaze never leaving mine.

I couldn't breathe beneath the weight of it. He captured me with his attention, and just that one searing look had me craving more.

Scythe disappeared from view, and War turned to me.

I blinked, trying to forget the feeling of Scythe's body on top of me and his gaze burning across my skin.

"What?" I attempted to straighten my clothes with fingers that didn't seem to want to work. "Why are you staring at me like that?"

"You really gonna let him walk away?"

I swallowed thickly. "I don't know what you mean."

He raised an eyebrow. "You looked like you were ready to come, and all he did was pin you to the bed. I don't think you're vanilla, Bliss. I don't even think you're strawberry. I think you want a whole lot more and you're too scared to say it." War cocked his head to one side. "You want me to say it for you?"

Oh God. Did I?

"Vincent," War called out, taking my silence as a yes.

Scythe's footsteps padded down the hallway, and he appeared in my doorway, leaning one shoulder casually against the frame. "Yeah?"

"You up for a threesome?"

"This is mortifying." I pulled a pillow out from beneath my head and slapped it over my face. My cheeks heated with embarrassment, but I held my breath, waiting for Scythe's response.

"She gonna have that pillow over her head the entire time?"

"Not sure. Bliss?"

I pulled it off. "I hate you both."

War laughed and took the pillow from my fingers, tossing it onto the floor. "Where's your phone."

"In my purse."

War nodded to Scythe. "Get it. Press record."

My heart thumped, and I turned huge eyes on War. "I don't know..."

He silenced me by planting his lips on mine. "That's why it's on your phone. Not mine. Not Vincent's. It's yours to do what you want with. You want to delete it, you can. You want to hold on to it and watch it only once you're eighty so you can remember what a hot piece of ass you were, then that's your call."

"Don't know about you two, but I'm still gonna be a hot piece of ass at eighty," Scythe quipped, propping my phone up on the chest of drawers.

War and I both ignored him. I didn't know what War was doing. He probably had threesomes every other day.

But I was pretty busy flipping out.

I didn't know how to do this.

Like he could read my mind, War placed a kiss on my temple. "Relax."

"The most unrelaxing word in the English language is 'relax.' You know that, right?"

He chuckled. "Just look at me. Pretend he's not here."

"Pfft. Insulting." Scythe dropped down on the bed beside me.

"You've had sex with both of us before," War reminded me. "This isn't that different."

But it was. It was so very different, and I thought he saw it on my face.

He nodded. "Okay, we're gonna play this different. Got a scarf?"

I nodded. "In the wardrobe. But—"

"Massage oil?"

Scythe groaned, getting up off the bed. "I'll go find some."

He disappeared out of the room again, and War found the scarf in my wardrobe, dropping it onto the bed. He kissed me roughly and then lifted my shirt over my head. "Gonna take your clothes off now, while it's just you and me."

He dragged my pants off, leaving me in just my underwear. I was suddenly glad I'd put on something pretty that morning. I hadn't for a second thought the day would end here, but I'd been trying to make myself feel better on a day where my emotions had been out of control.

They were still going haywire, but now for an entirely different reason.

War picked up the scarf, wrapping it over my eyes and tying it behind my head. The silky material blocked my view entirely, and instantly, a little of my stress disappeared. The darkness was comforting, and in it, I could pretend I wasn't nervous as heck.

Scythe let out a tiny groan as he returned, otherwise I might not have even known he was there.

"Lie down on your belly," War said quietly.

I reached out for the bed and crawled across it, lying in the center on my stomach with my head twisted to one side.

Identical dips in the mattress either side of me said the guys were both on the bed too.

My heart hammered. Two guys. And me. There were only so many places for *things* to go. And some of those places had never been explored before, and the thought had my heart slamming against my chest.

Warm, silky liquid dripped onto my back, and War rubbed the oil into my skin, unclipping my bra as he went. Each movement of his hands was heavenly after the day I'd had, and slowly, inch by inch, muscle by muscle, he worked the tension from my back and shoulders.

He acted like he had all the time in the world, his fingers kneading sore spots and smoothing down my spine until I was so relaxed, sleep started creeping in.

His fingers slipped beneath the elastic of my panties, waking me up again. "Lift your hips," he murmured, and I did as I was told, letting him slide my panties off.

His oiled-up hands slid over the globes of my ass, and then lower, massaging my thighs, dipping between them, spreading me just enough that his fingertips brushed over my sensitive places.

He didn't linger there long, though I wanted him to. He rolled his palms over my ass, feeling me up and groaning a little when I couldn't help but spread my legs for him, an invitation to touch me where I really wanted him.

He didn't though.

"On your back, baby girl."

I flipped over, pulling my bra fully off so I was laid out naked for him on the bed.

For them.

Though Scythe had been so quiet, I had almost forgotten he was there.

Maybe he'd gotten bored and gone for a burger. I had

no idea, and I didn't care, as long as War didn't decide to join him.

War went straight for my breasts with a new handful of massage oil, cupping me and smoothing the liquid over my erect nipples. His thumbs and forefingers pinched and played with me, until I was wriggling beneath him and desperate for him to move lower.

He didn't.

But somebody else did.

My legs were spread wide as a big body settled between them, and I gasped when his tongue went straight to my core.

He did it again, licking me from opening to clit, tasting how wet I was from War's hands on my body.

Tasting how wet I was because I'd known all along that Scythe wouldn't have left for anything. And that he was merely standing there, watching, waiting for his moment.

The moment was now.

He fit his mouth over my clit, sucking hard until I moaned, and War pinched my nipples at the same time, lighting up sparks of pleasure inside me.

"More," I moaned. "Sc—"

He froze between my legs, and so did I.

I yanked the blindfold down, and his gaze slammed into mine.

"What just happened?" War asked, complete confusion on his face, his hands still glistening with oil.

I shook my head. "Nothing. I just need to watch him."

I needed to watch him, because I needed the reminder that even when I was losing my mind over his wickedly talented tongue, I couldn't give up his identity.

Slowly, he lowered his head between my thighs once more, his gaze never leaving mine for a second.

It only made it better. He drove his tongue into my pussy, licking me relentlessly until I scratched my fingernails along his scalp.

He let out a guttural noise of pleasure and fisted the back of his shirt, whipping it over his head with one hand, only stopping for a split second to lift his mouth from my core before it was planted firmly back.

I loved looking at him. He was so damn sexy, with his tanned skin and dark hair. It was long enough that it fell around his face when it wasn't styled back, and his broad, muscled shoulders fit between my legs perfectly. He moved his tongue to my clit, teasing and taunting me with featherlight licks while he worked a finger inside me.

I moaned, arching my back at the intrusion, and War leaned down to kiss my mouth, stealing my noises of pleasure. His tongue delved past my lips, stroking mine with deep, drugging pulls that had new waves of arousal rushing through my body.

Scythe switched to two fingers, the second instantly coated by how turned on I was that he gave me a third.

It stretched me, until I was panting into War's mouth and grinding down on Scythe's hand.

"Not yet, baby girl." War stood, taking his shirt off his head. I recognized it as one of Scythe's when it hit the floor, but then he was dropping his shorts as well, and I was staring at his perfect cock, hard and ridged.

The fact I did that to him, my naked body, and his need for me, was overwhelming. I pushed Scythe back from between my thighs so I could sit up, though my core gave an unhappy throb at the loss of his tongue.

Scythe stood back as well, and I went for his shorts, dragging them down his thighs, so they both stood side by side, their matching erections right there, ready for me to take.

I gripped them both.

My inhibitions had all left the building. All I wanted to do now was make the two of them feel as good as I had felt when they touched me.

Scythe groaned when I pumped his dick and fit my mouth over his blunt head. I bobbed there for a moment, my breasts heavy and needy and arousal thick between my legs. I took him deep into my throat, taking as much as I could and jerking the base of him with my hand.

He gathered my hair up into a ponytail, wrapping it around his fist.

For a moment, he fucked my mouth, his hips driving back and forth, but then he pulled away, guiding me to War.

I loved sucking War off. I loved the way his eyes flared and the groans he made. I loved the way his abs flexed and how I already knew exactly what he liked.

His taste was familiar, a tang on the back of my tongue that I couldn't wait for more of.

I'd never wanted to swallow with Caleb. He'd forced me, and I'd hated it.

But it was a different feeling altogether to do it for someone who turned you on.

Or for two someones.

I changed back to Scythe, then War, switching

between the two of them, working their dicks until they were gleaming with precum and ready to roll.

Scythe was the first to move away, bending slightly to grab my knees and lift them, forcing me onto my back. His big body covered mine, and I stared up at him, drinking in his expression of pure lust and need.

I'd done that to him.

His lips dragged along my shoulder to my neck, eliciting goosebumps in their wake. "I want to be looking at you when I'm inside you, Bliss."

I wanted it too. So badly.

I lifted up on my elbows, connecting our mouths and tugging him down on top of me as he pushed inside.

"Oh!" I screamed. He was so big, he stretched me even though I was more than ready for him.

Scythe rolled us so I was on top, my legs straddled either side of his narrow hips.

Not all that long ago, this position would have had me cowering or begging for someone to turn out a light.

But not all that long ago, I wouldn't have ever let myself have this. I would have talked myself out of it, with my fears and body image issues and insecurities.

So I pressed my hands to his solid chest and rocked on his erection. He palmed my breasts until my nipples sang out in glory and my orgasm built within me.

War trailed his fingers up and down my back, still slick with massage oil. He gently pushed me down so Scythe could claim my lips, kissing me deeply while we fucked.

War's hands trailed lower, massaging my ass cheeks and slipping between them.

It was shockingly good. So much so it completely took me by surprise and threw off my rhythm.

Scythe picked it up for me, gripping my hips and guiding my movements, slamming his hips up to meet me while he kissed me stupid.

War's thumb glided over my asshole with every thrust of Scythe's hips, and then gradually, as he gauged my reaction, he upped the pressure. Every downhill slide on Scythe's dick, I took a little more of War's finger.

The pleasure was foreign but intense. He was gentle and moved slowly, never forcing me, and letting me set the pace.

"Fuck, your ass is tight, sweetheart. But you're taking it so well."

I loved when he talked like that. It was some weird mixture of embarrassment and heat, but it made me squirm in all the best ways, until I was craving more. I needed more of his mouth. More of the way he touched me.

"Spank me," I groaned, remembering how it felt the last time he'd done it. "Please, War."

He groaned, but then his palm slapped across my bare skin, and my pussy clenched down around Scythe's erection.

He let out a shout as he came, filling me with his cum while I rode his dick, taking everything he had to give. My orgasm spiraled out of control with the added intensity of War working my ass with fingers and slaps.

I moaned, biting down on my lip to keep from shouting out the wrong name. But it was all I could do. I buried my face in Scythe's neck, lost in the swirling sensations that sent trembles across my entire body. He thrust into me until we were both limp and spent and sweaty.

I was too busy reveling in the feel of Scythe's fingers trailing absently up and down my back. It took me a moment to reach for War, ready to make him feel as good as Scythe and I did.

Only to find Scythe's hand wrapped around War's dick.

War stared down at Scythe's hand, his finger brushing over his birthmark. "Never noticed that before. It's sort of like a curved L."

Or a scythe, if you were looking at it from the opposite angle. Which I was really glad War wasn't.

Scythe switched hands, tucking the one with the birthmark beneath the covers and pumping War's dick to distract him.

"Holy shit, that's so hot," I murmured, laying my head down on Scythe's chest and watching his grip move over War's erection.

"Should have seen the show we put on in the bathroom earlier," Scythe drawled.

I lifted my head and an eyebrow at the same time. "Seriously? You two...you know."

War grinned. "Depends on your definition of 'you know.'"

I had no idea why the thought of the two of them together was so incredibly hot, but it was.

It was good they were getting along. Maybe eventually, Scythe would tell War about Vincent, and I could stop chomping on my tongue in an attempt not to spill the beans.

"Someone needs to suck his dick," Scythe said to me. "Is it gonna be me or you?"

I grinned. "Most definitely me." I lifted myself off Scythe's fading erection and crawled across the bed on all fours to take War's dick into my mouth.

God, he was big. Thick and blunt and beautiful. My hand replaced Scythe's, and he shifted on the bed behind me while I drew my lips down over War's erection.

Scythe groaned, "Jesus fuck, Bliss." His hand smoothed up the back of my thigh. "Look at your pussy, all swollen and dripping with my cum while you take his dick. That's the hottest thing I've ever seen."

I panted around War's cock. I loved the way these guys talked, so openly and graphically sexual, always full of praise for everything I did.

I glowed under their dirty words and compliments. Each one filled me with a confidence I'd never found elsewhere.

When Scythe's fingers moved from my thighs to my swollen, slick slit, all I did was cry out my approval. Another orgasm rained down on me, and I reveled in it, sucking War harder and faster while my knees trembled and my arms shook because Scythe was a master with his hands.

War thrust into my mouth, pushing his dick deep so it hit the back of my throat. Every time it did, I drew closer to the finish line, riding Scythe's fingers. He pressed open-mouthed kisses up my spine until it was all too much.

"I'm going to come," I moaned, though he had to already know, with the way I was pushing back against him, taking three fingers and a fourth on my clit.

War's grip on the back of my head tightened, prickling my scalp deliciously. I sucked him hard, running my tongue along his sensitive head so I tasted his cum. He groaned my name as we both fell over the edge, him spilling deep in my mouth, while I came for a second time.

The pleasure was mind-blowing. Blackness flickered at the edges of my vision.

I almost laughed.

Never in my life had I come so hard I thought I might pass out. And yet here I was, with two of the most sinfully sexy men I'd ever seen, and I was on the verge of unconsciousness because they were that damn good at drawing pleasure from my body.

All three of us sprawled across my bed, a tangle of sweaty, naked limbs.

I'd never felt more fulfilled, more sexy, or more safe than I did in that moment.

We all breathed in unison, quiet and lost in our own thoughts.

It was Scythe who broke the warm silence, twisting his head to my phone still set up on the small desk. "So. Anyone want to watch the video?"

## 22

# SCYTHE

*L*ittle Dog's angry barking cut through my sleep. I blinked, trying to orient myself in surroundings I didn't recognize, before remembering I was in Bliss' room. I twisted to the left, my gaze traveling over the two other people in bed with me.

War was sprawled out on his back, still naked, his dick hard with early morning glory. Bliss was equally bare, her leg over his, her sweet ass round and so very fuckable it killed me not to reach out and run my hands over her bare skin.

I heard the knock this time, and Little Dog's new round of barking woke the other two.

"Is someone here?" Bliss mumbled sleepily.

"Looks like it." I got out of bed and pulled on the pair of shorts I'd worn yesterday. "Go back to sleep. I'll see who it is."

"If Little dog tries to bite—"

I grinned. "I'll kick her."

Bliss' mouth dropped open. "You would not."

I sniggered and jogged down the stairs, picking up the little yapper on my way to the front door. Checking over my shoulder to make sure no one was watching, I held her up to my face and kissed her furry head. "I would never," I murmured to her. "You cute little fuzzball."

She stopped growling and licked my face.

I hadn't told Bliss that I'd been secretly feeding Little Dog liver treats all week and that her love was easily bought.

It was too fun to tease Bliss to give up the game.

I opened the door in an obnoxiously good mood from a night of great sex and a feeling of belonging I'd never had before.

It died the instant I saw the person standing on the other side.

Little Dog bared her teeth and growled. I kind of wanted to do the same.

"Good morning, dearest. I've brought breakfast." Mother held up two plastic shopping bags stuffed with food.

But whatever she'd sourced from the local bakery wasn't of concern to me.

What was a concern was the young woman standing behind her. "I see you've brought a friend."

Mother smiled widely. "You remember Jezebel, don't you? Jezebel, this is Scy—"

"Vincent," I interrupted. "Her half-naked son because she doesn't know how to use this little thing called a telephone." I glared at my mother.

She stepped in close, edging through the doorway I was blocking. "She's the Montgomery girl. The one you need to marry before Vincent shows up again," she hissed.

I'd completely forgotten about this plan of hers, to marry me off so Vincent couldn't have Bliss.

It hadn't bothered me when we'd made the deal.

But now it bothered me greatly. "I'm not doing that."

Mother ignored me, brushing past into the house and singing gaily about getting us some plates. Which left me standing on the porch with the female version of myself.

I had no idea what I was supposed to say. So I went with what I knew. "So..." I said to her. "Knives, huh?"

She withdrew one from beneath her sleeve and flashed it at me. "Yeah. You, too?"

I bent to the potted plant at my feet, pushing aside a thin layer of dirt to pull out a small bone-handled knife.

Jezebel's grin grew wide, and she stepped past me, following my mother inside the house with a pat to my bare chest. "We'll get on just fine."

I groaned, closing the door behind her and following them through. "Mother, this is really not a good time. I have guests."

She looked over from where she was lifting plates out of a kitchen cupboard. "There's plenty of food for everyone. Invite them down, I'm sure they'd like to meet your future wife."

I wasn't so sure about that.

But the decision was taken out of my hands when a barely dressed War and Bliss arrived in the kitchen doorway, War's arm slung around Bliss' neck. They stopped abruptly, and I had to bite down on my lip from letting out a groan at the sight of Bliss in one of my oversized shirts.

I instantly wondered if she even had anything beneath it, or if she was still as bare as I'd left her, the remnants of what the three of us had done together still lingering on her thighs.

The way she tugged my shirt down made me think that maybe she didn't.

God-fucking-damn my mother and her lousy timing. And goddamn me for agreeing to this shit.

"Sorry," Bliss said, darting a glance in my direction, and then to my mother and Jezebel. "We didn't realize you had guests. We can go back upstairs."

I grabbed her hand. "Stay."

Her gaze held mine, and in an instant, she nodded.

Mom's disapproval was written all over her face. "Who are your friends, dearest?"

She already knew who Bliss was.

But I played along anyway. "This is Bliss. And that's War."

Mom's gaze studied War curiously. "War? Is that a nickname?"

"Yes, ma'am. My name's Warrick Maynard."

War answered so politely it shocked me. Who knew he had manners?

But I cringed at the look of recognition in her eye and the raised eyebrow she shot in my direction.

She knew who War was too, obviously.

And that I'd been responsible for his father's death.

That couldn't be a good thing.

Mom reached out to Bliss and War, playing the dutiful parent and shaking hands. With fake enthusiasm, she exclaimed over how lovely it was to meet Vincent's friends.

Bliss and War both smiled at her and engaged in conversation, like they couldn't see how very insincere the woman was.

She brushed past me on the way back to preparing her food and whispered, "The three of you reek of sex. Really, Scythe? I thought you had more sense."

I grabbed her arm, my fingernails biting into her skin, though I was sure War hadn't heard because he was busy introducing himself and Bliss to Jezebel.

"Don't call me that."

Her sharp-eyed gaze missed nothing, darting between me and War a few times, like she was putting the pieces together. "Interesting."

I sighed.

Bliss took up a stool next to Jezebel, accepting the muffin I put under her nose. We may as well eat my mother's food since we had to put up with her presence.

"So, are you visiting from out of town, Jezebel?" Bliss asked.

Jezebel shook her head, her long dark hair rolling down her back in soft waves. I frowned, hoping she tied it back when she was working on a kill. All that hair was an occupational hazard. It was too easy for the victim to become the attacker when there was something as easy as a ponytail to pull and control.

Though I supposed her love of knives made that a moot point. If she carried them around in her sleeve when she was just going to a casual breakfast, then she was probably armed to the hilt at all times. And nobody loved to get up close and personal more than someone who used a knife as their main form of execution.

"I'm Saint View born and bred," Jezebel answered

Bliss. "Don't get over to Providence all that much, unless my job brings me over this way."

Bliss took a bite of her muffin, chewing it thoughtfully before she asked, "What do you do for work?"

I froze, praying she understood that this wasn't the sort of company where she could share freely. But Jezebel simply took a sip of her orange juice, and without pause, said, "I'm a florist."

Bliss nodded. "Oh. Lovely. Do you have a card? We should really get some flowers delivered to the bar once in a while."

War scoffed. "What on earth for?"

She glared at him. "To make the place smell less like the bottom of a beer barrel and more like a welcoming place to hang out and spend money for the evening?"

I leaned over her, stealing a croissant. "I don't think flowers are gonna help."

She shook her head. "Fine. I'll put them in my office then, since the two of you are so opposed to having anything nice."

Jezebel smiled. "I'll drop some off for you next week."

"That would be lovely. Thank you."

"So do you think you'll do the flowers for your own wedding?" Mom asked Jezebel.

Bliss squealed and clutched Jezebel's arm like they were longtime friends. "You're getting married? How exciting! Oh, I bet you have a ton of ideas for your own wedding. Roses? Or are they too predictable?"

"I don't know." Jezebel glanced over her shoulder at me. "Do you have any preference?"

Oh, for fuck's sake.

War laughed. "Why would Vinnie have any preference on your wedding flowers?"

A frown of confusion formed between Bliss' eyebrows.

I didn't say a word. I didn't need to because my mother took great delight in filling them in.

She laughed, the sound grating and fake. "Well, because he's the groom, of course."

Bliss and War both turned to stare at me, their eyes wide.

"What?" Bliss eventually choked out.

I put my pastry down so I could explain. "Bliss... It's not what you think..."

She got down slowly off the stool and turned to Jezebel. "I...I didn't know. It was nice to meet you. I'm sorry." She turned and ran upstairs.

I groaned. I'd have put money on it that she was packing a bag right now and ready to run for the hills.

War just shook his head. "What the fuck, man?"

Before I could say anything, he swiveled on his heel and followed Bliss.

"Did you enjoy that?" I asked my mother.

The look of pure glee on her face said she very much had.

Anger boiled up inside me. "What's wrong with you?"

She scoffed. "I don't remember you being this soft. Once upon a time, you would have never even spared a thought for the feelings of a silly woman." She stepped in close and patted my cheek. "Don't let him turn you, son. You know you always were my favorite."

I pulled away from her. "Don't patronize me." I glanced over at Jezebel. "I don't know what she promised you, or more likely, what she threatened you with to agree to this, but this isn't happening."

For a tiny second, I was sure it was relief that flickered in Jezebel's almost violet eyes. But it was gone just as quickly, replaced with the same nonchalance she'd worn all morning.

I went to leave, needing to go explain myself to Bliss and War.

But my mother called after me. "It is happening. I'd prefer not to force my hand, but I will if I have to."

I stopped at the quiet threat in her voice and narrowed my eyes. "I'm not *him*, Mother. You can't threaten my dog and have me fall into line." I sniffed in the direction of Little Dog. "I don't even like his mutt."

I'd give her extra liver treats later for saying that.

Mother's shrewd gaze didn't miss a thing, and I fought to keep my expression neutral, when all I wanted to do was run upstairs and make Bliss understand.

Vincent's presence in the back of my mind was quiet, but it was there, urging me on.

And for once, I wanted to listen to it.

"People always have a soft spot. Even you. And you just gave yours up so easily, without even trying to hide it."

I ground my teeth, not saying a word, because I could tell she still had plenty.

When she patted my cheek this time, it was hard enough to sting. "Idiot," she hissed. "You act like you're the strong one, and yet there's a reason Vincent is the dominant and not you."

The words cut deep because it was a truth I'd always known.

My time was always limited.

Because I wasn't ever enough.

Mother's glare bored through me. "You'll marry Jezebel. And soon, because I can tell your grip is already slipping."

"And if I refuse?"

Her grin was pure evil. "I'll tell War exactly who you are, and exactly what you did to his father. Every. Horrific. Detail."

She had me and she knew it. Once War realized who I was, then so would Bliss.

All of this would end.

Permanently.

## 23

---

## BLISS

*I* was an idiot.

That was all I could think as the hot water streamed over my body. I squirted bodywash into my cupped hand and then added an extra two squirts for good measure to wash off Scythe's touch.

I'd spent all night in bed with a man who was engaged to another woman.

None of that sat right with me. I wasn't like that. I didn't take what wasn't mine. And now I felt like utter trash for poor Jezebel, sitting downstairs, trying to have breakfast with her fiancé while I wandered down, wearing his clothes and with his scent all over me.

I groaned into the water spray, letting it pummel me directly in the face.

The door opened a crack.

"Bliss."

I whipped around and glared at him, not even caring that I was fully naked. He'd spent all night inside my body, now was hardly the time to get shy. "Don't even, Scythe."

He shut the door quickly, and I knew it was because he didn't want War hearing me use that name, but I was too mad to keep his secrets in that moment. How many more were there anyway? Did he have a whole secret family I didn't know about?

This was my own fault, really.

He'd warned me.

This was what I got for trusting a psychopath. The fact I was surprised he'd lied to me so easily really said more about me than it did about him.

Hence, I was an idiot.

He folded his arms over his broad chest and stared at me through the glass of the shower. "She's not my fiancée, Bliss."

"Bullshit!" I shouted at him. "I saw your face back there when your mother dropped her little bomb. Your expression wasn't denial. It was goddamn guilt. Fuck you, Scythe. How dare you."

He groaned. "Could you stop yelling at me for a second and let me explain?"

I turned away, facing the wall so I didn't have to look at his stupidly handsome face.

God, it was hard though. I'd spent all night letting him and War make me come over and over, and each time, Scythe had been right there, kissing me deep, his gaze boring into mine, eliciting feelings for him that I didn't want to feel.

"Bliss."

I ignored him. I'd said all I wanted to say.

He let out a ragged growl, and the shower door

squeaked in protest as he jerked it open. He grabbed my arm and spun me around, his eyes dark with anger.

"Let go of me!" I demanded.

"Not a fucking chance, sweetheart." His voice was deep and gravelly.

Water fell over his bronze skin, sliding down his chest and abs in a waterfall and soaking his shorts. He grabbed my chin, forcing my gaze to meet his.

Our gazes clashed, both burning fiery hot.

"I've never even met that woman," he ground out through clenched teeth. "I agreed to marry her only because my mother insisted, and at the time, it didn't matter to me who I was with."

I gaped at him. "You don't seriously expect me to believe your mother arranged a wedding for you? In this day and age, without some sort of religious belief behind it?"

Water soaked the lengths of his hair, darkening the brown strands to black. "You think my mother's business isn't exactly like a religion? More like a cult when I think about it. But of course marriages are arranged. Our family is powerful. So is Jezebel's. We're a good match on paper. Fuck, we both even like knives."

I threw my hands up. "Well, I'm so glad you have something in common!"

He growled, the noise a deep rumbling in his chest. "I never asked for any of this, Bliss. In fact, the entire thing is your fault."

I widened my eyes at him, my mouth dropping open. "How on earth is this my fault? You're insane!"

"I'm well aware. But you're the one who made Vincent fall in love with you. You're the reason he wants babies, and a life with you as his wife, and to get out of the game altogether."

I blinked. "He's not in love with me."

He shook his head. "Yes, he is."

I mirrored his actions. "No, he's not."

"For fuck's sake, Bliss. Do you seriously not have eyes? Of course he's in love with you. Just like War is. Just like Nash is. Just like—"

My heart thumped against my chest. "Just like what, Scythe?"

"Nothing," he muttered, dropping his gaze to the floor. "The point is, you made him want those things. And Mother Dearest isn't going to let him go that easily. If I marry Jezebel now, while I'm in control, Vincent will have no say in it."

I gaped at him. "You can't do that!"

He sighed. "I have to."

I narrowed my eyes at him. "You're not a little boy, Scythe. You don't have to do what your mother tells you, you know?"

He laughed bitterly. "Except I do. Because there's always repercussions if I don't."

"Then suck it up and deal with them!"

"I can't!" he roared back. "She'll take everything I care about. Don't you understand that? She'll tell War, and then you'll know too, and then what do I have left? Nothing. If I don't have either of you, there's no fucking point in me being here."

His words hit me in the gut as hard as if he'd punched me. "She'll tell him what?"

He slowly raised his gaze to mine. "That I killed his father."

I squeezed my eyes shut tight. "No."

He didn't say anything, and when I opened my eyes again, I saw the truth in his expression.

He opened his mouth, maybe to explain, but I held a hand up in a stop motion.

"Don't, Scythe. Don't say another word."

"Bliss—"

"No. I can't deal with that. I don't want to know."

"You already do."

Emotions tried to rip me down the middle. My heart broke all over again for War. While anger swelled and stormed for the man standing in front of me. I just shook my head at him, turning off the water and stepping out of the shower to grab my towel. I wrapped it around my body, leaving him standing dripping in the shower.

"What are you going to do?" he asked when my hand was on the bathroom door, ready to escape.

I paused, refusing to look over at him, though everything inside me wanted to. "Nothing."

"I don't understand."

"What else is there to do other than nothing, Scythe? If I tell War what I know, he'll kill you."

"Yes."

"And you'll retaliate. Because I can't imagine that standing there while someone attacks you is really in your wheelhouse, am I right?"

The response was slower, but it still came, just like I knew it would. "Yes."

I pursed my lips and nodded. "And that is exactly why I can't say anything. Because you've put me in the worst position possible. Where if I tell the truth, I lose you both." I pushed down on the door handle, letting myself out.

This time, Scythe stayed quiet.

There was nothing left to say.

He was marrying someone else. He was already lost.

## 24

---

## WAR

My phone buzzed in my pocket multiple times on my ride back to my compound from Vincent's place in Providence, but I didn't stop to answer it. I needed the roar of the bike beneath me and rush of wind in my face.

A fucking fiancée?

Like I could talk. I was as good as married off to Siren.

Vincent and I were nothing to each other. So I shouldn't have been annoyed.

And yet, I was.

"Hypocritical bastard," I muttered, cussing myself out. He and I were as bad as each other. Neither of us deserved Bliss. The hurt on her face had gutted me.

Maybe that was why I was so drawn to him. Because we were two fucking peas in a pod, born into messed-up families and intent on screwing ourselves over. And over. And over.

I didn't even know what I'd been thinking last night. After the photos of him and I had spread around the compound, I should have been keeping a low profile. Staying away from him. Fucking some club women so everyone could be reminded where I liked to keep my cock at night.

*"You fuck your women out in the main room, where everyone can watch you dominate them,"* my old man had told me when I was barely old enough to get an erection. *"You make sure nobody thinks there's anything going on with you and Hawk. As the future leader of this club, those men need to respect you. They won't if they think you want to shove your dick in their asses."*

I'd listened back then. And I'd grown to like having an audience. Craved it, in fact. But my old man's warning was true. I hadn't heard from Hawk in days. And the other guys I'd run into had all eyed me awkwardly.

It had been a whole lot easier to hide out with Vincent and Bliss.

I loved her body. I was so fucking attracted to her it did my head in. And she was sweet, and smart, and fun to be around.

But I'd also liked his hand wrapped around my dick. I'd liked his tongue in my mouth.

I'd liked getting down on my knees for him and sucking him off until he'd come, his hand tight on the back of my head.

I groaned at the erection tenting my jeans and slowed my bike as I approached the compound gates. Fang was on duty again, and he had them open before I could come to a stop. I paused anyway. He was one of my best friends here, and I needed to know where I stood with him.

"You see the photos?"

He shook his head. "Didn't open 'em."

"Why not?"

"Don't care about who you fuck, Prez."

A grin spread across my face.

Fang didn't smile back. He never did. But the support was there anyway, and that meant something to me.

Was a shame I couldn't say the same for Hawk.

I hit the gas and steered through the opening, the gates creaking closed behind me. I pulled up out in front of the clubhouse, knowing I needed to face the music and have it out with anyone who felt differently than Fang. Bikes were parked out front, so I knew there'd be a crowd inside, even though it was barely four in the afternoon.

I got off, leaving my helmet on the handlebars, and let myself in.

Women filled the room, sitting and chatting on the couches and hanging around the bar making drinks. Somebody had made nachos, and I stole one as I passed, grinning down at Queenie when she let out a squeak of protest.

But then she saw it was me, and her squawk turned to an indulgent *humph*.

"Where is everyone?" I munched on my corn chip.

Her gaze darted to Siren and then back at me. She had an oddly guilty look on her face.

"Spill it, Queenie."

Siren did it for her. "They're in church."

I raised an eyebrow. "Excuse me?"

She lifted a dainty shoulder. "We tried to get a hold of you, but Hawk went and called it when you didn't answer."

I ground my molars. As the prez, I was the only one who could call church.

The fact they were all in there right now without me grated. I didn't fucking care if I hadn't answered my phone. Church was for decision-making. And no decision was being made around here without me.

I nodded at Siren and ignored their gazes on my back as I stormed to the room we used as a meeting spot. I threw open the door, and a dozen men swiveled in my direction.

I only had eyes for Hawk though.

The motherfucker sat in my seat at the head of the table.

"What the fuck is this?" I asked, leaning on the door-frame. It was a fake attempt to be casual when what I really wanted to do was slam a fist into someone's face.

Hawk glared at me. "We called you."

"And I didn't answer. So you went and called church without me?"

"Somebody had to. You ain't ever around lately. As VP, I took over. That's my fucking job, War. Don't give me a hard time about it."

"Bullshit," I spit the word in his direction. "What was so fucking important it couldn't wait 'til I got back?"

Hawk shoved to his feet, facing off with me across the length of the table. "How about the fact you've done nothing about your father's death? We know who did it. Why the hell aren't we moving on it?"

I glared at him. "You think it's that fucking easy? Scythe is a ghost. Most people think he's a myth. I can't exactly walk up to random people on the streets and say, 'Oh, hey, have you seen this random hitman for hire? Goes by the name of Scythe, but nobody knows what he looks like or his real name. Zero description or last known whereabouts.' How exactly do you think that's gonna go down?"

"Better than doing nothing. You're making us look bad. People are talking."

And there it was. The bullshit came unstuck and the truth came out. "I'm making us look bad because we haven't killed Scythe? Or because you saw a photo of me kissing another man, and now, you're afraid all the other clubs are gonna think I'm gay?"

"Not just you," he ground out. "All of us. Me especially. Everybody knows we're tight."

I shook my head. "You homophobic asshole. You think if I wanted to kiss you, I wouldn't have done it by now?"

He stormed around the table, his eyes blazing. "I'd like to see you try."

I cracked my neck, so fucking ready for a fight. I needed a place for all my anger and aggression to go.

Gus stood, putting himself between us. "Enough. Sit your asses down, both of you." He pinned Hawk with a glare. "In your own seat. Show some fucking respect."

I blinked, surprised at his support. But I nodded and went to sit in the seat Hawk had just vacated.

Gus and Hawk both sat back down, and everyone turned to me.

I sighed heavily. "First of all, who I sleep with is none of anyone's business. If you have a problem with it, like my supposed best friend here, speak now."

Nobody said a word.

"No, seriously. Speak now. Tell me how you really feel because it'll come out either way. Gunner?"

He shook his head. "Got a grandson who likes to wear dresses and have tea parties. If he grows up to like men, I'll paint my bike in rainbow colors."

I grinned at him. "You gonna do the same for me?"

He chuckled. "We'll see."

I looked around the table. "Aloha?"

He shrugged. "I got questions."

"Ask 'em."

"You gay?"

I shrugged. "If I had to label it, I'd say bi. Not gonna stop fucking women just 'cause one guy caught my eye."

Aloha nodded, satisfied. "Fair enough."

"Fact is, my sexuality has no bearing on whether I can lead this club. But your trust in me does. So take a vote. And let me know if I'm in or out. Because if I don't have unanimous support, I'm as good as done anyway. I'm not going into this war doubting that any one of you have my back. That's a real good fucking way to end up dead."

"We're going to war?" Gunner asked.

I scrubbed a hand through my hair. "Hawk is right. I've been sitting on the knowledge for too long. We have to make a move."

"So we go to war with the Slayers?" Hawk asked, his eyes gleaming.

I nodded. "They ordered a hit that took out our prez. We need to do the same to them. But I want more than just that."

"Scythe?"

I nodded. "I want his head on a spike. Find him."

## 25

# BLISS

*R*ebel floated around Psychos' party rooms like a cracked-out fairy. She moved at warp speed, running around, cleaning until the place sparkled, and then set up for what she'd informed me was going to be the party of the year.

I had no doubt.

It was good she was so busy. It meant she didn't notice I was quiet.

My mother did though.

To my surprise, she'd still been around when I'd gotten to the club in the late afternoon. George, Psychos' cook, had put her to work in the kitchen, and she'd been happily peeling potatoes or washing dishes every time I'd walked past.

Happy and my mom were two things I'd never associated with each other. I couldn't remember ever seeing her smile. Her life with Jerry had been one misery after another. But today, I'd caught a glimpse of one when George had sung off-key to an old Alanis Morissette song.

For a second, I'd thought Mom might join in, but instead, she'd smiled softly and gone back to her potatoes.

An hour before the party started, I pulled her aside and into my office. We'd stared at each other, her gaze full of hope. Mine probably full of doubt, though it softened by the minute.

"You've been working all day," I commented.

"I can keep going."

I shook my head. "You need to take a break before you pass out."

"I just want to be helpful." She took my hand, gripping it tightly between her bony fingers. "I'll do whatever needs doing. The floor is a bit sticky..."

"You know what's happening here tonight, right?"

"I do."

Heat flushed my face. "I can't work here tonight with you here. It's too weird."

Her eyes widened, but then she nodded quickly. "I understand. I can leave."

I caught her arm, scared of what would happen if I let her back out there. "Stay in my office. You can watch a movie on my laptop. Tomorrow, you'll work again. We'll have plenty to clean up. We'll also find you somewhere to live that's not in the center of a sex club."

Tears filled her eyes. "Do you mean that? You really want me to come back?"

"Are you going to keep working as hard as you did today?"

She nodded quickly. "I like it here, Bliss. It reminds me of Axel. And I get to be near you. I don't mind peeling potatoes or cleaning bathrooms. Whatever needs doing."

"You'll stay here as long as you hold up your end of the bargain. There's plenty of work here that needs doing, just not..."

She smiled conspiratorially. "Don't worry. I know it's Nash's birthday party and that you two have a thing. I'm not gonna spoil your fun."

The urge to hug her came on fast and strong, but I wouldn't. Today had been good. And I hoped like hell it was the start of something new. I'd never had a mother. Nichelle was barely older than me and hadn't come into my life until I was in my mid-teens. She'd never had any desire or need to parent me. This was the sort of conversation I'd always dreamed of, the kind mothers had with their daughters on TV shows. Talking about boys, or as the case was now, men.

But one good day didn't erase a lifetime of memories and disappointments. And I refused to let my heart be broken again.

But it was a start. A good one. She was trying, and so was I.

I left her in my office and ran into Scythe standing guard at the door.

"Bliss."

"No." I pushed past him, disappearing into the party room. If there had been any possible way of me running tonight without him, I would have sent him home, because I couldn't even bear to face him. He'd put me in the absolute worst position. I didn't want to lie to War. It had been bad enough calling Scythe Vincent, but at the time, I'd thought that was simply to make things easier for him. It wasn't my place to announce to the world that he had a split personality.

And I wasn't hurting anyone by continuing to call him Vincent.

Now I felt like I'd unknowingly been part of some big scheme the entire time.

The jealousy that flickered inside me told another tale.

"What did he do now?" Rebel asked, halting her whirlwind of activity to stand beside me.

"Who?"

"Vincent. If looks could kill, he'd be a dead man right now."

He watched us from the doorway, and I scowled at him, tugging her away so he was out of earshot. "I met his fiancée this morning. While I was wearing nothing but his T-shirt."

Rebel's mouth dropped open. "No!"

"I wish I was joking."

"You slept with him?"

Heat crept up my neck, but I was desperate to tell someone. "Him...and War...at the same time."

Rebel's eyes were the size of dinner platters. "Get the fuck outta town, Dis! You skanky ho bag! Well done! Was it good?"

My core clenched at the memory of just how very good it had been. And just how badly I wanted to do it again. "Yes," I whispered. "So good. But the fiancée..."

Rebel cringed. "Yeah. Not ideal."

"I feel like shit."

She squeezed my arm. "Hey. This is not your fault. You did nothing wrong. He's the asshole."

Except he wasn't. "He says it's an arranged thing. That he doesn't even know her..."

Rebel rested a hip on the back of a couch. "Except that doesn't matter to you...because you have feelings for him."

I bit my lip. "I think I'm jealous."

"I would be."

I shook my head. "That's irrational. I have no claim on him. We had sex a couple of times—"

"A couple of times, huh? You conveniently forgot to tell your best friend all the dirty, dirty details about that?"

"Stoppp." I laughed. "Be serious. I'm having a quarter-life crisis here."

She sobered. "Why wouldn't you be jealous? Any blind person can see there's more than just physical attraction between you two. You've been living together for weeks. Don't tell me that's purely platonic."

"I don't even like him sometimes. I think I actually hate him half the time we're together."

"You know what they say about fine lines, hate, and love."

"I don't love him. That's insane."

"Why?" She started ticking reasons off on her fingers. "One. The man has done nothing but protect you since the moment he came into the picture. He's let everybody in that bar know that if they so much as look at you wrong, he'll end them. Haven't you noticed the way you aren't getting 'accidentally' groped in there anymore? Two. He's sweet. In a scary, obsessive sort of way that I personally think is pretty hot. He follows you around like a little lost puppy dog, always making sure you have everything you need and want. Three. He let you move in with him. Four. The chemistry between the two of you burns me every time you're in the same room. Like, seriously, Dis. I have third-degree burns I'm sending the two of you the hospital bill for."

I laughed at her dramatics. "I'll admit I have feelings for him. I will not admit to those feelings being love."

Rebel shrugged. "Fair enough."

"But I'm also angry at him, and I'm gonna need a minute to get over that."

Rebel saluted me. "Also fair enough. This is Nash's party anyway. Might be a bit on the nose if you're off having sex with Vincent when the birthday boy is pining after you." She glanced over at the door. "Speaking of..."

My mouth dried watching Nash walk into the room. His black slacks were held up by a shiny black belt. They sat low on his hips, tucked around a pale-blue, collared, button-down shirt. Even from this distance, I knew it would perfectly match his eyes. His hair was freshly styled, and he'd rolled the sleeves of his shirt up to his elbows.

He strode across the room, gaze flitting around, checking everything was in place before landing on me. "Hey."

I drew in a deep breath, his cologne doing things to me that were entirely indecent. "Hey yourself. You look good."

He smiled, and it was devastating. I had to grip the back of the couch to keep my knees steady.

"Thanks. Are we all good to go?"

I shook my head. "Nope. I'm not talking to you about that. You are not working tonight."

"And neither are you," Rebel announced, eyeing me shrewdly.

I frowned at her. I'd done the roster. I knew I was scheduled on tonight. "Yes, I am."

Rebel sauntered off, calling back over her shoulder as she went, "Nope. I called in all the temp staff to cover you." She grinned at Nash. "That's my birthday present to you, Boss Man. You get the boss lady all to yourself for the night."

Nash's gaze rolled over me so slowly I instantly stopped arguing with Rebel.

Hell. If he was going to look at me like that, Rebel was going to have to run the place herself, because I was going to be taking care of some very real needs that sparked to life beneath his attention.

He leaned in close, fingers trailing up my arm in the lightest of touches. "That true, Bliss? Are you mine tonight?"

I closed my eyes for half a second, overwhelmed at the rush of feelings coursing through me. Before I could change my mind, I let instinct take over. "Yes."

He let out a groan. "Fuck. That's so hot. Tell me your limits."

I thought I would have had a list. And maybe a few weeks ago, I would have. But heat bloomed through me every time I saw Nash, or thought about his hands on me, or his lips on mine. I'd wanted him since the day I'd walked back into his life.

But more than that, I trusted him. I always had. He'd never let me down. He'd never hurt me. And now, standing in front of him, aching for him in a way that was entirely new, I knew I wouldn't stop him, no matter what he wanted from me tonight.

"I trust you." I turned my face into his thickly stubbled cheek and pressed a kiss there. "Happy birthday, Nash."

His arm clenched around my waist, drawing me in. "I don't want you to regret saying that."

"I won't."

He moved back, his blue-eyed gaze searching mine.

He obviously liked whatever he saw there because the corner of his mouth flickered. His fingers threaded through mine, and he pulled me down the hallway, past my office toward all the individual rooms that people could hire for private use. Beyond those was another large gathering room, one we hadn't set up at previous parties. But tonight, Rebel had gone all out, decorating it in red and black. Once the lights were out, it would be the stereotypical red room, roped off from the public with a thick red cord that we would have a bouncer on. People would be free to watch from behind the ropes, but to play, you had to pay a fee.

The tables were laid out with various sex toys and props, and anyone playing in here tonight was going to be putting on quite the show.

Right now though, Nash unclipped the rope himself and let us in. I glanced at him, and he nodded toward the tables. "See anything you like?"

My breath hitched. I trailed my fingers along the tabletop of floggers and ball gags, vibrators and dildos, silk ties and butt plugs. "Did Rebel rob a sex store?"

He grinned. "She talked one into sponsoring tonight. We've done it before. People get a chance to try things out. And when they like them, the shop gets all their repeat business. Works out nicely for both of us."

I couldn't stop looking at everything. There was more

than I'd imagined, and some of it I didn't even know what to do with.

"Still got no limits, Blissy girl?"

I glanced at him, and he was studying me intently. I very deliberately shook my head. "No limits."

"Good." He reached over and picked up a little oval-shaped insertable vibrator with a tail that was clearly meant to sit over your clit. He passed it to me, pressing it into my hand. "Put this in when you're getting ready."

My heart hammered, and my core lit up in excitement.

He took his phone out and grinned at me as he backed out of the room. "I've got the app that controls it. See you soon."

He left me gaping at him, with the hot pink vibrator firmly clutched in my hand. I started to question if I was really going to do this, but before I was even halfway through the thought, the device buzzed in my hand.

I stared down at it and knew instantly that yes, I was really going to do it. Knowing it was Nash on the controls only made it all the better. I grabbed a tube of lubricant from the table and hustled into the staff bathroom where I'd left my bag since my mother was occupying my office.

I had another set of lingerie picked out for the night. I'd showered right before coming in but hadn't wanted to put it on while I was busy setting up for the party. Now I slipped it from my bag and hung it on the back of the stall door. It was a lacy black one-piece that cut deep between my breasts and high in the back. It was simple but so incredibly sexy. The minute I'd seen it, I'd wanted to wear it and I'd picked it with Nash in mind. I stripped out of my clothes and then picked up the little wearable vibrator. I squirted some lube onto it, then worked the toy up inside myself.

I probably could have done without the lube. I was already turned on just from the idea of it.

It nestled inside me comfortably, and I fit the front of it to my clit. The tingle of excitement and anticipation ripped through me, and my whole body became aware of what I was doing.

Slowly, I dragged on the lingerie and checked myself in the mirror, marveling at the fact the sex toy was so small and discreet you couldn't even see it with the complete lack of clothes I wore. I took my makeup bag out and glammed myself up with more product than I normally wore and took my time curling my hair. Music started up outside in the main room, and a thrill of excitement rushed me, knowing that the room would be filling with people, each of them handing over stacks of cash for the privilege of being here.

Pride washed over me. Axel might have started all this, but I was upping the game, making it bigger and better. We might have been a dirty little secret to the people who turned up here, but these parties were a profitable business. One I owned. The extra drugs I'd ordered had shown up in a duffel bag on the front seat of my car, only discovered when I'd left Scythe's house this morning. They were now stashed in the safe. I had enough for several more parties, and theme ideas for each of them were ticking away in the back of my mind.

This was going to be my empire. It was going to provide for me, my family, and for my friends. A rush of power coursed through me, and I let myself feel it. I'd spent so long being walked all over. As well-meaning as he was, I'd been shoved into a box by my father, and the schools he sent me to. The friends I'd made had kept me there, and then Caleb had effectively sealed the damn box with tape.

I'd burst free and I wasn't going back. Not for anyone. Not now that Axel had given me this gift and a way of being the woman I'd always wanted to be.

I strode out onto the floor with my head held high.

All I needed was a crown.

The vibrator turned on, stopping me in my tracks. The internal part was pressed right up on my G-spot and that, in conjunction with the part that vibrated over my clit, had my mouth dropping open and a pant of need slipping out.

The vibrations stopped just as suddenly.

I straightened, sweeping my gaze around the room in search of Nash. The room was half full of people already, and waiters circled with welcome drinks. The stages were all set up, the gold cages glinting, and the performers already starting their acts. I'd grown used to the scenes they created, and I barely lingered on them now, more eager to find Nash than pay attention to their sexual acts.

I found him at the bar, watching me intently, a glass full of something dark in one hand, his phone in the other.

He raised one eyebrow at me.

I nodded, letting him know I'd liked it.

His returning smile was everything. My heart thumped unevenly, and the need to kiss him roared the closer I got. I sidled up beside him, taking a glass of wine when one of the temps we hired for parties passed it over to me. I took a sip, grateful for the cold liquid sliding down my throat that was suddenly as dry as the Sahara.

"You wear that for me?"

The heat in Nash's eyes was electric. It set off sparks within me that were very similar to the ones the vibrator had evoked.

"Yes," I murmured. "Do you like it?"

"I can't stop looking at you."

"I don't want you to."

He put one hand into his pocket, and the toy inside me started up again.

I gasped when the vibrations worked my most intimate areas.

"I like that you like me watching you." He moved in closer, his hand discreetly cupping me, pressing the toy tighter to my clit.

A moan fell from my lips as the vibrations increased, the pleasure concentrated on my sensitive bundle of nerves.

"I want to watch you come," he said in my ear. "But not yet."

The vibrations stopped.

"Dance with me?" he asked softly.

I nodded and let him pull me out onto the floor. It was already crowded with bodies in various stages of undress, each one moving to the rhythm of the music playing from hidden speakers.

Nash drew me in, and I wrapped my arms around his neck, letting his hands on my hips guide the way I moved. The song was sexy, slow, and sensual, and eyes turned to watch us move together.

I knew Scythe was one of them, and War was probably here somewhere, too, but I refused to think about it. I wasn't going to look in their direction when tonight was about Nash. I drank him in and was shocked all over again by how attractive I found this man. I desperately wanted him to turn the toy back on so I could come while staring into his eyes. There was a wealth of knowledge and experience behind them. I knew he was into things I'd probably never even considered, things that might push me right out of my comfort zone, but I wanted to try them all. With him.

"Do you know how turned on I am right now, knowing you have that inside you?" he whispered. "And knowing I'm the one who gets to control how it makes you feel?"

I trailed a hand down over his chest and abs and lower to feel his erection. He was huge soft, and even bigger hard. I almost wondered how the hell that would even fit inside me, but the thought washed away when Nash ground against my hand.

Anywhere else, it would have been completely indecent for the two of us to be feeling each other up the way we were, but here, it was encouraged. Women and men alike watched my hand rub over his pants, and I was rewarded with the vibrator coming to life once more.

He stroked my back, holding me close while the device did its job, sending pleasure through my entire body. A prickly heat settled across my breasts, my nipples going hard beneath the lacy material of my outfit.

"Oh God," I whispered, feeling the beginnings of an orgasm build.

Nash put his arm around me, drawing me in so my face was pressed against his neck. Waves of pleasure rolled through my body and at any minute, I knew he'd turn it off.

He didn't. He held me tight as I gasped into his neck, the orgasm taking hold. It wasn't strong, but it was pleasurable, and he dragged my head back so he could watch as I came. His mouth covered mine, and I kissed him back eagerly, accepting the plunge of his tongue and the sweet taste of the alcohol he'd consumed.

The vibrations stopped, and his lips traveled off my lips and up my jawline to my ear. "Take it out. I'm going to put my tongue in its place."

I stroked the nape of his neck, loving the feel of his lips on mine. "You aren't messing around tonight."

He pulled back, his gaze hot when it met mine. "I've waited weeks for this, Bliss. I've fought myself at every turn and denied myself what I really wanted."

"Are you done with that?"

He paused, watching me carefully. "For tonight, yes. I don't know if my answer will still be the same tomorrow. But right now, I need my tongue on your clit and my cock deep inside you."

I shivered at his promises, though I knew he was right. His sense of loyalty was so strong. It was one of the things I liked best about him.

It was also the thing that had stopped this from happening way earlier than now. But he was being honest. Telling me not what I wanted to hear but the truth.

I didn't care. I wanted Nash for as long as he'd let me have him.

## 26

## SCYTHE

*J* paced Psychos' parking lot, doing my job of only letting people into the party room if they had an invite, but my attention shot otherwise. I'd needed some air after watching Bliss come on the dance floor in Nash's arms. The jealousy in me had demanded I storm over there and throw her over my shoulder to lock her away until she forgave me.

Instead, I'd swapped posts with one of the other security guys and gotten the hell out of that room. I leaned back against the wall and lit a cigarette, inhaling the smoke and letting it take the edge off my feelings.

She was slipping from my grasp.

I shouldn't have cared this much. Not that she was with Nash and not that she and War were mad at me. Caring was a Vincent thing and had no place when I was in control.

I knew what that meant.

My mother was right. I was losing my grip. Vincent was quiet, and it had led me to believe that I would be able to hold on for as long as I had the last time I'd been dominant.

But I realized now that it was a false sense of security. He'd been there all along, just waiting for his moment to take back what had always been his.

I was always the outsider.

For a tiny moment, with Bliss and Nash and War and Rebel and the bar, I'd thought differently.

I didn't want to leave.

But I didn't know how to stop it.

I'd tried to talk to Bliss earlier, but she hadn't wanted to hear it.

Maybe War would.

I pulled out my phone and called him.

"Yeah?"

I drew in another inhale of my cigarette and let the smoke curl around my lungs. My dick stirred just at the sound of his voice. "How far away are you?"

"Not gonna make it. Something has come up."

I blew the smoke out in a steady stream and waved a middle-aged couple into the club without properly checking their invite, just because I didn't want an audience for this conversation. "What? I really need to see you."

"Club stuff."

My head thunked back against the wall. "Oh."

Disappointment flooded me. I wanted him here. But he had other people in his life. Other priorities.

Not like me with nobody but a mother who was more enemy than relative most of the time.

The was silence on War's end, then, "Are you okay?"

"Fine."

"You don't sound fine."

I was being a fucking pansy and I needed to quit it. If I was going out, and the fact I was all up in my feelings was a very strong sign that I was, there wasn't anything I could do about it. I just had to make the most of whatever time I had left. "I was just in the mood to have your mouth on my dick again."

War chuckled. "Bliss still too mad at you to do it, huh?"

"Something like that."

"I'll try to come late. But, Vincent?"

"Mmm?"

"If I'm coming all the way in there to suck your dick in the middle of the night, I'm not stopping there."

I groaned, blood rushing to my dick instantly. "Don't make promises you can't keep."

"That a yes?"

It was a yes. I wanted as much of him, and of her, that I could get because I had no idea how long it would be before I got to have them again.

Last time it had been years. Almost a decade.

Vincent was better at the game than I was. He always had been.

I was just along for the ride.

*H*awk walked into my cabin without knocking. Gus, Fang, and Gunner were all right behind him.

I ended the call with Vincent and put my phone down, looking to Hawk expectantly. "Well? You better have something." I would have preferred to be at Psychos with Bliss and Vincent, but the guys were right. I'd let myself be distracted by them for too long, and I'd shirked my responsibilities to my club.

As much as I didn't want it, I was the prez. There was no way around it.

I needed to step up and own it.

The first job of any new prez, taking the throne of one killed in battle, was to avenge his death. It had to be tonight, before my guys lost complete faith in me and I couldn't get it back. I knew how precarious my situation was, and that was only going to invite trouble.

Hawk slammed down a piece of paper onto my kitchen table and pointed at it with a finger. "Remember that Slayer who came here, spilling his guts about Scythe in the first place?"

"Winger? Slinger? Something like that."

He nodded. "He got us the number they used to put a hit on your old man."

"You sure it's legit?"

"No, but Winger knows he's not getting a cent out of us unless this pans out, and he seemed real eager for some drug money."

I frowned. "This could be his own number for all we know."

Gus folded his thick arms across his chest. "We don't have anything else to go on, do we? You're gonna know in a heartbeat if it's not for real. Winger said Scythe will only meet in person, and you text first to set up a time and place." Gus shrugged. "I dunno. Winger doesn't seem smart enough to set up anything of significance with that single brain cell rattling around his skull."

"Agreed." I pushed the piece of paper with messily scrawled digits in black pen back to Hawk. "Set it up."

He nodded, taking out his phone and copying the number in. His fingers moved rapidly over his screen, and then he sat it back down at the table. "Done."

We all went quiet, watching his phone.

It lit up almost right away with an incoming message, and Hawk snatched it up. "Meeting's in an hour."

"Where?"

"Saint View address. In the slums. Not too far from Psychos."

I pushed to my feet and eyed Hawk and the other men. "Load 'em up. I'll take my bike and meet with Scythe. You guys take the van. Find somewhere to park it so I have backup if I need it, but in my head, this is gonna be a one and done. He'll be dead before he even knows who I am. Everybody got it?"

The guys nodded and moved toward the door, Gunner cracking his knuckles with a big grin on his face. "'Bout time we got some action around here. I get twitchy when it's too quiet."

But Hawk shook his head at me. "No. You aren't doing it."

I narrowed my eyes at him. "Excuse me? Like fuck I'm not."

He narrowed his eyes right back. "Take your head out of your ass, *Prez*. This ain't about me challenging you. I'm looking out for your dumb ass. If this is a Slayers' setup, and you ride your bike on in there like you ain't got a care in the world, what do you think is gonna happen?"

I stared at him, knowing the answer.

"Yeah, exactly. You're dead before we can even get to you. I'll go. You watch from the van."

"So if it's a setup, I get to watch you die?"

"Better than losing another prez. We wouldn't ever come back from that."

"Fuck." He was right. Reputation was everything in this world. It was the thing you battled for until the very end. If we lost two presidents to local gangbangers who had gotten too big for their britches, then we'd never live it down. Other groups would stop working with us. The cash would dry up, and we'd all be fucking working behind the counter at McDonald's. "This is such a bad fucking idea. We're rushing."

Hawk shrugged. "Or, by the end of the night, we know who Scythe is and you get to put a bullet through his brain." He grinned at me. "Come on, War. Where's your sense of adventure?"

"That does sound appealing."

"We could be done in time to make a late appearance at Nash's birthday party."

An image of Vincent's and Bliss' naked bodies wrapped around mine popped into my head, and I threw caution to the wind.

Caution had no place in this life. If I was gonna be prez, I needed to prove I knew my place in it.

## 28

## BLISS

Nash's fingers slipped between mine as he led me down a hall, stopping at one of the private rooms and producing a gold key on a chain that would unlock it. This door wasn't one with a peephole, but I knew exactly what was on the other side and why Nash had chosen it.

My breath hitched as he dangled it in front of me. I took it eagerly, slipping it into the lock and twisting it.

It was one of the bigger rooms, with a large bed in the center, covered with silky black sheets and piles of throw cushions. There was a fresh, clean scent in the air, as well as a light perfume from candles that lined a shelf on the wall. Nash walked over to them, picking up a box of matches and lighting each one so they cast a soft glow around the room.

I shut the door behind me, blocking out the hallway lights, and the music from the main room. "The romance room, huh?"

He shrugged, setting the matches back down on the

edge of the shelf. "You know it's not necessarily as romantic as it might first appear."

I knew.

I bit my lip, hiding a smile. "You want to check it out?"

He laughed. "Hell yes." He pulled aside a curtain, revealing a floor-to-ceiling window.

There was another couple on the other side, in a room mostly identical to ours. They kissed deeply, her arms wrapped around his waist while he stroked his fingers up and down her back.

"So, do we just stand here and watch or..."

"We can do whatever we want to do. If they don't want us watching they can draw their curtain. Same goes for us."

I backed away, sitting on the bed and toeing my heels off. "Leave it for now."

He nodded, crawling across the bed after me when I scooted up it to plump the cushions behind us. We both settled in and watched the other couple. They were young, their bodies toned and taut. The woman's skin was a pale white, while the man's was a deep black, muscles rippling across his back. They were beautiful to watch and clearly very into each other as they slowly stripped each other of their clothes, each piece falling to the floor one by one.

"Want to play a game?" Nash asked.

"Like Uno? Or Monopoly?"

He laughed. "Whatever they do, we do."

I sucked in a breath. "What if they start having really horrible sex?"

Nash glanced over at the pair. The man's lips were on her throat, her back arched gracefully and her long hair dangling. "Do you really think those two are having bad sex?"

I giggled. "No. I don't. Okay, I'm in."

Nash pressed his lips to my neck, and I lay back on the cushions, tilting my head to give him better access. His tongue flickered against my skin as he trailed his way down my body, over my collarbone, and across the swell of my breasts. "She's very naked," he said into my cleavage.

The woman's small, high breasts were bare, and the man ran his palm along her naked hip and thigh. His clothes all lay on the floor as well. "So is he."

I undid Nash's top button and then quickly followed with the rest, my fingers working nimbly to shed him of his shirt. I shoved it off his arms, leaving his bare, tattooed skin for me to explore.

The muscles of his biceps popped while he pulled the straps of my one-piece down my arms, the material easily falling away from my breasts. He let it sit around my belly while he cupped both tits, pushing them up and together. His thumb flicked over one nipple while his mouth stole the other, sucking it into his warm mouth.

"Oh," I said softly, running my fingers over his shoulders.

"I haven't stopped thinking about what it would be like to suck your nipples since the last party, where you wore that top that just showed a hint of them."

"Does it live up to expectation?"

He grinned, switching to suck the other side into a stiff peak. "And more. Your tits are perfect. I can't wait to have them in my face while you ride me."

I'd never liked them. They were too big and not perky

enough. But the fact he was enjoying them made me suddenly appreciative. And I was certainly enjoying the way he licked every inch, running his tongue between them, and then lower, tugging my bodysuit as he went. His tongue circled my belly button, and he shifted, nudging my legs apart with his so he could kneel between them. He kissed the soft rolls on my belly, and I lifted my hips so he could remove the garment fully.

"Fuck," he swore, his gaze sweeping over my naked body in the soft light and coming to rest on the junction of my thighs, where the bright-pink clit stimulator still sat. "I love how that looks on you."

"I love how it felt."

"Watching you come out there with everyone around just made me want to get you in here alone so I could do so much more." His fingers trailed along my inner thigh. "What are they doing now?" He didn't take his eyes off me.

I peered around him. The man's head was buried between the woman's thighs. "He's going down on her."

"Man after my own heart." He put his fingers to the sex toy, gently pulling it from my body, and replaced it with his mouth.

I dropped back to the pillows once more as his tongue slid through my arousal and up over my clit. He did it again, and again, licking slowly, like he had all the time in the world.

My orgasm was impatient and needy though, taking up low in my belly and spiraling down and out, desperately waiting for him to let it free.

"You aren't coming yet. I haven't had enough."

He left my clit and moved lower, licking my pussy and

thrusting his tongue into my opening. I arched my back, loving the feel of him there. He tongue-fucked me so I was writhing and then licked me all over until I was sure he couldn't edge me any further.

He stared up at me, his eyes so piercing in his lust, that for a second, I forgot everything else.

He broke away first, peeking over his shoulder at the other couple.

"What are they doing?" I asked, trying to see around him.

But he put one big hand on my chest and pushed me down. "Nothing we need to do."

He went back to eating me like a starving man, and it was amazing, but his words niggled at me.

I frowned, lifting back up on my elbows to look over him.

The other woman was on her knees, ass in the air with her chest pressed down to the mattress, her face turned to us, but her eyes closed in pleasure. The man kneeled behind her, a silver plug in hand that he gradually worked into her ass while he rubbed her clit.

I flopped back down onto the bed.

"We don't have to do that, Bliss," Nash said between long licks. "Don't even worry about it."

I still remembered War's finger in my ass during our threesome and how much better it had made my orgasm. The dirty thrill of it sent a tingle through my spine, and I stole another peek at the other couple.

The woman's face was pure bliss, and I was pretty sure I could hear her moans even through the walls.

I put my hand on Nash's head. "I didn't quit the game."

He slowly lifted, eyeing me. "There are toys in the drawer over there. I saw Rebel stocking each room."

Swallowing down nerves, I nodded.

"You've never done anal before, have you?"

"Not much," I admitted. "But I want to."

"Don't do it for me."

"I want to do it for me."

He grinned. "Good girl. We'll go slow."

I nodded, some of my nerves slipping into eagerness. He padded across the room to the drawer, his torso so tightly cut it could have been stone. His erection tented his pants, and I really wanted him to take them off. I got up and moved in behind him, wrapping my arms around his waist to undo his belt while he searched the drawer.

His pants dropped to the floor right as he pulled out a plug, the base covered with a red gemstone. Though the base was wide, the plug itself wasn't terribly big. Definitely a lot smaller than the one currently inside the woman across the window.

"What do you think?"

"It's pretty for something that's going to go up my ass."

We both laughed at my awkwardness, and he kissed me again. "Lean over the bed."

Oh God. Nerves erupted everywhere, but I lay across the bed on my stomach.

I jumped a little as he spread my legs and ran his hands all over the globes of my ass, kneading and massaging. I swiveled my head to watch the other couple. They'd already moved on to him fucking her, the diamond-based plug glinting in the low lights.

I suddenly wished it was War and Scythe in the other room. Them watching us. Us watching them.

All of us coming together.

"Reach beneath you and rub your clit, Bliss."

I did, touching a finger to the already sensitive nub that sent a fresh wave of arousal through me. A moment later, his fingers worked their way inside my pussy.

"Nash," I moaned, rocking my hips back to meet his fingers.

"I want you dripping when I do this, Bliss. I want you begging for it."

I was already there, desperate for the extra pleasure point to bring back the orgasm that we'd let go earlier. "Please."

He moved his fingers, plunging the plug into my pussy and then dragged it back to my ass. "It's gleaming, Blissy girl. You're so wet."

My fingers were covered in my arousal too. But I didn't care. I just wanted to come. "More, Nash. Please."

"Fuck, I love hearing my name on your lips when you look like this." The plug ran over my ass again, slick with lube and my arousal. "Every time I watched you with War and Vincent, I had to hold myself back and remind myself you weren't mine to take."

"I am tonight," I moaned. "Nash, please."

He pressed the plug to my ass again, this time with a little pressure behind it. At the same time, he gave me back his fingers to grind on.

The women I went to school with and socialized with in Providence would be horrified if they could see us. Me dripping with desire and begging him to take my ass. His fingers thrusting into my pussy so deep and hard and fast that my breaths were noisy and wanton. He worked me with the plug, taking it slow and giving me time to adjust. It was foreign, but the added sensation was instant.

We both groaned when it slid all the way in.

"You should see yourself from this angle, Bliss. You're so beautiful."

"Have sex with me," I begged. "Nash, please. I need to come."

His fingers withdrew, and then a moment later, they were replaced by the thick blunt head of him.

"Oh, yes," I moaned, grinding back, taking what I needed.

We both stilled when he was inside me, and I yelled at the feeling of fullness. This had been so long in the making. There'd been so many days and nights of unfulfilled sexual tension. He was my brother's best friend, but there was no going back from here.

"Fuck me, you're so tight." He groaned as he withdrew and then pushed back in. "Dammit, Bliss. You need to come because I need to do this hard and fast. I can't be gentle."

"Don't be."

He grabbed my hip with a feral noise that came from somewhere deep inside him. He picked up the pace, fucking me hard, his hips slamming against my ass and thighs, the plug only making everything better.

My orgasm bore down on me, a culmination of all the edging he'd done so far. It hit me hard, an explosion of feeling that rocked my entire body. I turned my face into the mattress and screamed his name because it was all too much and yet perfect at the same time. My nipples slid along the silky sheets that we were messing up, each thrust from Nash rocking the bed until he bent over me, sinking his lips onto my shoulder.

My skin muffled the noises he made as he came, but they were music to my ears. He collapsed down on top of me, his weight warm and delicious, the two of us still joined so intimately.

I glanced over at the other couple who both watched us with soft smiles while they stroked each other.

"Uh, Nash?"

"Mmm?" He rolled off me, sounding totally blissed out.

"We still have an audience."

He lifted his head and looked over at the other side. "You want me to close the curtain?"

I probably should have been mortified, except I wasn't. If anything, the warm glow from my orgasm lingered, and I felt sexy with their eyes on me. "Leave it." I motioned him back to the bed. "Let them watch. It's your birthday after all."

# 29

## BLISS

Nash and I showered in the little private bathroom off the room he'd hired for the night. His hands smeared soap all over my body, paying particular attention to my nipples, until I was guiding his stiff dick inside me once more. He fucked me slow beneath the spray, every thrust eliciting a tiny gasp as he bottomed out inside me, his base grinding against my clit.

"I can't get enough of you," he whispered, water falling around us. "I want to do this again."

I ran my hands over his water-soaked skin, tracing the ridges of his muscles and swirling my fingers over his tattoos. "I don't know if I can have any more orgasms tonight. I think I'm broken."

He dropped to his knees, pressed his fingers between my thighs, and licked the tender flesh of my pussy. "I think you can come again."

"Nash," I moaned, half pushing his head away and half drawing it back. "I can't. I will fall over and die. I swear it."

Yet, I found myself opening up for him once more and accepting the pleasure he seemed so intent on giving me. Because I couldn't get enough of him either.

"I don't want you to go back to ignoring us." I leaned back on the shower wall and hooked one leg over his shoulder so he could plunge his tongue inside me.

He didn't answer, but then my orgasm was barreling down on me again, and all talk of the future disappeared from my brain in a poof of hormones and moaning.

Afterward, we dried off, pulling on our clothes again. I took a silky black robe with Psychos' logo embroidered on it, wrapping it over my underwear.

Nash took my hand and led me out to the main room, where the party was in full swing. I stuck close to him, letting him lead me through the crowd and eyeing other couples, threesomes, and more that we passed.

The scent of sex hung heavy in the air, and bodies writhed together, naked and glistening with sweat or oil or cum. Remnants of white powder lines marked the surfaces, and a young couple made a show of placing tablets on each other's tongues and swallowing them down as they kissed.

We finally reached the bar, where Rebel served drinks in her birthday suit.

She didn't have an ounce of shame when she noticed us, just wandered over and placed a cupcake with a candle in it in front of Nash. "Happy birthday to you. Happy birthday to you. Happy birthday, dear Boss Mannnnn..." She sang like a chipmunk on fast-forward. "Quick, blow out your candle before I have to make another round of drinks."

Nash leaned forward with a tolerant smile, puckered his lips, and blew out the little flame.

Rebel clapped him. "So. How was your birthday present?"

The corner of Nash's mouth flickered up. "Good."

I nudged him with fake outrage. "What we did in there was just good?"

He chuckled. "I was trying not to brag."

Rebel held her hands up. "Don't be modest on my account. I hope you blew my girl's mind. I mean, I'm rooting for you, but you got some pretty stiff competition in War and Vincent."

"You'd have to ask her."

Rebel raised an eyebrow in my direction.

"You have no idea. And yes, I'll fill you in later when he's not here to get an ego about it."

The self-satisfied grin on Nash's handsome face said it might have been too late for that. He'd blown my mind. Multiple times. We both knew it.

I leaned over to Rebel. "Hey, my mom hasn't come out, has she?"

Rebel shook her head. "Nope. Not that I noticed anyway. She's been very well-behaved in your office as far as I know."

I kissed Nash's cheek. "Eat your cake. I'm just going to go check on her real quick, okay?"

He fell back into conversation with Rebel, and I scurried around a very dirty threesome in order to unlock my office door. I slipped inside, closing it behind me.

Mom blinked at me from beneath a blanket on my couch, my laptop turned around and playing *The Notebook*. She sat up quickly when she realized it was me.

"Bliss. You're back." She patted the space next to her that her feet had occupied a moment earlier. "Do you want to sit? Tell me about your night."

I sat, but embarrassment flushed my cheeks. "It was very good."

"Is it too weird to tell me all about it?"

I laughed. "Yes. Very much so."

"But you and Nash? You're together?"

I lifted one shoulder. "We're...something."

She nodded. "I was wrong about him. I watched him all day, and he's so polite and respectful. Even to me, and I know I don't deserve it. He's changed. He's not the young man he once was. Jail changed him for the better, I think. I've never heard of him going back to it. Much to some of the girls' upset. They really liked him. Janice still talks about how he was the best pimp she ever had."

I blinked. "What?"

Her mouth pulled into a line, and the relaxed expression morphed into stress. "You didn't know?" She wrung her hands. "Bliss, I'm sorry. I didn't realize. I thought you knew. Everyone else around here does if they've been around for a decade or more. But I suppose that sort of thing doesn't touch all of you in Providence." She dug her teeth into her bottom lip. "And I'm real glad for that. I never wanted you to have this life. Please don't tell him I said anything."

There was so much deep-rooted panic and fear in her voice that wrapped its way around my gut and squeezed. It was the terrified babbling of a woman who'd spent her entire life being degraded every time she made a mistake.

I took her hand, trying to halt the tremors in it. "It's

okay. I won't tell him it was you. I just wish someone had told me earlier."

I understood now why nobody had wanted to tell me what he'd done to end up in jail. My stomach churned with the knowledge.

"There's something else you should know, Bliss."

I dropped my face into my hands. "Ugh. Is it better or worse than Nash selling women?"

"Maybe worse."

I jerked my head up to look at her. "Seriously?"

She cringed. "I think Jerry killed Axel."

I closed my eyes and tried to breathe calmly, though the storm of emotion that swirled inside me was nearly all encompassing. "Why?"

"We had a massive fight the night Axel died."

"What's new? You fight all the time. He's never tried to kill Axel any other time you've had an argument."

She picked at the edge of the blanket, pulling on a loose thread until it snapped. "I told him I was leaving. Him. Prostitution. All of it." She swallowed thickly. "I can't do it anymore, Bliss. I hate it. I hate him. I hate everything about this town and my life. The only good things in it were you and your brother, and I know I've so royally messed up with both of you, that you probably won't believe that. But Jerry knew."

My heart squeezed at the truth in her words. She'd never been able to show it, but in that moment, I saw its truth. She'd always cared. She just hadn't known how to be a mother. Or even a functioning adult. This life was all she'd known. It had broken her so many times, and each time, Jerry was the driving force.

"What happened?" I whispered. "Just tell me."

"We argued. He said I wasn't done until he said I was done, and that we both knew I couldn't make it without him. He'd heard it all before. I always told him I was leaving, and he never paid me any attention, because he knew I couldn't." She grabbed my hand, her eyes suddenly going fierce. "But I had a plan this time, Bliss. I swear it. I met a social worker on the streets one night. She paid for an hour of my time." She tucked her hair behind her ear and glanced down. "Some women did, you know? I used to like it better even, because they weren't normally so rough like the men are."

It was so hard to listen to. Her talk about being abused like it was no big deal because it was such an everyday part of her life.

"Anyway. She paid, but then she just bought me a cup of coffee at the diner, and we talked. She works at a women's shelter, and she said I would be safe there."

"Did you go?"

She shook her head slowly, her shoulders slumping again. "No. I never made it. I was stupid and told Jerry that I had someone watching out for me." She looked up, her cheeks stained with tears. "I never told him who. I didn't want him going after that lovely woman. But what if he thought I meant Axel? Jerry hit me. Over and over until I passed out. When I came to on the floor of the trailer, I saw him with his gun. He didn't know I was awake. He was cleaning it, and then he stashed it in the oven. The next morning, I had Nash's mom on my doorstep, asking for the gossip and wanting to know if it was true that Axel had been shot execution style."

Bile rose in my throat. "Did you tell the police any of this?"

She shook her head slowly. "I can't, Bliss. But I have the gun."

My eyes went wide. "Here?"

She nodded, leaning over to grab her purse. From inside, she took out a shiny gray handgun.

I stared at it in horror. "We have to take that to the police."

"There are warrants out for my arrest, and what if I'm wrong? What if he just went out somewhere and took the gun for protection? I'd never seen it before that night, but maybe he carries it with him. I don't know. But if the cops question him, he'll know it was me. Every time I've tried to report him, it's come back to bite me. He just pays the cops off and then takes his anger out on me." Her tears turned into sobs. "I can't do it, Bliss. I can't. I'm too old for him to keep hurting me like he does."

My heart ripped in two, and suddenly I saw all the years of my childhood in a different light. One where she wasn't the weak-willed woman who didn't care about her children. But one who loved them as best she could in the worst of circumstances.

"Shh. It's okay. We'll deal with it in the morning." Using the blanket to protect the gun from my prints, I took it from her trembling fingers, terrified she would accidentally shoot herself or me. I placed it in the safe, alongside the drugs and the leftover money from the last party and locked it again.

And then I pulled her into my chest, and like our roles were reversed, me the mother and she the child, she lay her head on my shoulder and cried.

My eyes were dry.

Every man in my life letting me down had left no space for tears. I was just done.

"This place is half yours, Mom," I murmured. "You're safe here. And I'll split the profits with you. It's what I should have done from the start."

To my surprise, she sat up quickly, wiping her fingers beneath her eyes. "No. I'm sorry I ever even said anything about it. I never wanted this place, but Jerry said I had to pay him out if I wanted to quit. Psychos is yours."

"We're both Axel's next of kin. Your name was on the paperwork too."

She shook her head. "We both know I can't run this place. I'm not smart like you and him. But I can work hard, Bliss. I swear it. I'll do my best. A job off the streets, and somewhere to live. That's all I need."

It was probably the saddest thing I'd ever heard, and it broke my heart all over again. They were such basic needs that had gone unmet. She wasn't asking for money or clothes or drugs. I prayed she was for real and that this wasn't a flash in the pan.

Because she deserved more.

She deserved to feel safe.

So did every other woman ever targeted by Jerry.

And by Nash.

## 30

# WAR

*S*hadows fell across the empty parking lot in the worst part of Saint View. It was Slayers' stomping grounds, and that didn't sit well with me. The entire thing reeked of a setup. Even if Winger was too stupid to come up with a scheme by himself, the Slayers' leader, Chaos, was not. We'd had enough run-ins in the past for me to know how smart the man was, even if we were on opposite sides of a decades-old divide that had started before we were even born.

Hawk rode his bike in idle circles, waiting for Scythe to show up.

I drummed my fingers on the steering wheel, edgy as fuck while watching from our concealed position. "If I'm sitting in this tin can only to watch my best friend take a bullet, I swear to you, Gus, you'd better be ready for a fight."

Gus sat in the driver's seat of the van we used for hauling guns. Or groceries, depending on the day. "You know I have your back. And Gunner and Aloha are around somewhere, though fucked if I can see them."

I peered into the dark night, but the other guys had done an A-plus job of concealing themselves. I only hoped Gus and I had done the same.

We waited in silence, watching the clock tick down to the meeting time and nothing happen.

I leaned back in my seat, letting out a breath laced with stress. "Sorry for being such an asshole lately."

Gus looked over at me, then turned back to staring out the windscreen. "Don't fucking apologize, War. Didn't your old man ever tell you that? Makes you seem weak."

I pressed my molars together. My father had told me that. Many times.

"I appreciate it though," Gus said without turning in my direction. "You're a mouthy bastard, but you'll make a good son-in-law one day."

I was glad we weren't facing each other. Because I was pretty sure my face would give away exactly what I thought about that.

It wasn't going to happen. It hadn't bothered me for the longest of times. I'd grown up knowing that Siren would be my old lady one day, and she was a good fuck and not bad to look at. For years, that was all I thought I'd wanted from the person I would marry.

Bliss had made me want more.

Vincent too.

Nothing between me and them was as simple as just pure attraction. There was something there with them that had never been there with Siren or any other woman.

But I knew Siren had her heart set on being my wife.

She'd patiently waited for years for me to propose. She'd watched while I'd fucked her, then shifted focus to other women the moment someone new turned my eye, always with the reassurance that I was hers for the long run. She would have my kids. She would be my queen.

I had to be the one to tell her I couldn't. That I'd made a connection with somebody else, and that any deal I might have gone along with was now completely off the table.

I could at least give her that much respect, even though I hadn't shown her much in the past.

So I said nothing and watched Hawk ride his bike beneath a pool of yellow light, cast by a solitary streetlamp.

Gus suddenly sat up straighter. "You hear that?"

I did, and a moment later, I saw the car the rumbling engine belonged to. A sleek, black limousine, completely out of place amongst the overgrown weeds, broken glass, and cracked sidewalks.

Hawk stopped his bike, putting his feet down on the concrete while the limo pulled to a stop.

The back door opened.

Gus frowned. "What the fuck? Scythe is a woman?"

I couldn't speak.

In the middle of the parking lot, exchanging details with Hawk, was the same woman I'd seen only that morning in Vincent's kitchen. The same one who shared his dark-brown hair and eyes and tanned complexion.

I'd been such a fool.

The mark on his hand. It wasn't an L. It had been an upside-down scythe. And then there were the times Bliss had started to call him something else, only to correct herself.

It had always started with a scy sound before she'd cut herself off.

They'd been playing me.

Him most of all.

The sense of betrayal hit me like a sledgehammer. "No," I bit out. "Scythe's not a woman."

Gus glanced at me. "How do you know?"

"You know that guy I was kissing in that photo?"

"Yeah?"

"That's his mother."

"That doesn't mean..."

I laughed bitterly. "That doesn't mean her son was playing me all along? Pretending to be interested so he could get close to me? Fuck, Gus! Is there a goddamn hit out on me too? Was he just biding his time, playing with his prey?"

Gus' face hardened. "Fucking asshole."

Anger roared through me, the betrayal and hurt stirring up a storm so powerful I couldn't contain it.

I didn't want to.

Gus' fingers clenched around the wheel. "You know what you have to do, right, son?"

My fingers tightened around the gun on my lap.

I nodded. "Kill him."

## 31

# SCYTHE

The sun peeked over the horizon, and yet Nash's party was only just beginning to wind down. The music still played from inside, but couples had started leaving in the last hour or two while I continued to stand guard at the door, half hiding because I couldn't stand Bliss' glare or Nash's hands on her body. The other half of me was waiting for War to get here.

Every engine noise from the street had me looking in that direction, and when he finally showed, it was minutes from closing time.

And not a moment too soon. I'd had enough of this fucking night. I needed to go home and lose myself in someone else.

I abandoned the door, shoving a rock against it to hold it open so people could stream out when the music cut out and the lights came on. "Hey," I called while he pulled his helmet off. "'Bout fucking time."

I stopped a foot away from him when I registered his expression. "Who shat in your cereal?"

"I don't know, Scythe. How about you tell me?"

It took me a moment to realize he hadn't called me Vincent.

Ice froze over my veins, a chill snapping my spine straight.

War laughed cruelly, unzipping his leather jacket and moving in my direction, his long legs eating up the ground between us. "You aren't even going to fucking deny it, are you?"

"No," I said quietly.

I'd always known it would come out. I didn't know how or why tonight was that night, but it had been in the cards the entire time. I'd played with fire, and I was about to get burned. You couldn't be mad about things that were inevitable. Not when you were aware of it all along. And when all of it was your fault.

War shook his head, reaching around to his back and pulling out a gleaming silver gun.

Without an ounce of fear or remorse, he pressed it up beneath my chin. His fingers bit into my biceps, holding me firmly in place, not giving me an inch to move.

The darkness inside me hissed, commanding me to pull the blade tucked inside my sleeve.

I closed my eyes and fought against the blackness, refusing to let him take control.

"Why?" War demanded, moving in so close there was no space between us.

"You know why. It was a job. It wasn't personal."

"It was fucking personal to me!" he roared, his fingers on the pistol readjusting.

I waited for it.

The blow that would end it all.

But I wasn't going out without saying my truth. "I followed your parents that night. They'd been out for dinner at a little Italian place on the border of Providence."

War's fingernails dug in so hard I was sure they were drawing blood. "Alberto's. My mother's favorite place."

"They do good lasagna," I murmured.

War stared at me, no trace of the good humor he normally showed at my jokes.

I sighed. "The minute I saw your mom with him, I decided I wasn't doing it. The hit was on him, not her. I wasn't going to take a man's life when he sat opposite his wife, sharing a bowl of spaghetti like they were Lady and the Tramp."

War shook his head. "And yet you did. You took my parents without a care in the world. Both of them, because she's probably never gonna wake up either. But you know the worst thing? You made me want you, and now you're taking that away too." His voice cracked, and he dragged me in close so our chests touched. "Fuck you, Scythe. Fuck you for making me want you."

I closed my eyes and breathed in the scent of him. I put one hand to the back of his neck, my lips hovering over his. "I put a bullet in your dad's head, but he was already at the bottom of the cliffs when I did it."

War jerked back, but I tightened my grip on his neck, refusing to let him go until I'd said what I came to say. "Listen to me! Your dad drove that car right over the cliff, War. I was behind him the entire way from the Italian place. He didn't brake."

War shook his head. "No. No. Why would he do that?"

I didn't know. And it didn't matter. Neither of us had

the answers to that. "I took the hiking trail that scales the cliffs to get down to them. Your mom was passed out but breathing. Your dad, though..."

"No," War gasped. "You're lying."

"He was in a bad way. There was a piece of metal through his chest..."

War shook his head, squeezing his eyes shut. But I had to keep going. I'd lied and covered up the truth for too long. If we had any chance of salvaging this thing between us, then he had to know exactly what had happened.

"He begged me, War. He begged me to end the pain. So I did."

An agonized scream ripped from War's chest, and he shoved me so hard I landed on the ground. I didn't try to get up.

The darkness roared within me, shouting demands laced with threats if I didn't comply. Vincent's voice swirled inside my head as well, but I couldn't make any of it out through the pounding inside my skull and War's shouts from the outside.

"Get up!" he screamed. "Fight back!"

"No," I forced the words out, though the darkness stole up my throat and swirled inside my mouth, tainting each word with evil.

War landed on top of me, his fists slamming into my face, though I barely felt the pain. The internal battle was infinitely more brutal, the darkness ripping at my insides, fighting its way to be free.

I couldn't stop it.

"I'm sorry," I whispered.

I gave in and pulled the blade from my sleeve, letting the darkness creep over me.

The scream of sirens had us both freezing.

It was only then I realized people ran screaming from Psychos, desperately trying to shelter in their vehicles after taking one look at War and me with weapons drawn.

Police cars swarmed Psychos' parking lot, megaphones blaring for everybody to get on the ground.

"Bliss," War and I said at the same time.

Our gazes locked.

Bliss had enough drugs in there to go away for years.

Both of us scrambled to our feet, people scattering away from us as we ran for the door.

The roar of bikes at our backs provided the distraction we needed. We put our heads down and sprinted, the first gunshot ringing out and a bullet whizzing over our heads. Pandemonium broke out, War's club and the police taking shots at each other.

I didn't care. Getting to Bliss was all that mattered.

Another shot flew by us, and a woman screamed as it hit her shoulder in a spray of blood and tissue.

Dread filled me, knowing the next one could be through Bliss if we didn't get her out of here. Psychos was a maze of rooms and doors. There were other ways out.

We just had to get to her.

"War!" someone shouted behind us.

War paused for the slightest second, giving me the chance to get ahead.

A figure moved out of the crowd around the door so seamlessly I didn't even notice him until he threw himself at my legs, taking them out from under me.

I went down hard, my head cracking off the cement. I couldn't even get my hands up to break my fall. Pain blinded me, my vision warping into darkness for a moment before I could regain my senses.

I blinked, rolling onto my back, my head pounding in agony.

A man towered over me, while others pinned down my legs and arms.

Tabor. The warden I'd escaped from at Saint View Prison

"Remember me, Vincent? Or should I call you Scythe?" His meaty fist flew into my face, punishing the same spot War had attacked earlier. My vision flickered again, and the darkness tried to claim me once more.

Except this time, it wasn't the evil that always lurked within me.

It was unconsciousness.

Something was wrong. I struggled to hold on to my blade, even though I knew it was the only option I had if I was getting out of this.

Through the haze of darkness and flashing lights, gunshots rained. The police and War's MC went to battle, no regard for the civilians trying to flee the scene.

Two men in MC cuts grabbed War and dragged him back, away from the club. He screamed for them to let him go, but they ignored him, hauling him away.

His gaze met mine, and the knowledge that we'd both failed to get Bliss to safety pushed down on my chest like an elephant until I couldn't breathe.

War turned around frantically as another round of cop cars flooded the parking lot, cutting off all the exits.

"Go!" I screamed at him.

It was too late for me. It was too late for Bliss and Nash. If they were trapped in the building now, surrounded by cops, there was no saving them.

All War could do was save himself.

He had friends. A family in his club, and they'd had his back. They'd protected him.

Bliss had Nash. Rebel. Even her mom.

It only made it all the more obvious that I had no one and nothing.

Tabor leaned down, smiling like the cat who ate the canary. "Got you now, Vincent. You aren't ever going to pull a stunt like that again."

"I got out once," I choked out around the blood pooling in my mouth. I tried to smile, because there was no way I was going to let him see the internal battle playing out inside me. I refused to give him the satisfaction. "I'll do it again."

Tabor chuckled and nodded to his friends, who I vaguely recognized as guards from the prison. I searched for Rowe, the one guard Vincent had liked, but none of them were him. They hauled me to my feet and dragged me back into the shadows, away from the cops and the swirling lights.

"You're right. You probably would." He patted my cheek with a glint of pure malice in his eyes. "But I won't be made a fool of twice. You aren't going back to prison, my friend."

His eyes turned as dark as I knew mine were.

There was an evil in Tabor too. One he kept hidden better than I did, but it was there all the same.

When he smiled, I saw the full extent of his evil.

His smile was manic, the man high on adrenaline and

power. "We have something much worse planned for you, Vincent. Much. Much. Worse."

THE END...for now.

Bliss, Nash, War, Vincent, and Scythe's story concludes in *It Ends With Violence*. http://mybook.to/ ItEndsWithViolence

Have you read the other Saint View trilogies? You'll see lots of cross over characters and storylines. Start with *Devious Little Liars.* There's a sneak peek at the first chapter on the following pages.

# DEVIOUS LITTLE LIARS (SAINT VIEW HIGH #1) SNEAK PEEK

# LACEY

*I* was about to be arrested.

That was my first thought when a flash of movement outside the window caught my attention.

Extreme overreaction?

Perhaps.

But when you'd illegally let yourself into your school on a Sunday, these were the worries that plagued a girl.

Acting on instinct, I hurled myself off the piano stool and onto the floor, scuttling to the windows overlooking the quad. Maybe they hadn't seen me yet. The late afternoon sun was sinking, and perhaps, if I was lucky, the glare would temporarily blind them. I could make my escape out one of the back doors. There was an exit in the administration hall. Others in the math and history wings. Of course, not one anywhere near the music rooms. Helpful.

Ever so carefully, I lifted to peer out the window, and yelped at the face on the other side. I ducked down again, though there was no chance he hadn't seen me, what with his nose an inch from the glass.

I was totally busted. But at least it wasn't the police.

Lawson's laughter on the other side of the window made me realize how ridiculous I was being. I stood, embarrassment heating my face.

"You want to let me in?" he yelled.

I squeezed my eyes closed but nodded. "I'll meet you at the door."

Scrambling down the hall, I tried to come up with a plausible story that would result in the least amount of trouble. I still had nothing by the time I pulled open the heavy, ancient oak doors of Providence School for Girls.

My uncle stood on the other side, boxes of his work balanced precariously in his arms. He shifted beneath their weight, sending a USB stick and a pile of papers sliding off the top. They fluttered down around our ankles.

I knelt hastily, tucking the USB stick into my pocket and gathering up the runaway pages. I glanced up at his familiar face. "Before you say anything, just remember, I'm your favorite niece."

"You're my only niece," he grumbled, but there was still a hint of laughter in his voice.

I put the papers back on top, then took the box from him, lightening his load. "Which means you won't have me arrested?"

He kicked the doors closed behind him. "Well, that depends on how quickly you start explaining why you're at school on a Sunday night, instead of at Meredith's, which is where you said you were going. How did you even get in here without tripping the alarm? If you broke a window, I won't be impressed." He walked toward his office.

I hurried to keep up. "No, no. All windows are intact. I used the code."

"What? How do you even know it?"

I snorted, then remembered I was probably about to be grounded until I turned eighteen. Which, admittedly, was only a couple of weeks away. But still. I tried to force my expression into something more suitably chastised. "Sorry. But you've been driving me to school and unlocking that door in front of me for the past three years. The code is my birthday. Just like all your passwords."

That resulted in a withering look, but I knew he wasn't really angry at me. We wove through the administration offices until we reached Lawson's, his gold-plated Principal nameplate on the door. He unlocked it, and we both dumped our boxes on the table.

Then he turned to me, folding his arms across his chest, giving me his best principal's glare. "How long have you been sneaking in here for?"

No point lying about it now. "Months."

His mouth dropped open. "To do what? Please don't say drugs. If you say drugs, I swear, I'm going to take you down to that police station myself."

I sniggered. "No. Something much worse."

"Sex? Booze? What could be worse?" He narrowed his eyes, but they crinkled at the corners. He was trying not to laugh. "Are you running some sort of illegal cock fighting ring out of the gym?"

I raised an eyebrow. "No, but wow. Thanks for the ideas. If college doesn't work out for me, I'll be sure to consider those options. I've just been practicing in the music rooms. All alone. No sex, drugs, or farmyard animals of any kind."

My uncle frowned and grumbled. I'd won him over. He knew how important music was to me. "So. No police?"

His expression morphed into fatherly affection. He put his arm around my shoulders and kissed the top of my head. "What do you think? I'm hardly going to call the police when I'd be the one to pay your bail. I've got work to do. Go on, go do your thing. But set your alarm and meet me back here in two hours. You know how you lose track of time when you play."

I breathed a sigh of relief. He so rarely lost his temper, and almost never at me. I couldn't have stood it if he were angry. I kissed his stubbled cheek. "Love you..."

Not for the first time, the word 'Dad' formed on my lips. But at the last moment, I swallowed it down. Instead, I gave him a grateful wave and hurried back to the music rooms.

When I got there, I shut the door behind me and made a beeline for the piano, running my palm over its gleaming black surface. This was my happy place. And it filled something inside me in a way that nothing else did.

Pulling my phone from my pocket, I set the alarm so I wouldn't be late.

Then I pressed my fingers to the keys and closed my eyes, the first lilting notes lifting to the air. Time ceased to exist until a blaring alarm cut through my bubble.

I lost focus, hit the wrong key, and the entire song unraveled. "Dammit!" I slammed the keys hard.

I glanced at my phone and silenced the obnoxious

beeping. In the blink of an eye, two hours had passed, and the real world came rushing back in. The sun had set, leaving me in near darkness, and I hadn't even noticed. Patting the top of the piano like it was a dog who'd just completed a new trick, I murmured, "Until next time."

In the corridor, I stopped dead as I caught a whiff of something unpleasant. "What the hell..." I murmured, wrinkling my nose. I took a few more steps, then froze.

Smoke.

I peered into the darkness, trying to remain calm while my brain scrambled to find logical conclusions. It was nearing the end of summer. People could be having barbecues nearby, and the smoke might have just blown in on the breeze. Or perhaps a wildfire had started. The smoke alarms weren't going off. Nor were the sprinklers. I picked up the pace, heading for the admin offices. The entire time, I scrabbled with my thoughts, fighting against the obvious. Pushing myself to believe those excuses, because what was right in front of my eyes was too scary to comprehend. I rounded a corner and stopped dead.

There was no denying it anymore.

The building was filling with thick, acrid smoke.

Something instinctual pushed me forward, and my feet went with it, instead of listening to the panicked voice in my head screaming to turn and run in the opposite direction. I fumbled for my phone, pulled it out, and dialed nine-one-one. Smoke invaded my chest and eyes. I coughed, trying to clear it while fear clawed its way up my spine.

"Fire!" I gasped when the operator answered. "Providence School for Girls." Racking coughs took over. I hung up, but the farther I got, the thicker the smoke became, until it didn't matter if I spoke or not. I held my arm over my mouth and nose, trying to keep it out, but it was a losing battle. My lungs protested, but I moved on, my pace increasing until I was running. I skidded around the corner, bashing my hipbone on the wall. The darkness was disorienting. The visibility next to nothing. I couldn't see farther than a few steps ahead of me.

"Lawson!" I yelled, immediately regretting it when smoke filled my mouth and nose. It got thicker with every step. I coughed again and ran my hands over the wall where I thought the light switch should be. I came up empty, my nails scratching over nothing but drywall.

I spun around, confused now at exactly where I was. I needed to get to my uncle. I knew, that if there was a fire, he would have come for me. Called me. He knew where I was. And there was only one way to get there. We couldn't have missed each other. I pushed my legs harder, not certain that I was even heading in the right direction, but I had to try.

Suddenly, the room around me opened up, and I nearly wept with relief as I recognized the foyer. But there was no time for that.

I'd found the source of the smoke.

Flames licked the walls.

"Lawson!" I yelled again, tasting ash. Panic surged, adrenaline kicking in and powering my movements. My brain short-circuited, whether from lack of air or fear, I didn't know. The one thing I was certain of was that I couldn't lose another parent. I couldn't add my uncle to the broken part of me that had existed ever since my birth parents' disappearance. He was the only father I really remembered. And he wouldn't have left without me. I knew that without a doubt. He wouldn't have left me there to die.

Which meant he was still inside.

I ran in a crouch toward the flames. They grew with every second that passed. "Laws—" I couldn't even get his name out this time before the lack of air stole my voice. I held my breath and rushed toward his office, throwing open doors as I went and dodging the deadly heat.

I skidded to a stop at the glass window of the principal's office. A scream curled up my throat but came out silently.

Lawson's still form lay facedown on the floorboards.

Flames billowed up around him, higher in here than anywhere else. They crawled across the ceiling, like slithering beasts of orange fury. I bashed on the window so hard it should have broken, desperately yelping my uncle's name between racking bouts of coughing.

Overhead, a beam cracked.

Sparks flew and I flinched away. I tried again, lunging for the door, but the heat drove me back. Tears streamed down my face. "Help," I croaked.

I couldn't save him alone. He was right there, the flames getting ever closer, and I couldn't reach him. I stumbled back the way I'd come, dropping to my knees and crawling when my feet wouldn't take another step. My eyes stung. My gaze flitted around the smoke-filled room, but my head grew cloudy.

With a sudden certainty, I realized we were both going to die.

There was no way out.

I closed my eyes. At least the last thing I'd done was something I loved. I remembered the way it felt to have my fingers flying over the piano keys, the song soaring, not only in my ears but in my heart. When the flames took me, that's where I'd be in my head. In the place I was happiest. The only place I had true peace.

Something grabbed me.

Not something, someone.

I dragged myself back into the present. There was somebody else here. Someone who could help. Hope surged within me.

"My uncle," I choked out.

Startled by hands on my bare skin, and my body being lifted from the floor, I tried to force my stinging eyes open. But my vision was so blurred I couldn't make out a face. I turned into the person's chest, and my gaze focused instead on the thing closest to me. Letters floated across my vision, a mere inch from my nose.

The man—it had to be a man, his body had none of the softer curves of a woman—didn't say anything, but gripped me tighter while he moved through the crumbling building. Heat seared at my legs, my arms, my face. I couldn't do a thing but fist my fingers into the material of his shirt and hold on. The embroidered feel of the letters scratched, in contrast with the softness of the fabric.

He muttered something that sounded like, "Hold on, Lacey."

A thought floated through my head, but it was too hard to grasp. I wanted to chase it, grab it, and force it to make sense. But I was too tired. I watched it go, disappearing into a smoke tendril.

My body jolted against his with each step. I wanted him to run. I wanted him to get me out of this place, but it all just seemed impossible now. Everything hurt. My lungs screamed in pain. It was too hard to hold on. My grip on his shirt loosened.

"Lacey!" he yelled, but his voice was far away.

I closed my eyes and let the darkness take me.

Keep reading here: https://mybook.to/DeviousLittleLiars

# WANT SIGNED PAPERBACKS, SPECIAL EDITION COVERS, OR SAINT VIEW MERCH?

Check out Elle's new website store at
https://www.ellethorpe.com/store

# ALSO BY ELLE THORPE

**Saint View High series (Reverse Harem, Bully Romance. Complete)**

*Devious Little Liars (Saint View High, #1)

*Dangerous Little Secrets (Saint View High, #2)

*Twisted Little Truths (Saint View High, #3)

**Saint View Prison series (Reverse harem, romantic suspense. Complete.)**

*Locked Up Liars (Saint View Prison, #1)

*Solitary Sinners (Saint View Prison, #2)

*Fatal Felons (Saint View Prison, #3)

**Dirty Cowboy series (complete)**

*Talk Dirty, Cowboy (Dirty Cowboy, #1)

*Ride Dirty, Cowboy (Dirty Cowboy, #2)

*Sexy Dirty Cowboy (Dirty Cowboy, #3)

*25 Reasons to Hate Christmas and Cowboys (a Dirty Cowboy bonus novella, set before Talk Dirty, Cowboy but can be read as a standalone, holiday romance)

**Buck Cowboys series (Spin off from the Dirty Cowboy series)**

*Buck Cowboys (Buck Cowboys, #1)

*Buck You! (Buck Cowboys, #2)

*Can't Bucking Wait (Buck Cowboys, #3)

**The Only You series (complete)**

*Only the Positive (Only You, #1) - Reese and Low.

*Only the Perfect (Only You, #2) - Jamison.

*Only the Truth - (Only You, bonus novella) - Bree.

*Only the Negatives (Only You, #3) - Gemma.

*Only the Beginning (Only You, #4) - Bianca and Riley.

*Only You boxset

Add your email address here to be the first to know when new books are available!

www.ellethorpe.com/newsletter

Join Elle Thorpe's readers group on Facebook!

www.facebook.com/groups/ellethorpesdramallamas

# ACKNOWLEDGMENTS

So....Who switched to Team Scythe? *raises hand*

I can truly say, Scythe is my all time favorite character that I've ever written. He cracked me up from page 1 and I've loved every minute of writing him. I hope you guys loved him, and the other guys, as much as I do.

Thank you to Jolie Vines, Emmy Ellis, and Karen Hrdlicka who make up my stellar editing team. Thank you to Jo Vines, Zoe Ashwood, Sara Massery, DL Gallie, Lissanne Jones, and Kat T Masen for all the chats and support. Book writing is hard and can be lonely, but you guys make long days fun. Thank you to Shellie, Dana, Louise, and Sam for your early feedback. A massive thank you to my promo and review team for always being there for me. Thank you to the Drama Llamas for being my honorary extended family.

And as always, a huge thank you to my family. To Jira, Thomas, Flick, and Heidi. You four are the loves of my life and I couldn't do any of this without you.

Love, Elle x

# ABOUT THE AUTHOR

Elle Thorpe lives in a small regional town of NSW, Australia. When she's not writing stories full of kissing, she's wife to Mr Thorpe who unexpectedly turned out to be a great plotting partner, and mummy to three tiny humans. She's also official ball thrower to one slobbery dog named Rollo. Yes, she named a female dog after a dirty hot character on Vikings. Don't judge her. Elle is a complete and utter fangirl at heart, obsessing over The Walking Dead and Outlander to an unhealthy degree. But she wouldn't change a thing.

You can find her on Facebook or Instagram(@ellethorpebooks or hit the links below!) or at her website www.ellethorpe.com. If you love Elle's work, please consider joining her Facebook fan group, Elle Thorpe's Drama Llamas or joining her newsletter here. www.ellethorpe.com/newsletter

facebook.com/ellethorpebooks

instagram.com/ellethorpebooks

goodreads.com/ellethorpe

pinterest.com/ellethorpebooks

Made in the USA
Monee, IL
18 March 2024

55257877R00194